BLACK
TUESDAY

NEW YORK TIMES BESTSELLING AUTHOR
BOB MAYER

AREA 51
A TIME PATROL NOVEL

BLACK
TUESDAY

47NORTH

Published by 47North, Seattle

www.apub.com

Amazon, the Amazon logo, and 47North are trademarks of Amazon.com, Inc., or its affiliates.

ISBN-13: 9781503946637
ISBN-10: 1503946630

Cover design by Jason Blackburn

Printed in the United States of America

"The only reason for time is so that everything doesn't happen at once."

—Albert Einstein

WHERE THE TIME PATROL ENDED UP THIS PARTICULAR DAY

ON MAPS OF OLD, THOSE BLANK SPACES BEYOND THE KNOWN WORLD WERE MARKED: *HERE THERE BE MONSTERS.*

Off the East Coast of England, 999 AD. 29 October

Roland was ready for battle, a sword in his hand rather than a machine gun, but the general concept was the same: fell deeds awakening against the forces of darkness.

And here be the monster as a thick, ropy tentacle lunged up out of the water. At the tip was a mouth fringed with sharp teeth, snapping, searching for flesh. It hit one of the Vikings directly into the chest, the teeth boring deep. The man slashed at the creature with his sword even as he died.

The Viking leader was fast to the defense with Roland at his side, almost as fast. They battled desperately as more tentacles came out of the water. Roland sliced through one, stomping down with his leather boot on the snapping end, crushing the teeth. To his right, another Viking was lifted into the air, tentacle wrapped around his chest. The unfortunate warrior was pulled down into the black water, disappearing. The man never cried out in terror or for help, swinging his sword even as he was taken into darkness. It was the way a Viking should be taken, weapon in hand, guaranteeing a place in the hall of Valhalla.

If such a place exists.

But warriors need to believe in something beyond themselves, whether it be country, flag, unit, comrades, or Valhalla.

Neeley had told Roland of these creatures, the kraken.

He was elated to finally meet one.

Roland jabbed the point of his sword directly into the mouth end of a tentacle, right between the teeth, as it came straight for him. The sword went in and then farther in, the teeth snapping down on the steel, getting closer and closer to his hand, finally stopping at the cross-shaped haft before the tentacle pulled back, dripping gore.

It is 999 AD. The last year before the turn of the first millennium *anno Domini.* In another part of the world, the Samanid Dynasty, encompassing parts of Iraq and Afghanistan, ceases to exist after crumbling under an invasion from the north. Not for the first time and not for the last time, that region of the world is convulsed in conflict. Across the sea to the west of England, Christianity is being officially adopted in Iceland. Gerbert of Aurillac becomes Pope Silvester II, succeeding Pope Gregory V. He is the first French pope and introduces the western world to the decimal system using Arabic numbers. He would thus be accused of studying magical arts and astrology in Islamic cities, with charges that he was a sorcerer in league with the devil.

Some things change; some don't.

And here, on a Viking longship, Roland was facing creatures of legend while on a mission whose objective he wasn't exactly certain of. But he had a shield and a sword and he was in the company of fierce warriors in the midst of a battle.

Roland was at home.

Los Angeles, California, 1969. 29 October

Shifting her focus, Scout caught her reflection in the mirror and grimaced. Her hair was brown, very brown, with no colored streaks, because the hair-streaking business was still in the future. She had a part in the middle. Most unattractive and nondescript. But one did have to fit in. Her thin little peasant top revealed she was braless, but her breasts were small, so no issue there.

So. She was a feminist. Victoria's Secret was still a few decades down the road too and maybe braless was the way to go until someone thought up a pretty bra. She checked the waistband of her low-riding jeans and sighed. Yep. Cotton bikini panties. Gross, but thongs were as far off as pretty bras. And thus is the place of underwear in history, she thought.

The sacrifices she made for her duty.

It is 1969. The first man walks on the moon. Joe Namath leads the Jets to a shocking Super Bowl win. The first Led Zeppelin album is released. Faced with pressing needs from the Vietnam War, the first draft lottery since World War II is held. Nixon becomes president. A teenager in St. Louis dies of an undiagnosed disease and it would be fifteen years before it's realized he was the first confirmed death from AIDS in the United States. The Beatles are photographed crossing Abbey Road. *Scooby-Doo* airs for the first time. And *Monty Python's Flying Circus.* Fourteen men, nine of them Jews, are executed in Baghdad for spying for Israel. Woodstock.

Some things change; some don't.

As she went toward the door of the small room, it also occurred to Scout that this was the era of free love, which Scout doubted was ever free.

But still. She was only here for a day and then she would be gone.

Scout had a strange feeling. It took her a moment to recognize it: excitement. This could be interesting.

She was sure her mother wouldn't approve of the feeling or the thought.

London, England, 1618. 29 October

Mac shivered as much from the night air as the pronouncement of the pending execution.

The Lord Chief Justice took a step forward. "Sir Walter Raleigh, you must remember yourself; you had an honorable trial, and so were justly convicted; and it were wisdom in you now to submit yourself.

"I pray you attend what I shall say unto you. I am here called to grant execution upon the judgment given you fifteen years since; all which time you have been as a dead man in the law, and might at any minute have been cut off, but the King in mercy spared you. You might think it heavy if this were done in cold blood, to call you to execution; but it is not so, for new offenses have stirred up His Majesty's justice, to remember to revive what the law had formerly cast upon you. I know you have been valiant and wise, and I doubt not but you retain both these virtues, for now you shall have occasion to use them. Your Faith has heretofore been questioned, but I am resolved you are a good Christian, for your book, which is an admirable work, does testify as much. I would give you counsel, but I know you can apply unto yourself far better than I am able to give you."

Raleigh's head drooped down, the messy hair falling over his face and mostly hiding it. But Mac caught the hint of a smile on Raleigh's face through the hair.

The Lord Chief Justice continued. "Fear not death too much, nor fear death too little; not too much, lest you fail in your hopes; not too little, lest you die presumptuously. And here I must conclude with my prayers to God for it, and that he would have mercy on your soul." He paused, and then announced: "Execution is granted and will be carried out later today."

As the guards stepped up next to Raleigh to escort him away, he lifted his head and looked at the man next to Mac. "Will you be present at the show later this morning, Lord Beeston?"

"I hope so," Beeston said. "If I can find a place in the crowd."

Raleigh smiled. "I do not know what you may do for a place. You must make what shift you can. But for my part, *I* am sure of having a place."

The guy had guts, Mac had to grant him that.

And with that, Raleigh was hustled away.

Beeston edged close by Mac's side and spoke in a low voice. "You are here to help save him. Say the word is yes. I will lend my sword to yours, as will those who have gathered. Surely history cannot allow such a man to suffer this fate. It is not in the prophecy."

It was also not stated as a question to Mac.

Mac looked at the old man, well dressed for the time period, sporting a wig that didn't quite hide his baldness. He had a wicked rapier scar slashing across his left cheek, a piece of nose missing, and a gash ending above the right side of his mouth. The wound had not healed well. And his eyes glittered, in which Mac recognized the confidence of a fellow warrior.

Nope, Mac thought, *I'm not here to save him.*

It is 1618. The Thirty Years' War, one of the longest and most destructive conflicts in European history, begins when two Catholic lord regents are thrown out of a window in Prague; they land unharmed. Pluto reaches its aphelion, coming closest to the sun, and will not do so again until 1866 and then 2113. Kepler discovers harmonics law. The Truce of Deulino ends the Polish-Muscovite War, until it resumes fourteen years later.

Some things change; some don't.

But then the question Mac pondered was: Why *was* he here?

Andes Mountains, Argentina, 1972. 29 October

Moms had done a lot of hunting in her time, but she'd never seen a track like this. Large, over six inches wide by sixteen inches long. Almost human shaped, but different. "What made that? What did we shoot?" Moms asked.

"A monster," Correa said. "We did not kill it, as you could tell. It has gone off to nurse its wounds. It has had many names, in many lands. Yeti in the Himalayas. Abominable Snowman. Sasquatch. Bigfoot. Ts'emekwes among the Native Americans of the Pacific Northwest. Here in the Amazon and Andes it has been called Mono Grande, or Large Monkey." He shrugged. "I prefer Yeti. Much simpler." He slid the FN FAL rifle onto his shoulder. He coughed, hard, for several moments, turning partly away from Moms and bending over.

"Are you all right?"

"A touch of the flu," Correa said, straightening up. "Nothing to worry about."

Moms didn't care for the cold. Early in her career she'd served in a Special-Ops unit that was oriented toward Winter Warfare training. That meant she was prepared, which was both a good thing and a bad thing. It was good that she knew what she was doing here at 13,000 feet in the Andes in the middle of the fall.

It was bad in that she'd learn to hate being cold.

It is 1972. According to Coordinated Universal Time (UTC), this is the longest year ever, with two leap seconds added. The Nightstalkers close a Rift near Hoover Dam. Nick Ut takes his Pulitzer Prize winning photo of a naked nine-year-old Vietnamese girl running after being bombed by napalm. A Japanese soldier is discovered hiding on Guam, twenty-eight years after the end of World War II. A Serbian flight attendant survives a fall of 33,000 feet in the tail section of a plane that explodes midflight. *The Godfather* is released. Nixon orders Haiphong Harbor mined. Watergate. Atari releases Pong. The last manned moon mission, Apollo 17, is launched. We've never been back.

Some things change; some don't.

Her mission had just begun, and already Moms had battled a creature of legend.

Nothing but good times ahead.

Not.

1

Eglin Air Force Base, Florida, 1980. 29 October

"Lots of history at that there airfield," Hammersmith told Eagle, while pointing with the end of a twig at the triangle of runways on the map. "March of '42, ole Doolittle hisself brought his raiders there. Trained them to take off in a short distance, just like they was gonna do the next month off the *Hornet* when they bombed Japan. Can still see tire marks where they burned rubber on the tarmac, cranking those old birds to full power, then releasing the brakes. Those marks have lasted longer than the men who made them.

"Then right after the Big War, they tested some flying bombs they copied off the German V-1, launching them in this field, here, off the airstrip. Abandoned now, but some rusting launchers are still there. Use them as objectives sometimes for the students. Those old-timers used Nazi scientists for that 'cause after the war, the Russkies were the enemy. Kinda strange ain't it, how yesterday's enemy is today's buddy, eh?" He didn't wait for an answer and Eagle began to suspect there was more to Hammersmith than his first impression. "Airfield been abandoned for a long time though." He looked up at Eagle. "Until lately. Been off-limits for a bit."

"So," Eagle finally said, "you're my contact."

"Yeah. Surprised, ain't you, son? Takes all kinds to keep the timeline ticking. I ain't gonna ask you when you come from. I don't want to know dick about the future. That would fuck with my head and my head's already kinda fucked up. I done two tours in 'Nam and sometimes I don't think so straight. And I know you're here only for twenty-four hours, so let's not be dicking around. Let's get this done. I don't suppose you know what this is about?"

"You know what's happening at Wagner Field?"

"Yeah. They're testing a modified C-130 for short landings and takeoffs. Almost Doolittle like, which I kind of find interesting. I gotta assume it's got something to do with the cluster fuck in the desert back in April. Know some fellows from the Battalion who were in on that. So maybe we're going to be trying again? And you're here to make sure that happens."

The last sentence was said not as a question, and that was enough warning for Eagle to keep the details of today's history from Hammersmith.

"Sort of," Eagle said.

"Fuck me to tears," Hammersmith said, and Eagle could only think of Nada saying the same thing, so many times. The Ranger Instructor was no fool.

"We gotta stop it, don't we?"

Okay, Eagle had seriously underestimated the Time Patrol agent. "Yes."

Hammersmith was silent for several long seconds. "Then that's the mission." A soldier accepting his duty. "Do we have to kill any of our own?"

"No." *Hope not*, Eagle amended silently.

"All right." Hammersmith nodded. "I can live with that. Time to get real." Hammersmith shrugged off his rucksack and opened it. He dumped a sack on the ground. "5.56. Live ammo. Take the damn blank adapter off your weapon and lock and load. I'll be your assistant patrol leader and I'll navigate for you. The rest of the men have live ammo in their rucks and I've already passed the word to load up." He slapped his own rucksack. "We got one

M60 with eight hundred rounds of 7.62, claymores, some LAWs, grenades, pistol ammo. One of the fellas got an M21 if we need to pop someone at distance. Oh yeah, two M203s with fifteen HE rounds each." He held up a shotgun with a short box magazine. "And I have my Lola. SPAS-12 shotgun, loaded with slugs."

Eagle processed the inventory: Claymores were anti-personnel mines; LAWs were light-anti-tank weapons; an M21 was a sniper rifle. Live ammunition. The M60 was a medium machine gun, good firepower. The M203s were M16s with a 40 mm grenade launcher slung under the barrel. And there was Lola, a semiautomatic shotgun.

So they were prepared for battle.

Eagle was starting to feel better about this mission, but Hammersmith put an end to that flicker of optimism. "We might not have to kill any of our own, but that don't mean this is going to be a cakewalk. I been in these swamps for years, sonny. Grew up down here. Walked many a patrol so I can get us the airfield. But things ain't right." He nodded out toward the dark swamp. "There's something out there. Something that don't want us getting to that airfield. Something bad, real bad. Evil-like. And it's between us and the airfield and whatever it is you gotta do." He paused. "I don't suppose you can tell me what it is *exactly* you gotta do?"

"No, Master Sergeant."

Hammersmith sighed. "Figured." He turned off the flashlight. After a moment, they emerged from underneath the poncho and stood up.

Hammersmith became formal. "Let me know when you want to move out, sir."

It is 1980. President Jimmy Carter decides to boycott the summer Olympics in Moscow in response to the Russian invasion of Afghanistan. Mount St. Helens erupts, killing fifty-seven people.

CNN goes on the air. John Lennon is shot and killed. The Iran-Iraq War drags on. Operation Eagle Claw, intended to rescue the American hostages in Tehran, fails. There are 226,545,805 Americans registered in the census. A Norwegian oil platform collapses in the North Sea, killing 123 of its crew and spilling oil. Reagan defeats Carter in the presidential election.

Some things change; some don't.

Eagle took a deep breath.

This was going to suck worse than doing Ranger School again.

───────────

AND THEN THERE ARE THE MOST DANGEROUS MONSTERS: THE ONES DISGUISED AS HUMAN.

Manhattan, New York, 1929. 29 October

Ivar was startled as a man darted out from an alley and ran into him. He felt wetness on his face and realized it was blood as the stranger collapsed to the ground. There was blood everywhere and Ivar's instinct was to flee, but his Special-Ops training upon "joining" the Nightstalkers allowed him at least to stand his ground for a moment.

"Are you him?" the man gasped.

Ivar knelt, trying to find the source of the blood, but it was everywhere and he hadn't taken the emergency medical training as seriously as he should have. Then his hand sunk into the guy's stomach, intestines like soft, warm snakes, and Ivar realized the man had been gutted. And there was a gurgling noise and Ivar knew the guy had been stabbed several times, including at least once in the lung as the sound indicated a sucking chest wound.

So some of the training had stuck.

The stranger held out a canvas bag. It was smeared with blood, but Ivar automatically took it. *Might be a bomb,* he heard Nada warning, but Nada wasn't here. Wasn't around in the then (or was it now?) either.

"What is it?" Ivar asked.

The man was looking over his shoulder. "Run. Run. They're coming."

"Who's coming?"

"Them."

"I'll help you."

The man winced in pain. "The mission is more important. Go!"

Ivar looked past the man and saw no one, but he had no doubt that whoever had wielded the blade would be following the blood trail.

Every instinct he had pressed Ivar to run away and leave the man as requested.

Ivar ripped off his overcoat and tied the arms tightly around the stranger's chest and stomach, partially staunching the flow of blood.

"Come on."

There was no protest. Ivar wrapped his arm around the man's shoulder and headed down Wall Street. Past the statue of George Washington, marking his inauguration at this very spot where slaves had been bought, sold, and rented. He turned into a dark alley, searching for a door or window.

It is 1929. The British High Court rules that Canadian women are persons. The first Academy Awards are given out and *Wings* wins Best Picture. The *Graf Zeppelin* flies around the world in twenty-one days. Stalin sends Trotsky into exile. *All Quiet on the Western Front* is published. Popeye appears for the first time in a comic. The Dow Jones peaks at 381.17, which it will not reach again until 1954. The first patent for color television is submitted. Rioting breaks out in Jerusalem between Arabs and Jews over access to the Western Wall.

Some things change; some don't.

The world was indeed never, ever, going to be the same.

BEFORE THE TIME PATROL ENDED UP THERE AND THEN

The Possibility Palace

"You know the Nightstalkers as well as anyone," Dane, the Administrator of the Time Patrol said. "You were a major part of their initial selection and assessment and are responsible for their psychological status. Who do we pair with which year?"

"Should we even call them Nightstalkers anymore?" Frasier asked. "Wouldn't Time Patrol be more appropriate?"

Frasier tended to disconcert those who sat across a table from him, but Dane wasn't the type to get disconcerted. Frasier's left eye was solid black, the implant surrounded by scar tissue. It was a very sophisticated device, capable of measuring the slightest of changes in body temperature of whomever it observed, zero in on the beat of a pulse in a person's throat, and scour other data, effectively making the cybernetic eye a lie detector. His left arm, covered by his black suit, was also artificial.

"What we wish to call them isn't important right now," Dane said. "I need to make some decisions on these assignments. Quickly."

They were in a bland, off-white square room, a door in the center of each wall. A wooden table was set in the middle of the space, and Dane was on one side, Frasier on the other.

Frasier looked down at the single piece of paper in front of him. "Obviously, Doc would be best suited for the California operation, but—"

"I have other plans for Doc," Dane said. "He won't be deploying. Choose among the remaining six."

Frasier's voice showed the slightest taint of irritation. "As I was going to say, that means he *shouldn't* be the one for it. It's about computers and science and Doc gets too caught up in the technical aspects of his surroundings, so he would lose sight of the mission." Doc had a number of PhDs, a topic he managed to insert rather quickly into conversation with anyone who wasn't already aware of that, and sometimes with those who were, on the off chance they might have forgotten. His parents had emigrated from India when he was young and he'd immersed himself in the academic world until the Nightstalkers, perhaps now the Time Patrol, came calling. Frasier shook his head. "We need someone who will find the era interesting and will fit in. Someone young, since it will be on a college campus."

"Scout," Dane said. Not a question, as he wrote down her name on his own single sheet of paper.

Scout was the youngest member of the Nightstalkers, recruited by the team two years ago when they parachuted into a gated community in North Carolina to battle Fireflies, energy creatures that had come through a Rift. She was just past her eighteenth birthday, and while her recent Special-Ops training had tried to shake off her rebellious edge, it hadn't taken. She colored her hair depending on her mood, and then put streaks in it to rebel against her own rebelliousness.

"Although she's the youngest, Scout is the most astute of them," Frasier said. "She has an instinct that,"—he shrugged—"well, I can't explain. Intuitive."

Dane nodded. "All right. Next. Elizabethan England."

Frasier took the opposite reasoning on this one. "First, who can't go? Moms. Female; a second-class citizen in that era, even though the recently deceased Elizabeth had ruled for decades. Eagle is African American and that's a no-go for that time and place. Roland? This mission requires some subtlety and let's say that's not Roland's forte. That leaves two. Ivar, but his ability to blend in is doubtful. That leaves us Mac. It's a perfect fit for him. He's been acting all his life and this will be no different." Frasier smiled. "A critical moment in Mac's life occurred when he was in high school. He landed the lead in his high school play. Shakespeare. The second his father saw him in costume, he lost it. Called him all sorts of things. Made what he considered derogatory comments about Mac's sexuality, which, actually, were rather on the mark, but even Mac suppressed that."

"Won't that be a problem then?" Dane asked.

"Mac isn't suppressing that part of himself anymore. He's accepted who he is."

"Fine." Dane wrote the second name on the sheet. "The Andes mission?"

Frasier didn't hesitate. "Moms. It has nothing to do with her personality, although I do have some concerns after her recent foray to Kansas. She has the training for the weather and the altitude. I think that trumps everything else."

"What happened in Kansas?" Dane asked, obviously not overly curious.

Frasier sighed. "She corrected some trauma from her childhood using her training. Killed a man who had assaulted her mother many years ago."

"Is the Cellar after her?" Dane asked, now concerned about losing an asset to the organization that policed covert organizations and rogue operatives.

"No," Frasier said. "It was a justified kill. Long overdue. I haven't had a chance to follow up with her to see what the psychological ramifications have been, but we don't have the time for that. Bottom line, she's trained in Winter Warfare, which requires a specific set of skills. Perfect for the Andes."

"All right." Dane wrote down the third. "Eglin Air Force Base?"

"Eagle," Frasier said immediately, referring to the Nightstalkers' pilot and resident genius.

"Good." But then Dane frowned. "That leaves two missions and two names."

"That's the math," Frasier said, which earned him an irritated look from Dane.

"Manhattan?" Dane asked.

"Ivar. Process of elimination." Ivar was on the team by default, a former graduate student who'd been used by his professor to help open a Rift at the University of North Carolina. Ivar was the only member of the team to go through a Rift and come back, although no one, even Ivar, was quite sure *who* exactly had come back. "We haven't quite been able to"—Frasier halted as he searched for the right words, an unusual sign of uncertainty on his part—"determine how he was affected by his experience, but he proved capable on the last mission into the Space Between. Besides, Foreman requested him for the Manhattan mission."

Dane raised an eyebrow. "Indeed? Why?"

"Foreman has his own reasons," Frasier evaded.

Dane didn't have time to probe deeper. "That leaves Roland going to England, long before Mac's mission. But it's also the vaguest mission. Is it wise to send Roland on the one with the most possibilities?"

Frasier almost laughed. "Roland is gifted with the least imagination on the team. Psychologically, it actually makes sense to send him on the mission with the greatest number of variables. He won't be overwhelmed. He won't overthink it."

Roland was the Nightstalkers' weapons guy. A huge, musclebound man, he was, as Frasier said, not overly gifted in the thinking department. But he had other talents.

"Roland is going into a violent era," Frasier said. "Of all the members of the team, he is the most capable once blood is drawn. And I would make it a safe bet that blood will be drawn quickly and often during his twenty-four hours in the past."

A door behind Dane opened and a woman dressed in a bland gray jumpsuit walked in. She leaned over and whispered something in the Administrator's ear. He nodded. The woman left, and then Dane stood. "I'll keep your recommendations in mind. They'll be here shortly."

New York City, The Present

Cleopatra's Needle was bathed in sunlight and Edith Frobish took the extra moment to circumnavigate it, checking all four sides of the obelisk in Central Park with more than the usual perusal. It was as it always had been.

For now, Edith thought as she turned for the Met with a bounce in her step. For now. Who knew? Some day Caesar might just turn out to be alive and ruling in Egypt. She was pretty sure Dane had gotten that little wrinkle from some other timeline for Foreman to play on the Nightstalkers.

With extra vigor, Edith shoved open the blank metal door.

"Hello, Burt. Beautiful day outside." She held up her badge, but the guard didn't even look at it.

"Hey, Edith. It sure is."

She walked down the hallway, turned right, past the CLOSED FOR CONSTRUCTION sign, and got on the OUT OF ORDER elevator.

She rode down patiently.

The doors opened and Edith walked out. She came to the guard post and the heavily armed man did his checks without a greeting or how-do-you-do. But Edith looked at him differently now, recognizing his real job. So she paused, and graced him with a smile and a "Have a wonderful day" before breezing down to the next steel door.

She stepped in and waited for that door to shut behind her. Passed the DNA test. Then opened the next door.

A spotlight was focused on the HUB. The gate was where it should be. And standing by it were Moms, Eagle, Mac, Roland, Ivar, Doc, and Scout. The Nightstalkers. And now also the Time Patrol. Edith Frobish walked across the cavern floor to the gate and joined them. She paused, as she always paused. "Are you ready?" An unfair question, Edith knew, because they still really didn't know what they needed to be ready for. They walked up next to her. And then they all stepped through . . .

. . . into a bland room with a wooden table in the center and chairs surrounding it.

The gate they'd come through faded out of existence.

The walls were off-white, a color a shrink might recommend if you want no reaction at all from people suddenly appearing in the middle of the room. There were no windows. But there was a door centered on each wall. Four ways to go. Who knew what lay beyond each?

"This way," Edith said, leading them to one of the doors. She pushed it open and they were immersed in the quiet hum of a lot of people working without some of the sounds one would be used to, like phones ringing or music being piped in.

They were on a wide balcony that extended left and right, curving, overlooking a massive space.

"Whoa!" Scout said.

"Organized madness," was Eagle's take. "*Ascending and Descending*."

"What?" Roland said, clueless as to who and what Eagle was referring to.

As usual.

But there was a pattern amid the chaos. The basic structure was a huge, ascending outward spiral from a center pit, so far down and away they could barely make it out. A single ramp rose along the edge, going clockwise, with different widths and angles in places, circling again and again, rising up over three thousand feet from the bottom and crossing over itself, wider and wider, dozens and dozens of times. The track was sometimes accentuated by overhanging balconies of various sizes. Desks were crowded along the track and on the balconies, manned by personnel in various outfits. Along the outer edge of the apparently unending spiral were filing cabinets stacked precariously high.

Ladders ascended and descended here and there. Staircases cut through spots with no apparent rhyme or reason.

"Check it out," Scout pointed, as someone rode a zip line on an angle from one part of the ramp to another.

Overhead, the ceiling arced high above them. The entire area was so large, it was generating its own weather system with wisps of clouds. It was as if someone had taken the largest quarry on the planet and turned it into a madhouse with a purpose.

"Welcome to the Palace," Edith said.

"Palace of what?" Scout asked.

"Possibilities," Edith said. "The Possibility Palace."

"Are you serious?" Scout asked.

Edith looked insulted. "Of course."

"I think she's always serious," Mac noted.

"I have a sense of humor," Edith said without much conviction.

"Right," Scout said. "Keeping it close, aren't you?"

"No computers or phones," Doc noted, indicating the ramp and the desks.

"No," Edith said. "We don't use computers. And there's no need for phones since everyone is here in the Hall when on duty; messages are sent on paper through pneumatic tubes. This is the brain of the Time Patrol. And the repository of all our knowledge."

"*Battlestar Galactica*?" Scout asked.

"Excuse me?" Edith was confused. Besides humor, she also didn't have cable TV.

"You don't use computers because the Cylons can hack into your system?" Scout asked. "Or the Valkyries in this case."

Edith shrugged. "We just don't use them. I suppose the people are the computers."

"Like you?" Moms asked.

"I suppose." Edith didn't seem very interested in pursuing that line of questioning. She was a tall woman, just shy of six feet, with short hair. Lengthy and lean described Edith, from her form, to her face, to her slightly too-long nose. She pointed down to the barely visible bottom three thousand feet below. "It begins there."

"What begins there?" Mac asked.

"History," Edith said. "And then it spirals upward and outward along the ramp. The timeline. And the people who study it."

"Is there a desk for every day?" Doc asked, grasping the geometry of time laid out in front of them.

"No." Edith shook her head. "That would be too much, although there are some days in history, significant ones, with a single desk assigned to them. There are actually long stretches of history when not much happened. But then . . ." She peered out, and then pointed at a particularly large balcony not too far below. It looked jury-rigged, with cables stretching back to bolts on the wall and several ladders hanging over the edge to the spiral level below. A staircase cut through the ramp, then zigzagged up to another portion of the ramp above. "That's World War Two."

Looking more carefully, they could now see that many points along the spiral were accessorized by the people who worked there, manning various times and various places.

Eagle spoke up. "How are these people part of the Time Patrol?"

"We're *all* part of it," Edith said. "We all have different roles to play in the larger scheme of things."

"How do the people down there," Scout asked, "get up here? Or we get down there?"

"We don't and they don't," Edith said. She pointed to a round tube on the wall. "Old-fashioned, for our present: pneumatic delivery. The folders go back and forth inside little tubes. Intelligence."

"What's in all the rooms up here?" Mac asked, pointing at the numerous doors off their overlooking balcony.

"Some are rooms for Time Patrol agents and teams. Some are for supervisors. Some contain other things."

"Vague much?" Mac said.

Doc had a question. "Where and when is this place?"

"Ah," Edith said. "That I don't know. And even if I did know, I could never tell you. The location and time of the Palace is the most heavily guarded secret and our ultimate defense."

"Has to be in the past," Doc said. "Right? You said that we can't travel forward in time, so this has to be some time in the past. And the location has to be hidden from those in the local time." He had a thought. "Unless we're in prehistory."

Edith ignored him and gestured out to the Palace. "We track our timeline's history here. Operatives like me come and go from various times and deposit our summaries. Six pages. No more; less is preferred. It's all catalogued and cross-referenced. I suppose one reason we rely on people rather than computers is that some of the connections between ripple events aren't logical, but they are there. You get a feel for it after a while. And there are patterns. Patterns that—" She suddenly halted, as if she'd said too much. "I'll let the Administrator explain that to you."

"Dane?" Moms asked, referring to the man they'd met in the Space Between who'd given each of them a choice. The ultimate choice: whether to move forward and be part of the Patrol or go back and change something in their past.

Only Nada had gone back.

And Moms missed him terribly, with a depth of feeling she'd never experienced before for a fellow warrior. His calming presence, his Nada Yadas, which had preceded her—and every other member's—time on the team.

"Yes," Edith said. "He'll be with us shortly."

"What's that?" Scout asked, pointing to a large, six-foot-high hourglass that stuck out from the balcony they were on, suspended over the floor. Sand was slowly running down from the top to the bottom. It was almost done.

"Time," Edith said. "The only time we keep here. Six shifts of the glass, four hours each. Equals a day." She pointed. "Watch." The last of the sand ran through, and the glass slowly rotated and the sand began its tumbling again. From just below, a bugle rang out, announcing the change. The call was picked up by other instruments: other bugles, horns, drums, even someone yodeling . . . a cacophony of sound that lasted almost a minute and then faded away.

Doors opened on the outside of the ramp and people streamed in, replacing a sixth of those on duty.

"We maintain continuity through shifts," Edith said.

"Where do they go?" Scout asked.

"To their quarters," Edith said vaguely. "They stay among those from their own era." She changed the subject. "We track not only our timeline here, but what we can gather on other timelines. Especially the ones that don't make it."

"What do you mean 'don't make it'?" Moms asked.

"They end," Edith said. "For humanity that is. The planet is still there." She paused. "Usually."

Everyone digested that for a few seconds.

Edith continued. "We need to understand how they failed. Where they went wrong. Whether they ended internally, which means without interference from other timelines. Such as all-out nuclear war. Sadly that's a rather common occurrence since it appears almost every timeline moves into the nuclear age if they make it to the twentieth century. Or a plague with one-hundred-percent kill. That's ended a line or two even before the twentieth century. Or simply destroying the planet's infrastructure to the point where human life isn't sustainable. Much more likely to happen than most people believe; in fact, almost inevitable, we're afraid. Before we concern ourselves with external attacks from beyond our timeline, we must guard against our own flawed humanity."

"That was our mission also," Moms said.

"It was in the present," Edith agreed. "You were on the forward edge of the time wave as it evolves. But we, and now you, cover the entire timeline, a much broader spectrum." She spread her hands, taking in the entirety of the Possibility Palace, and that punctuated her statement with an exclamation point. "And then there are the timelines harvested by the Shadow."

"Harvested for what?" Eagle asked.

"Everything and anything." Edith paused. "Some timelines have been entirely stripped of natural resources, particularly air and water. You saw how the Valkyries controlled by the Ratnik were reaping humans for their body parts? The Shadow reaps entire planets for their resources.

"It's troublesome. We used to think the Shadow was a single timeline. And perhaps it is, but we're starting to suspect that the Shadow is some larger entity than just a timeline and has corrupted *several* timelines to do its bidding because the attacks are not consistent. The goals of the harvesting are often widely variable. The vagaries of the variables as the Administrator likes to say. Possibilities."

"How do you learn about these other timelines?" Doc asked.

"Refugees who make it to the Space Between," Edith said. "The Amelia Earhart you met, for example. She was not from our timeline. She was a survivor from a timeline that is no longer viable due to the Shadow. Which is why she can't go back."

"What happened to the Amelia Earhart from our timeline?" Scout asked.

Edith shook her head. "As best we can tell, she really did crash on her round-the-world flight and died."

"And you don't know who or what this Shadow is?" Moms asked.

"No." Edith seemed troubled by the question. "The Administrator will brief you shortly. Please come with me."

"What's that?" Scout asked, pointing to the right and down at the ramp just below the balcony. A grayish-white fog obscured one end of the ramp as it ascended.

"That," Edith said, "is the present, leading into the unknown future."

EVEN BEFORE THEN: THE DISTANT PAST

Approximately 10,000 BC

A thousand men and women manned the fortress walls, waiting to die bravely. They were the elite of the Atlantean army,
handpicked for this last mission. The survivors of a seven-year
war against an enemy none had ever returned to describe, but
there were rumors of monsters and worse. They were armed with
spear, sword, and bow, and knew these weapons would be useless
against what the approaching darkness was bringing. There were
persistent rumors of other weapons that had been developed, but
the rumors were bitter because the weapons were not to be used
to save them or their home, but the future.

Such is the nature of true sacrifice. Still, they stood tall on
the ramparts and looked out to the sea from which their doom
would come.

The fortress was set on the smallest of thirteen volcanic
islands in the middle of the Atlantic Ocean. Although the smallest, this island, centrally located, was the most important, as it

was the seat of power for the Empire of Atlantis. The fortress wall surrounded a magnificent city, consisting of more than forty square miles of homes, temples, government buildings, and businesses constructed from a fine white marble that gleamed in the late afternoon sun. In the very center of the city, a huge pyramid had hurriedly been constructed. It was more than three hundred feet high with a level top twenty feet wide. Contrasting with the rest of the city, it was built of black stone.

On the top of the pyramid stood the High Defender. She was a tall woman with short red hair and pale skin, clad in a white robe with red trim and wore a crystal amulet around her neck as a sign of her special position.

Her eyes were icy blue, and they were currently scanning to all points of the compass from the center of Atlantis. In every direction, darkness covered the ocean, a black wall over a mile high of undeterminable depth: the Shadow's domain. The circle of black was slowly closing on the center island, the capital city that had once ruled the other twelve islands in the middle of the Atlantic and colonies on both sides of the ocean. The twelve islands were uninhabited now after having been overrun, year after year, two by two, for the past six, by the Shadow.

It had started seven years ago to the day. Two islands to the west had been consumed by the unknown darkness in just twenty-four hours. When the Shadow lifted, no one was left. No one alive, no bodies, nothing. Then exactly six years ago, two islands to the south suffered the same fate. Then five years ago, on the same date, two to the north.

There was nothing special about this particular day of the year as far as the Atlanteans could determine. But by the third-year anniversary, the assault was anticipated. Nevertheless there was nothing that could be done to avert the same result as islands five and six were consumed. Most had escaped beforehand, warned by the Defenders of the coming doom, their ships spreading out across the ocean before the darkness finished encircling. The twelve tribes of Atlantis sought haven far over the seas, carrying with them the legend of their kingdom and the knowledge that had been given in visions to the Defenders by the Ones Before.

Years four and five saw two more islands wiped out.

The islands were covered in darkness. Once more, when it withdrew, there was no sign of the handful who had remained behind out of sheer stubbornness and despair. There were always those who would refuse to leave their homes, no matter what was coming.

Now as the seventh-year anniversary of doom approached, all knew it would be time for their capital, the last of Atlantis, to suffer the same fate.

Just after midnight, the blackness had appeared, closer than ever before, completely encircling the capital island. As dawn approached so did the darkness. Ahead of the darkness were monsters of the sea—kraken—attacking ships that were futilely trying to fight the inevitable.

A man stood by the High Defender's side. He was dressed in the plain leather of an ordinary warrior, although he was anything but ordinary. He was the Administrator. Next to him was an obsidian, three-foot-high triangular column. Gathered behind him were six men, dressed similarly, with an identical device next to each one of them. Each of the men had a bulging pack slung over his shoulder containing scrolls.

After the second-year attack, a select few among the Atlanteans, all women, began receiving visions and hearing voices from some unseen entity calling itself the Ones Before, warning them about the nature of the force behind the darkness—the Shadow—and telling them ways to combat the threat. At first, the visions and voices were ignored as the warriors tried to use traditional means to fight the Shadow, but when all those attempts became abject failures, the people were forced to turn to these seers.

Thus the Defenders were formed. The darkness over the two islands the previous year was destroyed by a pyramid and the sacrifice of a Defender and several warriors exactly as the Ones Before instructed. But the islands were devastated by the defense, stripped bare of life, and all involved were killed. It was hoped that this disaster might mean an end to the Shadow, but now they knew that hope was in vain. Meanwhile, the Administrator and his select people worked on another possible means of fighting the Shadow based on information gleaned from the visions sent by the Ones Before.

For the past year, desperate visions warned of the coming threat and now it was here, on schedule. Pri Tor shifted her gaze to those gathered on the broad stairs of the pyramid: twelve priestesses like her, one Defender survivor from each island who'd been at the capital in service and thus escaped the destruction of her home. Two warriors stood by, the taller of whom held a staff, one end of which was a razor-sharp spearhead and the other a seven-headed snake—the Naga. Behind her was a large slab with the contour of a human etched into its stone surface.

Pri Tor spoke in a low voice that only the Administrator could hear. "I regret to say that I tremble at what is to come."

"Your visions are incomplete," the Administrator said.

"I do not understand what these Ones Before want from us," Pri Tor said. "I thought we could defeat it," she added, nodding toward the approaching darkness.

"We will," the Administrator said. "But apparently not here and, more importantly, not now." He waited a moment. "You can come with us."

"My place is here and now," Pri Tor said. "I only know what must be done now to save the rest of the world in this time. We will take this attack with us into oblivion and save the possibilities for the future. It is time for you to escape and live in that future. I do not know where your travels will take you." She nodded toward the horizon. "I sent my other priestesses away last month. Spread to the far seas. Some will survive. Some will keep the bloodline of the Defenders viable. Keep the Sight viable. I have kept only the handful needed."

"You are the ruler of the twelve here and now," the Administrator acknowledged.

"And you will take the six over the paths of time," Pri Tor acknowledged. "Let us hope one of us ultimately succeeds."

"We have a little bit of time," the Administrator said, with a glance at the approaching darkness.

"Time." Pri Tor shook her head. "I do not understand it. I do not understand why it is this day, of all days, every year now."

The Administrator had no answer because he didn't understand either.

The High Defender reached out, lightly touching the Administrator's leather armor over his heart. "Believe here, before you think here," she pointed at his head. "That is the one message the Ones Before have sent consistently. Good must triumph over evil. Love over hate. We cannot think our way into that."

The Administrator bowed his head for a moment. "That is how it shall be and how we shall teach those who follow us."

Pri Tor's attention was elsewhere now. She called out to her priestesses. "It is time."

The dozen priestesses bowed their heads in prayer for several moments.

"Go," Pri Tor ordered. The priestesses made their way down the stairs and then scattered to the twelve positions on the walls that Pri Tor had chosen as a result of the vision she had been given. Meanwhile, Pri Tor took a dark red cloth from her pocket and draped it over her shoulders. It was inscribed with hieroglyphic writing, a gift from the Ones Before, one of the few substantial things received via a gate besides the triangular pedestals. As far as Pri Tor and the Administrator could tell, both the Shadow and the Ones Before used the gates, although no human had ever entered one and come back to tell of it, and no representative of either side had ever come out of the darkness of a gate into light.

Pri Tor glanced at the Administrator standing next to the short, black triangular column and amended that thought: so far.

Pri Tor walked to the slab and climbed onto it, standing tall, where she could see all of the capital of Atlantis spread out around her, a halo of captured sunlight surrounded by a tower wall of darkness. She saw the chosen thousand on the walls. *Would they be enough?* she wondered briefly, and then dismissed the doubt. It was one of many decisions she'd had to make in the past week as the inevitable drew near. They had to be enough. The plan she'd "heard" from the Ones Before had indicated a thousand should be sufficient and she had to trust in it.

Pri Tor raised her gaze beyond. The Shadow was closer. Pri Tor looked at the fortress walls. The thousand warriors were ready. At the twelve designated points along the walls, her priestesses stood.

Pri Tor felt a trembling beneath her feet. The ground itself was unsteady, a result of the Shadow's power.

She signaled and the two warriors came up the stairs and joined her.

"Be ready," Pri Tor ordered. One of the warriors put the spearhead into a slit next to the slab. His steady hand rested on the snakeheads.

Then Pri Tor lay down, her body fitting into the outline. She felt more tremors. High above, all she could see was blue sky. A single seagull flew overhead. She felt a tremendous wave of sadness knowing this was her last day. There would be no more beautiful dawns and wondrous sunsets. The simple joys and the pains of life were all to be ended, and she didn't understand why.

"How close?" she called out.

"Just about to touch the walls," the warrior informed her.

She could feel the sheer evil of the darkness that approached. Of that, there was no doubt. Theological questioning and reasoning aside, there was the reality of the threat that had proven itself again and again over the past seven years.

"At the walls," the warrior announced.

Pri Tor could hear the screams of the warriors at the city's outermost defenses as the darkness slid over them and they encountered what was inside. She closed her eyes. She "felt" a wave of bravery mixed with despair from the warriors.

With great effort, Pri Tor lifted her head and looked toward the walls. Darkness had encompassed the southwest part of the structure, but she could see the two priestesses who had been overrun as deep blue silhouettes in the blackness, a beacon of positive power. Their skulls were absorbing the same thing her mind was feeling, the raw power of the warriors' emotions, and the energy that was pouring through them to the pyramid.

The Administrator gave a signal and as one, the six men behind him placed their hands on top of their columns and they snapped out of existence in the here and now. His own hands hovered over his column. He gave one last look at the approaching darkness, back to Pri Tor, tears in his eyes, and then placed his hands on the flat surface and was gone.

A third and fourth Defender on the wall fell into the darkness. Bolts of blue, from the four now covered, flickered out to the others arranged around the wall, but most of the energy flew to the pyramid.

Pri Tor felt the power in her head building, almost unbearable. "Now," she ordered.

The warrior turned his spear.

The pyramid began to vibrate. A blue glow suffused the slab and Pri Tor's body. Energy from the outlying Defenders came toward her, adding to the power. Her mouth opened in a silent scream. The skin on her face began rippling as if there were something alive beneath it. Then her flesh began peeling away as her eyes turned into two blue glowing orbs.

The darkness was closer now on all sides. Seven of the twelve Defenders were covered, sucking in power from the doomed warriors' minds. Pri Tor had a moment of clarity when she realized what was happening—the absolute desperation of the warriors, combined with their bravery in the face of it, was tapping something primeval and very powerful, and the nearby Defenders were able to channel it to her.

Still the Shadow closed in.

Deep inside Pri Tor, she felt the darkness slide over the top of the pyramid and her body. She was still alive, her head the focal point of the skulls of twelve priestesses, the twelve Defenders, who had already given their all in the battle against the Shadow.

Her body felt faint and far away. She distantly heard a warrior shout something and then scream in agony. More power flowed in. All the Defenders were active now.

There was a pause and with a moment of clarity, she saw the lines of connection in the future: the descendants of her Defenders who had already left and spread out. Planting the seed of their line into their new lands. Moving forward into something she couldn't see. A bright light. The future.

Bolts of blue shot out of Pri Tor's head into the encompassing shadow.

Again and again, blue lightning burned off the top of the pyramid into the darkness. The consistency of the darkness began to change, swirls of blue mixing with the black, spinning about the top of the pyramid.

Pri Tor's head was now a clear crystal, suffused with blue. The power from the twelve Defenders still poured into the pyramid, their heads also crystallized, still channeling raw emotion from the dying warriors.

Neither Shadow nor Defender would yield.

So the Earth did.

The explosion centered on the pyramid, on a scale not seen since meteors battered the planet. A tidal wave more than a mile high spread outward from the center of the Atlantic, so powerful it circled the entire globe before slowly subsiding. Atlantis's thirteen islands were gone so completely, with no indication there had even been land in the center of the mighty ocean, no ruins for later civilizations to find.

And so it begins.

THE POSSIBILITY PALACE, HEADQUARTERS, TIME PATROL

When: Can't Tell You. Where: Can't Tell You.

"Forget everything you were told," Dane said to the Nightstalkers. A mousy woman in a gray suit handed him a manila file folder and waited. Dane was an average-sized man with thick hair that was prematurely gray. His beard was a few days removed from the last touch of a razor and there were deep bags under his eyes.

"Just great," Scout muttered.

"Roland already did," Mac said. "Never need worry about that."

"Told by who?" Moms asked. "You? Amelia Earhart? Her?" she added, with a nod toward Edith Frobish.

Dane was looking inside the folder. He frowned, pulled a pen out of his pocket and scrawled something inside, and then handed it back to the woman. "Okay. Maybe not *everything*."

"Too late for that," Mac said. "Roland just dumped what little he had."

Roland glared at Mac, not quite accepting the ribbing. It was somewhat astute of the big man to be defensive because underneath

Mac's comments, there was a pain. Unfortunately, Roland wasn't astute enough to recognize that pain had nothing to do with him. Neeley could have reassured Roland, but she wasn't here, so he was on his own, ill-equipped to handle a verbal assault but disciplined enough not to respond.

The woman in gray left, a door shutting behind her, cutting off the low roar of noise from the Palace. They were in a small room found through one of the many doors on the balcony. There was a wooden table in the center and lockers along the far wall. The wall behind Dane was covered with a large blackboard, imperfectly cleared of whatever had been written on it before with large smears of chalk going this way and that.

"Take a seat," Dane suggested.

The Nightstalkers, along with Edith Frobish, settled down in wooden chairs around the table.

"This will be your team room," Dane said. He pointed past them to another door. "There are sleeping quarters back there, but you won't be sleeping for a bit."

"Of course not," Scout muttered.

"We don't know how many parallel Earths there are," Dane began. "Amelia Earhart, from her position in the Space Between, has encountered people from what she believes are thirty-two different timelines, including her own, which is not ours. But it's a rather unscientific survey as it consists of her checking a particular history and seeing if it's radically different from other timelines. We believe the differences between timelines are often much more subtle. Some could seem exactly the same, but have differences that aren't immediately obvious."

"Infinite," Doc said. "There can be infinite timelines."

Dane nodded. "Theoretically, there *can* be. But how many are there really? If I make choice A instead of choice B, have I created a new timeline on my own? Are *my* choices that important? Are any of our choices that important to an overall timeline?"

"Probably not," Doc said. "You'd still have the one timeline, although your life might turn out a bit differently."

Dane nodded. "Correct. It is very, very difficult for a new timeline to split off; it requires a time tsunami. But it has happened. At least thirty-two times."

"How did the first split occur?" Ivar asked.

"You're asking how did the multiverse begin?" Dane said. It was obvious it wasn't a question he expected answered.

But Doc gave it a shot. "Perhaps at the bottom of the Possibility Palace. The start point of the spiral ramp. Isn't that the start point of our timeline?"

Dane sighed. "It's the start point of the Time Patrol. We're not even certain when our universe began. Maybe the multiverse started at the same time?

"Let's deal with the problem, not the theory. The problem is *our* timeline has been attacked and continues to be attacked, in various ways. What you just experienced with the Ratnik in our timeline was a test based on a real problem, an introduction to a concept many can't grasp. But it was also real. The Ratnik, the Russian Time Patrol, were a problem, one from our own timeline."

Moms spoke up. "Are there any other Time Patrols from our timeline, like the Ratnik?"

"Not that we're aware of," Dane said.

"Great," Scout muttered.

"One of the problems," Dane said, with a glance at Scout, "is that our timeline, and others, are not unified entities. We have wars and competing superpowers. We do not present a united front against the assaults from the Shadow even inside our own timeline, never mind across timelines."

"Like the United Nations," Doc observed.

"Indeed." Dane sighed. "Listen. We don't understand a lot of this. We do the best we can."

"And what's the best you expect of us?" Moms asked. "You've got all those people out there. You have other time travelers working for you. What do you want from *us*? You didn't randomly pick us and test us."

"No," Dane agreed. "We didn't. There's a new threat that we have to counter in a new way. Which is why we recruited you specifically." He nodded to his left, where Edith Frobish sat. "Some of what she told you is indeed true. The concept of time ripples, shifts, and a possible tsunami which could alter our timeline, or even wipe it out. However, we've learned of a new threat in terms of that. A more focused one. A potentially more dangerous one."

"Cutting to the headline," Scout said.

Dane graced her with a patient smile. "Sometimes a buildup is necessary. There is a paradigm called the Rule of Seven. This applies to a time shift occurring; in fact it applies to a lot of things. For time, it takes six ripples or changes, with the seventh one being the shift. We call these ripples 'cascade events.' Six cascade events lead to the seventh: the shift."

"And how many shifts to a tsunami?" Doc asked.

"We don't know," Dane said. "And we don't want to find out. We've been studying the Rule of Seven and we've found it applies to almost every manmade catastrophe or disaster. Six things go wrong, minor things, things most people never even notice, but the seventh is catastrophic. Plane crashes, for example. You can have five things go wrong and the plane is still flying. You don't even know how close you came to disaster. But when the sixth happens, that causes the seventh, cataclysmic event, the crash."

That caught Eagle's attention. "True. As a maintenance test pilot, I've had to study almost every major crash. None just happened without precursors. And pretty much every one could have been prevented if someone had paid attention to the events leading up to it."

Dane agreed. "And human error is always a factor. Thus these disasters can be prevented."

"And we're here for?" Moms prompted, getting back to her original question. "To pay attention?"

"Let me diagram this for you," Dane said. He turned to the board, shook his head at the mess, and then found a relatively clean area. He picked up a piece of chalk and drew three horizontal lines. He put an arrow at the right end of the center line. "Right here," he pointed at the arrow, "is the front of our timeline. The leading edge. When you came from. We can travel to anything before that. But not ahead of it; i.e., not into the future. That's the unknown."

He began making small x's above and below the central line but inside the top and bottom line. "These are ripples, cascade events. Changes in our history. Initiated by the Shadow. If we get six"—he began connecting the x's—"that are uncorrected, we get the seventh." He put a large X above the top line. "A shift outside the parameters of our timeline. History will change, which means our present will change in some way. We fear that a couple of shifts could send a time tsunami and wipe us out."

"You said this was a new development," Moms said. "How do you know about this Rule of Seven?"

"The Rule of Seven is old," Dane said. "But this mode of attack, using it in a specific way, is new." Dane turned to Edith. She pulled a scroll out of her leather briefcase.

"This is ancient," Edith said, laying the scroll on the table. "We believe around twelve thousand years old."

"Whoa, hold on," Doc said. "First. No paper would survive that long."

"It's not paper," Edith said. "Feel."

Doc reached across the table and slid his finger along the edge. It had a plastic texture, but it was thin and flexible. "What is it?"

"We don't know what the material is," Edith said. "And that's not really important. What's important is what's written on it."

Doc got to his feet and leaned over, looking at the scroll. "That's hieroglyphics."

"Yes," Edith said. She nodded toward the door that led to the Possibility Palace. "That's what we use as our common written language. We cover all eras and all times out there. Thus we need a common way to record what we know and communicate. These hieroglyphics are the oldest known language and surprisingly easy to learn."

Doc shook his head. "There wasn't even civilization, never mind writing in ten thousand BC."

"There *was* civilization," Dane said.

"Atlantis," Eagle said. "Earhart mentioned it in the Space Between."

"Indeed," Dane said. "The myth is based on reality." He pointed at the document Edith had unfurled. "That's from Atlantis and the original writing of mankind."

"What happened to Atlantis?" Moms asked.

Edith tapped the scroll, bringing attention back to it and her. "This partially explains things. It's the oldest document we have.

The foundation of the Time Patrol. It was brought here by survivors just prior to the destruction of Atlantis by the Shadow. It
tells how their empire was assaulted by the Shadow for six years;
six cascade events. And then in the seventh year, the final assault
came. The people who brought this document escaped via time
travel, back to an earlier time, and then relocated here."

"The bottom of the Possibility Palace," Ivar said.

"Correct," Edith said.

"So we must be in prehistory," Doc said. "Prior to the destruction of Atlantis?"

Dane and Edith ignored that.

"And you're not going to tell us where here is," Moms said.

"I'm not," Dane confirmed. "Nor when," he said, with a glance
at Doc.

"Why didn't the time travelers go back and save Atlantis?" Ivar
asked.

"It was too late," Dane said. "The six cascade events had
already occurred and they were in the midst of the seventh before
they were able to move through time."

"And how did they discover that little feat?" Moms asked.

"They didn't," Dane said. "They were given it."

Everyone waited for an explanation. Edith shifted uncomfortably in her seat.

Moms finally spoke up. "One of the tenets of the Nightstalkers
is that everyone knows everything possible about a mission. What
we don't know can get us killed."

"I understand," Dane said. "I served in MACV-SOG during
the Vietnam War."

That got the attention of those Nightstalkers who'd come out
of Special Operations. MACV-SOG stood for Military Assistance
Command Vietnam—Studies and Observations Group. It was a

rather innocuous title for a unit that conducted numerous covert, and often illegal, operations during the Vietnam War, including a number of cross-border missions.

Dane continued. "We've got a short fuse on this mission, folks. I know you're frustrated with a lack of information, but the reality is, there's a lot we don't know. We inherited time travel from the Atlanteans; we didn't invent it. How the Atlanteans got it: we don't know exactly."

"Pants on fire," Scout muttered.

"So," Mac said, focusing on the tactics, "six attacks and then the last one destroyed Atlantis."

"Exactly," Dane said. "A major shift in our timeline. But not a fatal one. Mankind survived and eventually flourished. The curious thing is, *every* timeline we've encountered records the destruction of Atlantis, even if only as a myth. It is the one commonality."

"Wait a second," Doc said. "That could be where the first timelines split off. The beginning of it."

"It could be," Dane admitted. "It's a theory our scientists argue. But no one knows for certain."

"And now?" Moms asked.

"And now," Dane said, "we think the Shadow is trying to shift *our* timeline again. Not in the way we're used to: trying for a major ripple or two, trying to cause a shift with a single bold move, but a more coordinated attack, similar to what happened to Atlantis, but still different."

"Different how?" Moms asked.

"More subtle," Dane said. "And following the Rule of Seven. The Shadow is going to infiltrate six points in history and try to change events, leading to the shift."

"And you want us to stop these changes." Moms didn't phrase it as a question.

Dane turned to Edith. "Tell them the key."

Edith tapped the scroll. "When Atlantis was first attacked, no special focus was paid to the day. But the second attack occurred exactly a year later. Then the third, a year to the day later. And the fourth. Fifth and sixth. And the final assault. All on the same day."

"What date?" Doc asked.

"We don't think the exact date matters," Edith said. "We believe what matters, according to what's written here, is that it's the exact same day of the year."

"Why?" Doc asked.

Edith shook her head. "If we knew the answer to that, we'd understand this all a lot more than we do."

"Could be celestial," Ivar said. "Same location in the orbit of Earth?"

Doc shook his head. "A year isn't perfectly exact. That's the reason we have leap years. It's not celestial. Besides the orbit isn't exact. The physics don't work out."

Dane sounded weary. "Again. We don't know *why*. And while Atlantis was attacked in roughly the same location, in successive years, the intelligence our operatives have picked up indicates that though the attacks will occur on the same day, they are years apart and spread out around the planet." Before being assaulted by more questions, Dane held up his hands in defense. "We don't know how the HUBs work. We don't know how other equipment we have works, such as the memory block-slash-download device that was used on Edith during your test."

"And on my team sergeant," Moms said, a tint of anger in her voice.

Dane pursed his lips at the chill that blanketed the room at the mention of their former team sergeant. "Nada made his choice. We all did."

"His freedom of choice was taken away from him for a long time," Moms said.

"For his own good," Dane replied. "And that wasn't my decision. That was a decision inside the present by your own people." He waved a hand, forestalling Moms's next words. "This is not the time or place to discuss this matter. We're on the clock here."

"How so?" Scout asked, with a glance at Moms.

"We're getting indications," Dane said, "that some of these ripples are in the process of occurring. We believe some are pending. The key is that there's been no shift yet, so we still have time to stop it from happening. But it has to be coordinated. All the missions inside the same twenty-four-hour window on that particular day, whatever year it happens to be."

"I'm confused," Doc said, speaking for the rest of the team.

"My head hurts," Roland said. Doc and Roland both being confused was like cats and dogs living together, a sign of the Nightstalkers' universe being out of balance.

"I'm not far behind you," Moms commiserated. "Let me see if we can get past the theory, or more appropriately leave it behind. You want us to run six concurrent ops to the same day in the past?"

"Same day, different years," Dane said.

"What day?" Moms asked.

"The twenty-ninth of October. Most famously known as Black Tuesday in 1929, but we also have five other years."

"What years?"

Dane glanced over at Edith. She opened up a file folder next to the scroll. "All AD. 999. 1618. 1929, of course. 1969. 1972. And 1980."

Moms stood. "When do we deploy?"

"In three hours," Dane said. "There's much to be done between now and then. Edith will take each of you to a team that will outfit you in the appropriate clothing and with the gear you'll need. Then we will have a mission briefing here in an hour."

The White House

"So the world wasn't at stake?" The President made her words both a statement and a question, a skill any good politician needs to have.

"Apparently not, Madam President." The Keep had the leather-bound Book of Truths open. A quill pen, once wielded by Thomas Jefferson, was in her hand and a small bottle of ink awaited its dip. She looked at the President, who was seated across from the Keep's tiny desk.

They were in the Keep's office in the attic of the White House, a tiny cubicle most who worked in the building weren't even aware existed, tucked away among the offices for housekeeping and other maintenance staff. The only person in the entire building who knew what the Keep did was the President. Everyone else thought she worked for someone else.

The Keep's job was maintaining the Book of Truths.

And briefing the President when there were incidents from the world of secrets that were beyond the province of the CIA,

NSA, and the rest of the alphabet-soup agencies. There were a few more of those than any head of state ever liked, and they inspired additions to the gray hair one can track spreading on the president's head as they made their way through terms in office, wrestling with the secrets the public is never privy to.

"Nothing at all in there about the Time Patrol?" the President asked.

"No, ma'am."

"That's not good," the President said.

The Keep had no opinion on that. That wasn't her job. She was a tiny woman, slender, with short black hair. There were a few more strands of gray sprinkled about in that black than there had been just a week ago.

Such was the effect of the revelation of the Time Patrol and Foreman's ruse that the world would end in twelve hours if the Patrol wasn't "rescued." That hadn't quite been the truth. While there had been a real problem with the Ratnik, the reality was that Foreman had used the incident to test the Nightstalkers in order to recruit them into the Patrol.

"But there should be something in there now about the Time Patrol." The President wasn't asking, but the Keep answered anyway.

"Yes, ma'am." She held the pen, waiting for the words, but they didn't come. Not yet.

There was a knock on the door and a Secret Service agent popped his head in. "He's here, Madam President."

"Send him in."

The small office got tighter as Foreman entered the room. The old man used a cane, a concession to his age and bad knees. He wore a suit that was out of style at least a decade ago and held a porkpie hat in his other hand. Covered by a fedora, his once-thick white hair was now thinner and he was rail thin, the kind of weight loss that wasn't healthy.

"Nice of you to make it," the President said in a tone that indicated she didn't think it was nice of him at all.

"I work for you, Madam President," Foreman said with a slight bow of his head.

"Do you?" the President asked.

Foreman eyed the third chair in the room, but the President didn't give him permission to sit. Power hath its privileges and anger hath its petty revenges.

"Of course," Foreman said. Before the President could say anything, he quickly followed that up, lest she misinterpret and think she had "hand." "I work for the office, ma'am. Majestic-12 was formed by presidential decree after World War Two. My office was a spin-off from that. I understand you feel blindsided by recent revelations, but believe me, there was no intent to deceive you. No president has been aware of the existence of the Time Patrol. It's not personal."

"I'm not taking it personally," the President said in a clipped tone that her husband could have told Foreman meant she was indeed taking it personally. "Truman formed Majestic-12. It's in the book." She nodded toward the Keep. "But the Time Patrol isn't mentioned. The Nightstalkers are, among other groups such as the Cellar. Was Truman aware of the Time Patrol?"

"He didn't have a need to know," Foreman said.

"The president didn't have a need to know?" The President was not pleased.

"You have to remember," Foreman said, "that Truman didn't know of the Manhattan Project until after FDR died. Compartmentalization is the key to secrecy."

"And abuse of secrecy," the President said. "Doesn't the revelation that time travel exists change our framework of reality?"

"Not really," Foreman said, once more eyeing the seat.

"Oh, sit down," the President said in exasperation.

Foreman settled into the seat with a grateful sigh. He put the cane across his knees and rested the *Breaking Bad* hat on top of it.

"It changes *my* perception of reality," the President said. "How about you?" she asked the Keep.

The woman was startled to be asked something so bluntly. "I always thought that if time travel existed, then it must exist in the present, if that makes sense."

The President blinked, processing that, but Foreman graced her with a smile.

"An excellent observation," Foreman said. "And it makes perfect sense. Even if we didn't have time travel today, if someone in the future invents it, then it exists now. Takes a moment to wrap one's brain around it. Except time travel has existed for a very, very long time."

He shifted back to the President. "Madam President, the thing to remember is that we, our time, goes on as usual. The purpose of the Patrol is to ensure that. We are the front of, shall we call it, a time wave. The future is unknown." He paused, looking between the Keep and the President. "You are aware, of course, that we cannot time travel into the future?"

"Yes," the President snapped. "So I've been told."

Foreman smiled. "Then the Time Patrol really is of no consequence as long as it does its job and maintains the integrity of our timeline."

"And if it doesn't?" the President asked.

Foreman shrugged. "There's not much we can do about it in the here and now. Your job, and everyone else's who has power, is to maintain our timeline and look to the future. To keep ourselves from blowing our world up with nuclear weapons. To prevent climate change from devastating the planet. You take care of the present and the future. The Patrol takes care of the past."

"You're telling me my job?" The President glared at Foreman.

"Madam President, I'm simply telling you the way things are."

"I don't like being played, Mister Foreman. I had the Keep deploy Furtherance to New York City," she said, referring to the Keep's placement of a nuclear weapon deep underneath the Metropolitan Museum of Art in the center of Manhattan. "And it was armed and ticking down. Not a great example of taking care of the present, but I did it because I was kept in the dark about your little test."

"I'm aware of that," Foreman said. "I was there. But, remember, it didn't go off. Everything worked out fine."

"I don't like you, Mister Foreman," the President said.

A muscle twitched on Foreman's face, but that was the extent of his reaction.

She continued. "What a president gives, a president can take away."

"I'm just a part of the machinery," Foreman said. "The Patrol goes on with or without me."

"Its funding doesn't."

"I'm afraid, Madam President, that it does. That appropriation is grandfathered into the budget so tightly, you'd have to reveal everything in the Black Budget to the world. And we certainly can't do that, can we?"

Foreman didn't smile, but there was a relish to his words. A satisfaction of old age and experience versus youth and pettiness. Foreman had lived through many presidents. He'd outlasted every other bureaucrat in Washington. He'd faced down chiefs of staff, generals, senators, admirals, and more. "And besides," Foreman added, almost as a taunt, "we have our own internal funding as needed."

The President didn't rise to the bait; she had her own set of skills. "I need more information, Mister Foreman. Since the Time Patrol has been such a big secret, why reveal it now? Just to test the Nightstalkers? Take down the Ratnik? And, by the way, did the Soviet government know about their own time patrol? And that it went rogue?"

Foreman tackled the questions backward. "There was a man in the Soviet government who held a position similar to mine. He was the liaison to the Ratnik. He is long dead. The program is long dead. Once Chernobyl went critical, that was the end of that. The Ratnik escaped into the Space Between, their base in our time was destroyed, and now they no longer exist. The Nightstalkers saw to that."

"So the Chernobyl meltdown happened because of the Ratnik and time travel?" the President asked.

"The Russians had a base near Chernobyl," Foreman said, "named Duga 3. We knew they were doing something strange there. The unofficial secret rumor was that it was part of an over-the-horizon radar system, part of an anti-ballistic-missile warning setup. It wasn't. We learned, too late, that the Russians had stolen information about time travel from us. And were trying their own experiments. It didn't work out quite right for them."

"Who is this 'we'?" the President asked. She glanced at the Keep. "Anything in the Book of Truths about that? I don't remember you telling me anything."

"Negative," the Keep said.

"So who is 'we'?" the President asked Foreman.

"I was using the pejorative," Foreman said.

"I think you're full of shit," the President said.

The Keep's only reaction was to raise an eyebrow.

"The Nightstalkers were needed," Foreman continued. "There is a new threat with a short fuse, one it was felt needs to be dealt with. And you need to be warned about."

"You just told me that the Time Patrol is of no consequence to our time," the President said.

"If it fails in the face of this new threat, it is."

That brought a few moments of silence before Foreman continued.

"Our enemy, the Shadow, is trying a new tactic. Or perhaps resurrecting an old tactic. We're really not sure." He went on to explain the Rule of Seven to the President and the Keep.

"The good news," Foreman said, "is that the odds are in our favor. The Shadow has to change all six events in order to cause a shift."

"How do you know this?" the President asked.

"It's how Atlantis was destroyed," Foreman said.

"'Atlantis'?" the President repeated. "Are you serious?"

"And," Foreman said, "we've received several reports of this tactic being used on other timelines."

"I'm still on Atlantis," the President said.

"You know as much as I know about that," Foreman said. "It existed. It was destroyed by the Shadow."

"I doubt that I know as much as you," the President replied. "Where was Atlantis? It's a myth. Mentioned only by Plato."

"Your schooling in the classics is correct," Foreman said, "but I assure you, Atlantis did exist. And it was destroyed."

The President scrunched her eyes shut and then rubbed them. Her husband could have told both Foreman and the Keep that this meant she was on the verge of either exploding in anger or accepting defeat, rarely the latter. She opened her eyes. "If there's nothing I can do about the Time Patrol, I ask you again: *Why* are you telling me this?"

"Because you need to prepare contingencies in case the Patrol fails and we get hit with a time tsunami."

"And what will happen if such a tsunami hits?"

"At the very least," Foreman said, "civilization will collapse. We're more vulnerable than ever before in our history to a tsunami. Most people don't realize it, but we're only about a week away from the collapse of civilization if the delicate infrastructure that supports it is broken. The world has become so much smaller and interdependent than ever before. With greater advancement comes greater danger."

"What about at the very worst?" the President asked.

"Our timeline will blink out of existence," Foreman said.

"Not much I can do about *that*, is there?" the President said.

"No. There isn't."

The President stared at him for a few moments. "You're lying to me. I've been in politics long enough to recognize that. I've been around some of the greatest bullshitters there are. And you, Mister Foreman, rank up there."

Foreman got to his feet with difficulty. "Is that all, Madam President?"

"You tell me," the President said. "Is that all you're going to tell me?"

"Yes, ma'am."

"Get out of here."

With a slight bow, Foreman left the Keep's office.

The President turned to the Keep. "What do you think?"

The Keep shook her head. "I'm still processing time travel and Atlantis."

Surprisingly, the President laughed. "I've given up trying to understand any of this. When you briefed me shortly after I took office from that book on the Nightstalkers and Rifts and the Cellar and all that other incredible stuff, I think my mind either broke or expanded to accept pretty much anything. We don't have to process this stuff. We need to deal with it.

"I want to talk to Hannah."

THE POSSIBILITY PALACE, HEADQUARTERS, TIME PATROL

When: Can't Tell You. Where: Can't Tell You.

Roland laughed, pointing at Mac. "Nice legs, dude."

"Shut up," Mac snapped.

"Oh come on," Roland said. "You're kind of cute and—"

Mac whipped a rapier out of his belt. Roland was almost as fast with the longsword already in his hand. Each blade came to rest on the opposing man's throat, pressing against the skin.

The fact each went on the offensive and for the throat, rather than trying to block the other, said everything there was to know about the mentality of the Nightstalkers. The fact neither would ever follow through said everything about teamwork.

"Easy," Moms said. "Easy, men."

Roland pulled the sword away, always obedient to Moms's slightest command. Mac gave it a second, and then pulled away the rapier. Mac was dressed in Elizabethan garb, the tight leggings below the short pants the prompt for Roland's comment. He also had on a "puffy" shirt underneath a doublet and a cloak.

His natural good looks were actually enhanced by the clothes; he could step on any stage and be considered a Tom Cruise look-alike.

Roland *wasn't* looking better in worn leather pants and tunic. His large arms were bare, along with most of his chest, making him a perfect candidate for a romance novel cover.

Moms stepped between them, outfitted for cold weather, pre-Gore-Tex and all the other high-speed gear that had been developed in the last couple of decades, her outfit consisting of mostly wool with white camouflage outer garments. An M14 with a bulky suppressor on the end of the barrel was slung over her shoulder.

"Play nice," Moms said. "Roland. Say you're sorry to Mac."

"I'm sorry," Roland murmured, his face red from Moms's rebuke.

"Mac?" Moms said, feeling like she was shepherding kindergartners.

"Yeah, okay."

"You look very nice," Moms said to Mac, who twitched a smile in response.

The door opened and Eagle walked in wearing Vietnam-era OD green jungle fatigues with an old external-frame rucksack over one shoulder and an M16 with a blank adapter on the end of the barrel over the other. He had on a patrol cap, which he took off.

"We were out of Vietnam by 1980," Moms said to Eagle.

He nodded. "Got to be something else. Somewhere else. The blank adapter suggests a training environment." He looked at Mac. "1618. Looks like England for you." Then Roland and his large sword. "Perfect fit. Looks like you get to kill someone or something, big man."

Roland nodded, eager to be out of there and into the action. He twirled the sword, belying its weight. "It has good balance.

Good steel." He sounded like a man talking about a woman he loved, but that was Roland's way with weapons.

And he'd never talk about Neeley in front of the team because he truly loved her and that was locked deep into his heart.

"You're going someplace cold," Eagle said to Moms.

"No frak, Sherlock." Moms looked none too pleased by the prospect.

Ivar walked in, appearing as if he might be auditioning for a gangster movie in the roaring twenties. He had a fedora pulled down low over his eyes and wore a sharp suit.

"Yours is the easiest," Eagle said, nodding at Ivar. "October 29, 1929 was Black Tuesday. 10-29-29. The stock market crash that brought on the Great Depression."

Ivar took off his hat. "Seems like we ought to be stopping the Great Depression."

"Not the way it works," Moms said. "We maintain history."

"Yeah," Ivar said, "but—" He stopped as the door opened and Scout came in, followed by Edith Frobish and Doc.

"Well," Moms said as she took in Scout. She couldn't find the words to say anything more. The rest of the team was similarly dumbstruck.

Scout was ready for Woodstock. She wore low-riding jeans sporting a wide leather belt and a peasant top that bared her midriff. Her hair was parted in the middle and lacked its usual streaks of color. She didn't look happy.

"Nice threads," Roland finally said.

Scout gave him the stink eye. "Right." But she followed it with an appreciative smile, because, like Moms, she knew Roland had a good heart. What he said, he meant.

"1969," Eagle said. "A time of great turmoil. But also exciting."

"Right," Scout repeated, clearly uncomfortable in the outfit.

"Your clothes are authentic," Edith said. "Supplied by agents from the era you will be infiltrating."

Roland scratched underneath his armpit.

"You stink," Mac noted.

"The clothes stink," Roland said, taking a deep sniff.

"Again," Edith said, failing to see the humor, "the clothes are accurate and well worn."

"What about me?" Doc asked.

"You're staying here," Edith said. "There's some data that we would like you to look over."

Doc didn't seem overly disappointed.

"Sir Walter Raleigh," Eagle said, looking at Mac.

"What?" the team's demo man said.

"October 29, 1618," Eagle said, drawing on his massive memory. "On that date, Sir Walter Raleigh, favorite of Queen Elizabeth, was beheaded. Seems to be the most likely event on that day in that year for you to be dealing with."

"So I make sure this guy Raleigh gets his head chopped off?" Mac asked.

"It might not be that simple," Edith hedged. "Wait until Dane gets here and can brief you." She turned to the rest of the team. "Next we—"

"Hold on," Moms said. "There's something the team has to do first."

Edith opened her mouth to say something, but Moms's tone stopped her.

"We take care of our own," Moms said.

The team gathered round her and linked hands, leaving Edith standing nervously near the blackboard.

Moms continued. "It is Protocol for us to acknowledge the death of a Nightstalker because no one else will. We must pay our respect and give honors.

"He was named Nada by the team," Moms said, "but in death he regains his name and his past. Sergeant Major Edward Moreno, US Army Infantry and then Special Forces, Delta Force and Nightstalker, has made the ultimate sacrifice for his country, for his world, and for mankind. We all speak his rank and his name as it was."

The team spoke together. "Sergeant Major Edward Moreno."

Edith Frobish had seen this before, in New York when the team paid its respects to Kirk after he was killed by a Valkyrie. She bowed her head out of respect.

"We, the Nightstalkers," Moms continued, "have seen many things and been many places. We don't know the limits of science and we don't know the limits of the soul. If there is some life after this, or some existence on a plane we can't even conceive of"—at that, Moms gave a glance toward Edith—"then we know Nada is there, in a good place. Because that is what he deserves for performing his duty without any acknowledgment and for making the ultimate sacrifice. If there is nothingness in death, then he is in his final peace and will not be troubled any more by the nightmares of this world having fought them to his death."

There was a moment of silence before Moms continued.

"He is buried at Arlington, in a place of honor. He died on a mission for the Time Patrol. Changing an event in the past so the present would be a better place."

When she paused, Eagle spoke up. "He died so that Kirk could live. A different life, but a life where Kirk takes care of his family."

Moms continued. "He leaves behind a wife and daughter we never knew of. As Nada always insisted, we take care of our own.

His family will not do without. They will be protected by the Nightstalkers to our death."

There was a silence, broken only by Scout sniffling and holding back her sobs. Finally, the youngest member of the team spoke through her grief. "All we can do is keep him in our hearts."

"In our hearts," the rest of the team, and Edith, murmured.

Then Moms did as she regularly did. She reminded them. "Why are we here? Because someone has to man the walls in the middle of the night. The walls between the innocents who go to sleep each night with only the troubles they see in their lives. Normal troubles. Who know little, if anything, of the dangers, the nightmares, surrounding our world. Who need people like us to stand watch over them. To protect them from"—Moms paused— "the Shadow. And the forces it sends against our timeline. Trying to obliterate us and everyone we know, and everyone we love, from existence.

"We fight against things like the Valkyries and the kraken and whatever else is sent against us. We've defeated Fireflies and shut Rifts. We've stopped the folly of man destroying our own world with nuclear weapons."

And then she intoned the lines that the deceased Ms. Jones used to remind the team of every time they came back from a mission when they were battered and hurting and wondering if it was all worth it.

"We are here," Moms said, "because the best of intentions can go horribly awry and the worst of intentions can achieve exactly what it sets out to do. It is often the noblest scientific inquiry that can produce the end of us all. We are here because we are the last defense when the desire to do right turns into a wrong. We are here because mankind advances through trial and error. Because nothing man does is ever perfect. And we are ultimately here because there are things out there, beyond mankind's current knowledge level, which man must be guarded against until we can understand those things, as we finally understood the Rifts and the Fireflies and our role in that. We must remember this." Moms took a deep breath. "Can we all live with that?"

Everyone, Edith included, nodded.

"Impressive," Dane said. He was in an open door on the other side of the room, entering unnoticed during the ceremony. "You have my condolences on the loss of your teammate. He died bravely and for good cause."

"I saw his grave," Scout said, surprising everyone.

"When?" Moms asked. "How did you make it—"

"In a dream," Scout said. "I saw it at Arlington. A young girl was there. Isabella. His daughter. She was grieving. It was in 2005."

An uneasy silence settled over the team room.

Dane was the first to speak. "Sin Fen said you had a touch of the Sight."

"And what is that?" Scout asked.

"To see things others can't see," Dane said. "To see back in time. Sometimes even get visions of what might be. To see possibilities and realities and memories you shouldn't have."

"Where does it come from?" Scout asked.

Dane shrugged. "We're not sure."

"Bull," Moms said. "You know more than you're telling us."

"Let's focus on the mission," Dane said, once more raising the shield of mission first, information second. "We don't have much time before launch."

Moms indicated the team members and their outfits. "Just because we're dressed right doesn't mean we're going to fit in."

"True," Dane acknowledged. He held up a device they had all seen before—the memory blocker Frasier had used to unlock Edith's memories, and Nada's. "This does more than block memories and restore them. It also downloads knowledge. Language, directly into your brain so that you can immediately understand and speak a particular tongue. All you'll need to know about the place and time you will be going to. It can be a bit overwhelming, but remember, you should have an agent in place who will assist you. Each agent is from the time and place you'll be going, so that gives you extra cover."

"Should we know each other's missions?" Moms asked. "Doesn't that violate security?"

Dane shook his head. "Your missions run simultaneous to each other. And"—he paused, as if considering how to broach the subject—"the Shadow is already ahead of you. We know the date and the years because agents close to the years have reported the beginning of ripples. Your job is to stop those ripples."

"I don't get it," Mac said. "If the Shadow has already changed things, aren't we too late?"

Dane sighed. "There's a lot we don't understand. The best I can explain these ideas are in the way the scientists explained them to me, and I don't think they know as much as they think they know."

"Ain't that always the truth," Roland said with a glance at Doc, a rather amazing cutting observation coming from Roland.

"The day each of you are going to," Dane said, "is like a bubble. A bubble in time. It doesn't matter what happens during the actual day; what matters is the result at the end of the day. Is the result the same or is the result different? Right now, agents are picking up ripples of possibilities. But the bubble is still there."

"That's why this is called the Possibility Palace," Edith threw in, gaining her an eye roll from Scout.

"Your job is to make the result the same as history recorded it," Dane said.

"We just show up?" Ivar asked. "Isn't that going to be obvious?"

"No," Dane said. "It's a bubble where all before and all after are question marks. You'll arrive being part of what you come into. The only one who will know you're 'new' will be the Time Patrol agent who should be there to meet you."

"'Should'?" Scout said.

"Should," Dane said. "The vagaries of the variables."

"You sound like a politician," Scout said.

Dane stared hard at her. "I do the best I can." His head dropped for a moment, as if accepting Scout's take on things. "The problem is, we're not sure exactly what the Shadow is doing to change the past. We're pretty sure of the events for each of you. Well, almost all of you."

"Which are?" Moms asked.

"That's the briefing I'm going to give you now," Dane said. "Before you go to get downloaded and infiltrated through time to your objective."

"Isn't that backward?" Eagle asked. "Shouldn't we be downloaded before you brief us? That way we have the knowledge base?"

Dane shook his head. "And that way you start heading down the wormhole overwhelmed with information. Remember, information is not intelligence. We know where and when you're going so that gives us the most likely key event the Shadow will try to manipulate, but I want to emphasize that you must keep an open mind. If we cloud your brain beforehand, there's a danger you'll get tunnel vision. Also, you won't know how to sort the information that's going to be poured into your head into intelligence you can use."

That satisfied Eagle and the rest of the team.

Dane walked to the blackboard. He wrote:

1618 AD—ENGLAND

He pointed at Mac. "As you already guessed, Elizabethan England. The 29th of October, 1618, is the date on which Sir Walter Raleigh was executed. You'll get all the details on the execution and why it happened and his background during download. The most obvious thing the Shadow could do is prevent the execution. So it's possible that isn't its plan at all. It could be misdirection for a number of other things on that day, like an attempt on the life of King James the First, who succeeded Elizabeth. Also, that year was the start of the Thirty Years' War, which ravaged Europe. It's doubtful any single event occurring on that day could stop that war, but who knows?"

"Helpful," Mac said in a tone that indicated it wasn't helpful at all.

Dane gave a wry smile. "It's why we recruited the Nightstalkers. The best of the best and all that."

"Blow smoke somewhere else," Moms said.

"It's not smoke," Dane said. "You're Special Operations, and as Nightstalkers you've been involved in events far beyond that which ordinary people can even fathom as you yourself just said in your touching ceremony honoring your team sergeant. We trust your judgment. It's why we recruited you." From anyone else it would have seemed patronizing, but they could all sense Dane's sincerity. He was a warrior like them, tested and forged in combat.

No one had anything to say to that, so Dane wrote on the board:

1972—ANDES MOUNTAINS

"Moms, as you can tell by your outfit, this is yours. On the 13th of October in 1972, Uruguayan Flight 571, carrying forty-five passengers and crew, crashed in the Andes. Twelve died immediately in the crash and five the day after and another on the 21st. On the 29th, your day, an avalanche sweeps over the crash site, killing another eight."

"*Alive!*" Eagle said, emphasizing the word, and referring to the bestseller written about the event.

"Indeed," Dane said. "Two of the survivors eventually make an epic ten-day journey over the mountains to get rescue."

"You're skipping over the anthropophagy," Eagle said.

"Huh?" Roland said.

"Ditto," Scout added, earning an appreciative glance from Roland.

"Cannibalism," Eagle explained. "They ended up having to eat their dead in order to survive."

"Oh," Roland said, and it was obvious he was ponderously rolling the implications of that around in his brain.

"I don't get it," Moms said. "Am I supposed to stop the avalanche? Actually, make sure it happens? Isn't it an act of nature?"

Dane shrugged. "Again, your call once you're on the ground. We know the avalanche happened. Perhaps it's the goal of the Shadow to stop the avalanche? Keep one of those who died alive? Or something completely different. Make sure none of them survived the avalanche?"

"Great," Moms said.

Dane ignored that and wrote on the board once more:

1929—NEW YORK CITY

"Duh," Ivar said. "That was the easy one."

Dane agreed. "Black Tuesday. The implications are huge. The world, not just the United States, plunged into the Great Depression that lasted until after World War Two."

"I doubt the Shadow could stop that from happening," Eagle said.

"Wait a second," Ivar said. "What if it could? Would that be a bad thing?"

Dane stared hard at Ivar. "When we recruited you, I gave you a choice. Whether you would go back and change something in the past if you could or whether you were willing to move forward. That was a personal choice. You have no choice now. Our timeline must be maintained no matter what you think or feel.

"Additionally," Dane continued, "our timeline exists and is functioning. Maybe not perfectly, but let me tell you something." An edge had crept into his voice. "We've learned what happens when things *don't* work. Worlds where humanity has been wiped out. We'll take what we have right now over possibilities of making things 'better.' Because you have no idea what changing things will unleash. Say the Shadow stops the Great Depression? What then? Maybe there's no World War Two. Or maybe there's a delayed World War Two and both Germany and the United States develop nuclear weapons. But the Germans have the rocket capability to reach targets in America and the US can't reach Germany?" Dane shook his head. "Maybe this and maybe that." He pointed at Ivar. "The creed of the Time Patrol is to maintain our timeline at any cost. If you don't like that, you can remake your personal choice and be gone from here."

Ivar put his hands up defensively. "Whoa. Listen, I was just throwing out an idea."

Dane took a deep breath, and then turned back to the board, ending that discussion. He wrote:

1980—*EGLIN AIR FORCE BASE*

"Not Ranger School," Eagle said. "I did it once. Not again."

"I did it too," Dane said. "A long time ago. And it kept me alive in Vietnam. You *will* be going to a Ranger patrol, but only because your objective is on the Eglin reservation: Operation Credible Sport."

The team turned to Eagle, expecting his vast trove of information would spill forth with what Dane was referring to, but for once he came up blank.

Dane continued. "Earlier in 1980, on the 24th of April, an attempt was made to free the hostages in Tehran."

"Operation Eagle Claw," Eagle said.

"Yes," Dane said. "It failed. Eight servicemen were killed."

Every member of the team who'd been in Special Operations before the Nightstalkers knew about Eagle Claw. It was the start of the Special Operations Command and many other changes in the military. It was part of their legacy.

"Even though it failed," Dane said, "the military did not give up. A task force was—" He paused as a door opened and one of the nondescript people in gray came in without a word and handed him a thin folder. Dane opened it, read, grimaced, wrote something, gave it back, and then the person was gone.

"Bad news?" Moms asked.

Dane ignored her. "A task force was formed to come up with another mission to rescue the hostages. Operation Credible Sport was to be that second rescue attempt."

"But there wasn't a second one," Eagle said.

"Exactly," Dane said. "Credible Sport failed during preparation. Because of the helicopter failures of Eagle Claw, Credible Sport involved retrofitting a C-130 transport plane with rocket engines to allow it to land and take off from the short field inside a soccer stadium across from where the hostages were being held. On the 29th of October, they were conducting the last test at Wagner Field on the Eglin Reservation. Up to that point, everything had worked perfectly. Every takeoff and landing on spot. It looked like the plan was a go.

"As the plane was attempting to land on this last test, the

braking rockets were fired too soon while the plane was still in the air and the vertical rockets didn't fire. The plane slammed into the ground and the right wing broke off. The plane caught on fire. No one was killed, but the project was scrapped. There was no second rescue attempt and the hostages were released just after President Reagan was inaugurated later that year."

"So the Shadow is going to try to make that last test a success?" Eagle asked. "Have the rescue mission be a go?"

"Again," Dane said, "we don't know. But it's the most likely scenario. We've projected several possibilities: What if the second attempt succeeded and the hostages were rescued? What if the second attempt failed during the mission in a disaster that dwarfed Eagle Claw? The plan called for gunships to support the assault. There is the possibility hundreds, if not thousands, of Iranians might have been killed in the attempt along with the hostages and the rescue forces."

"How did the braking rockets get fired too soon?" Eagle asked, focusing on the technical aspect and leaving the what-ifs to Ivar and Doc.

"Two versions," Dane said. "One is that the flight engineer manually fired them too soon. He denied that, of course. Lockheed engineers working on the project claim it was an electrical malfunction, which caused the braking rockets to fire early and the descent-braking rockets not to fire. Regardless, the plane crashed."

"All right," Eagle said.

"Again, though," Dane said, "stay open to possibilities."

"Of course," Eagle said dryly. "Possibilities. Vagaries."

"Listen," Dane said, "most people think history is written in stone. But history is part of perspective. You've heard the saying that the victor writes history? Expand that to realize that humans write history. And those doing the writing are rarely objective. They approach it with an angle. Sometimes we know what happened but we don't know *why* it happened. Sometimes we don't know *how* it happened. Does that make sense?" Dane looked around the room, meeting each member of the team in the eyes. He got a nod from each one, some more reluctant than others.

"So keep an open mind."

Dane looked at Scout, a faint smile on his lips. "I remember when women wore clothes like that. It was a different time. An exciting time, but also a time filled with tragedy, especially after all that happened in 1968—Robert Kennedy and King assassinated. Tet. That was a bad year." The smile was gone and his gaze was a bit unfocused, but he quickly got back on task. He wrote on the board:

1969—UCLA

This time Eagle beat him to the punch. "ARPANET."

"Most likely," Dane acknowledged.

"English," Scout said.

"Advanced Research Projects Agency Network," Eagle said. "Established under DARPA."

"Oh," Scout said. "I get it now. Not."

Dane explained. "ARPANET was the first data transmission project. A way to get computers to talk to each other."

"The Internet," Eagle clarified. "It started with ARPANET."

"And on the 29th of October, 1969," Dane said, "the very first Internet message was sent from a computer at UCLA to one at Stanford."

"I don't know much about computers," Scout warned, already dreading this.

"You will soon," Dane said. "The Internet was initially funded by the Department of Defense. Some say it was because they wanted a way to communicate in case of nuclear war, but that's not correct, at least not initially. The focus was on getting computers, often very different from each other, to communicate with each other. That night, the first message was sent. It wasn't exactly mind-boggling, like Morse tapping out 'What hath God wrought' or Bell saying 'Come here Watson, I need you.' The man at UCLA, Charley Kline, was typing in 'LOGIN.' He got to the G and the system on the other end, at Stanford, crashed."

"Exciting," Scout said. "So what would be the problem? The thing didn't even really work."

"It worked," Dane said. "And from it, we've got the Internet we know today. Do you realize how much of our infrastructure relies on the Internet?"

"So the Shadow wants to stop this message from getting through?" Scout asked. "That stops the Internet? Wouldn't they try the next day?"

"Again," Dane said, with a bit of exasperation, about as much as the team was feeling, "we don't know what the Shadow is trying to do. But who knows what even just a day delay in the development of the Internet would do? And maybe the Shadow has its sights set on something bigger than just stopping that message?"

"Okeydokey," Scout said. "Why do I get the nerd mission?" She nodded at Doc. "Seems he should be dealing with the computer eggheads."

"It's yours," Dane said with a finality that silenced Scout. He turned back to the board and wrote:

999 AD—ENGLAND

Dane pointed at Roland. "That's you. It's also the vaguest mission."

"Given to the vaguest guy," Mac said.

Dane ignored that. "You'll infiltrate onto a Viking ship that's just off the coast of England."

"Cool," Roland said.

"Beyond that, we really haven't a clue what your mission is," Dane said.

"That's okay," Mac said. "Roland doesn't either."

Roland was still focused on the Viking aspect so he barely heard Mac.

"Nothing significant historically on that day?" Moms asked.

"Not that we've been able to uncover," Dane said. "October is late in the season for a Viking raid. We're hoping there's an agent on that ship who can brief Roland."

"You better—" Mac began, but a sharp glance from Moms shut him down.

"I'll make it work," Roland said, having no clue what the *it* was.

Dane nodded, realizing Frasier had been right in the choice. "Good. The next step is for all of you to get downloaded."

"Is that all that's going to happen?" Moms asked. "Are you going to block certain memories also? Is that why it doesn't matter that we know what each other's mission is?"

"Perceptive," Dane said. "We will block certain information about this place and the Patrol. And our timeline. The less information the Shadow gets, the better."

"'Gets'?" Ivar repeated. "How would it get information from us?"

"If we're captured," Moms said. "Remember what the Ratnik were doing to those people in the Space Between?"

"Oh," Ivar said.

"Let's move out," Dane said, indicating a door.

The Cellar

Hannah looked across her desk at Neeley. "Why didn't you go with the Nightstalkers?"

"My place is here," Neeley replied. "And my time is now."

They were in Hannah's office deep underneath the National Security Agency headquarters at Fort Meade, Maryland. Hannah ran the Cellar, a unique organization tasked with policing the world of secret organizations and the spies and operatives who dwelled there, in the shadows and the darkness.

But the realization that a Time Patrol existed, that there was time travel, that our world was under threat from other timelines and other times, had caught Hannah off guard.

"Besides," Neeley added, "you need me."

Hannah smiled an acknowledgment. She was in her late forties, her brown hair well styled, her skin smooth, her eyes dark and bewitching. If this conversation had been taking place at a country club, one might think her either a well-maintained housewife, or, more likely, a powerful woman capable of holding her own. She'd been the former, and now she was one of the most powerful people in the government, capable of ordering Sanctions where her operatives, such as Neeley, were judge, jury, and executioner.

Officially, no one had oversight over Hannah and the Cellar. Unofficially, the President's recent phone call was a reality that had to be dealt with.

Neeley fit the role of judge, jury, and executioner as Hannah needed. Statuesque and slender, she was dressed in black slacks and a black turtleneck. Her hair was cut short and there was more gray each time she came back to see her boss and friend.

Such is the price of being in reality.

Hannah leaned back in her chair and let out a deep breath. "I suppose I do need you, except—for once—I don't know what for."

"Foreman," Neeley said, referring to the old spook who'd been aware of the Time Patrol, controlled its funding, and tricked the Nightstalkers into becoming involved in stopping the Ratnik.

"What about him?" Hannah asked. "I've run a background on him since this started. His story is what he claims it is. We at least have records of that."

"But is he what he appears to be?" Neeley asked. She didn't wait for an answer. "He lied to us. He knew more than he told us. He played us into thinking the fate of the world was at stake simply to test the team. Taking down the Ratnik was surprisingly easy after the huge buildup. And he's been keeping the Time Patrol secret for decades."

Hannah shrugged. "We keep secrets too, Neeley. And we play people."

"It doesn't feel right," Neeley said.

That got Hannah's attention. The two of them had survived in the covert world for a long time, often trusting to instinct over knowledge.

"And there's another factor," Neeley said. "Foreman's dying. Being aware of that, a clock ticking on one's life, can change anyone."

Hannah considered that, but her next question was about something completely different. "And Roland?"

Neeley's left eyebrow went up, the only indication of her surprise. "What about Roland?"

"Do you miss him?"

Neeley sighed. "Yes. I do."

"That's good," Hannah said. "It's better to miss someone than have no one to miss."

The room was silent for a few moments. "Check into Foreman," Hannah finally said. "I agree with you. He played all of us and players always play."

IN THE PAST: PART ONE

Off the East Coast of England, 999 AD. 29 October

Roland wasn't there, and then he was there, but he'd sort of always been there. It was the best way to explain how he arrived, becoming part of his current time and place without fanfare or excitement among those around him. He was in the bubble of this day, not before, and hopefully he wouldn't be here afterward.

Roland was holding onto a wooden pole and it took him a second to realize it was an oar. That moment of confusion was enough for him to get out of rhythm with the others and earned him an earful of curses that, despite being in a foreign tongue, he could understand. The usual: things to do with bowel movements, his mother, his masculinity or lack thereof, and various sexual acts, most of them anatomically impossible but quite imaginative.

Some things never change among warriors.

Roland caught the beat quickly and lowered his heavy oar into the water in sync with the others. Satisfied he could perform this mindless task—even for him—he took a look about. He was cold and wet, but that didn't bother him. The human body is waterproof. The Ranger Instructors at Fort Benning, then in the mountains of Dahlonega, and finally the swamps of Eglin Air Force Base, had shouted it at him enough times that it was now a part of him. His attire of dirty leather trousers and tunic was completely inappropriate for the damp and cold, but quite right for manly Vikings.

Roland could almost hear Eagle: Manly men doing manly things with each other and the goats running scared.

He missed his team, but being with real Vikings, well . . .

A wooden shield hung over the side of the boat next to Roland. At his feet lay his sword, a very long and heavy sword with something inscribed on it. An *Ulfberht* sword, made from fine steel imported from Central Asia via the Volga trade route, a long and dangerous journey that made it quite valuable.

Roland blinked. This download stuff was cool.

Still, his head hurt from the download, but he liked the sword. Even more, he liked the idea of wielding the weapon in battle. It was a different form of combat from that of bullets and air strikes and artillery. More personal. Close range. Mano a mano.

Roland looked up from the sword. It was night, but there was a cloudless sky and the stars were out and the moon was half, giving plenty of light. The Viking longship was a *skeid*, with thirty benches for rowers. It was over eighty feet long by fifteen feet at its widest. Open to the elements, the emphasis was on functionality, not comfort.

Roland smiled at the information his brain was supplying. The team would be pretty damn impressed, even Eagle. The ship was narrow and double-ended, which meant the rowers could simply swing in the opposite way and the boat was just as quick in that direction, although the rudder was only at the stern, so maneuvering would be a little difficult. Still, Roland knew tactics, and usually if one had to beat feet, or in this case, row a retreat, a straight line was always the quickest.

In Viking fashion, the keel was hewn from a single large oak tree and curved. It was carved in a T shape, the narrow side projecting down into the water to aid in steering a true course. The ribs of the ship were made of solid oak and the hull built with overlapping strakes. It was a strong and flexible vessel designed to handle the pounding and waves of the open ocean while also able to navigate shallow waters and be drawn up on a beach as needed.

Necessity breeds innovation.

Roland vaguely remembered watching some History Channel show about Vikings in the team room back at the Ranch near Area 51 (definitely one Eagle had tuned in to as Roland preferred wrestling, mixed martial arts, or those puppy shows). He knew this information wasn't coming from memory, though, but from the data downloaded into his brain prior to infiltration on this mission.

Roland looked up. The mast was twenty-five feet high. The wide sail hung limp, the air still.

Too still, Roland knew. They were in the midst of an unnatural calm. Never good. Roland's warrior instincts were tingling.

In the scant light, he could make out that a large hand silhouette had been imprinted into the sail's cloth with some red dye.

A man came down the center of the ship. He was very large, two inches taller than Roland's six foot four inches, which made him a true giant in this day and age, a year before the turn of the first millennium. He was carrying a Danish axe with a haft over four feet long. The base of the haft had a metal point so it could be used on that end if needed, but the true working axe end was broad, consisting of a finely honed edge for cutting on one side and a thick blunt end made for crushing on the other.

Roland felt a pang of envy as he eyed the weapon. The sword at his feet looked pretty cool, but that axe was awe inspiring.

Mental note, Roland made, focusing hard, because sometimes he had a hard time remembering mental notes: *Next Viking trip, get a big axe.*

Long dirty, dark hair tumbled over the man's shoulders. He had a square face with a thick, poorly healed scar running down the left side, from temple to jaw. Unlike most of the crew, he sported no beard, just a few days' growth of stubble. He knelt on one knee next to Roland and looked at him with surprisingly blue eyes.

He spoke in a whisper only Roland could hear. "I am Ragnarok Bloodhand."

"Roland." Roland considered adding something cool to his name, like Roland the Slayer or Roland the Badass, but it just didn't fit.

"Roland is a good name," Ragnarok acknowledged, which made Roland feel better. Ragnarok looked Roland over, noting the scars. "You are a warrior."

It was not a question.

"That is good," Ragnarok continued. He nodded toward the bow of the ship. "We are only a few hours from England. The sea has been strange along with the winds. We are trusting to the gods that our course is true." Ragnarok smiled. "And to Hrolf the Slayer who steers the ship. He has never let me down."

Roland was still marveling he could understand the man, the words falling on his ears in Norse but processed automatically into English. He looked to the rear of the ship and saw a much shorter man but very broad in the chest with a large belly. He had a hand on the tiller and was peering ahead, as if he could see through to their destination.

Roland the Slayer, Roland thought, glad he hadn't tried it out on Ragnarok. They already had one. Figured. Frakking Vikings. Acted like they had a monopoly on the crazy warrior thing.

Roland looked at the hard men around him and had to admit: Maybe they did?

Ragnarok put a hand out and tapped Roland on the shoulder. "Do you know what you are to do?"

Roland shook his head and decided to try his tongue. "No. I am supposed to watch and see. But it will be done today."

Ragnarok nodded. "We're heading toward a monastery near a village. There shouldn't be any Saxon troops." He paused as a slight figure wrapped in a black cloak came down the center of the ship. The other Vikings shifted uncomfortably as the figure passed, as if it were a dangerous spirit.

"The Disir desires to speak to you," Ragnarok said in a low voice. "She's been waiting for you. She met us before we sailed. She claims to have traveled half the world, from beyond the steppes of Russia to be here. I am not certain whether to believe her." He said the last hurriedly and in a whisper as the figure arrived.

Roland processed that with a tumble of information that overwhelmed him until he simply focused on the keys: A Disir was a spirit or seer in Norse mythology. A cousin to the Valkyrie in some ways, which caused Roland his own unease.

The figure knelt next to Ragnarok and pulled back the hood. Roland was surprised to see a woman obviously from Southeast Asia. Her hair was shocked pure white and Roland knew that whatever had caused that change was something very terrifying indeed.

"I am Tam Nok. I am here to help you in whatever way I can. I have been waiting all my life for this day. It is my calling."

For some reason, her eyes reminded him of Neeley, and he felt a pang of distance and longing.

"Do you know what it is I am to do?" Roland asked. His brain did a double backflip as it translated what he'd just said, and he realized he sounded more sophisticated speaking in Norse than he did in his native English.

Too bad no one else on the team back in his time spoke Norse.

Tam Nok shook her head. "Not yet. I have not been given the vision with my Sight." She nodded toward the bow. "But I know where we are to land. Mighty Ragnarok Bloodhand, wielder of Skullcrusher, has graciously consented to take us there."

Roland glanced at the Viking leader.

"You have paid us well," Ragnarok said, indicating the extent of his graciousness.

"You said it was a monastery," Roland said to Ragnarok.

The Viking nodded. "Yes. I've been along this coast before. Eight years ago I was with Olaf Tryggvason and his fleet. We killed many Saxons. Three years ago I sailed up the Thames with Svein Forkbeard and we forced a ransom from London. But the Saxons have little left to pillage."

"It is not about pillaging," Tam Nok said.

Ragnarok sighed, somewhere between disgust and frustration. "When you know what it *is* about, let me know. You've paid well but once my men smell blood, I will not be able to hold them back. We take what we take. For now—" He suddenly paused and turned his head, sniffing like a dog. He sprung to his feet. "Half force to arms! Fast beat rowers!"

Every other rower locked down his oar and grabbed shield and weapon. Those still on the oars increased their cadence.

Roland hefted the sword, adjusting to the weight of it and the shield combined. He peered about but couldn't see what had caused Ragnarok's alarm. But he could sense it. He'd felt this before: danger close.

Ragnarok glanced over at Roland. "Stay with me." He smiled. "I sense the opportunity for glory." He pointed at Tam Nok. "Stay behind us."

And here be the monster as a thick, ropy tentacle lunged up out of the water. At the tip was a mouth fringed with sharp teeth, snapping, searching for flesh. It hit one of the Vikings directly into the chest, the teeth boring deep. The man slashed at the creature with his sword even as he died.

The Viking leader was fast to the defense with Roland at his side, almost as fast. They battled desperately as more tentacles came out of the water. Roland sliced through one, stomping down with his leather boot on the snapping end, crushing the teeth. To his right, another Viking was lifted into the air, tentacle wrapped around his chest. The unfortunate warrior was pulled down into the black water, disappearing. The man never cried out in terror or for help, swinging his sword even as he was taken into darkness. It was the way a Viking should be taken, weapon in hand, guaranteeing a place in the hall of Valhalla.

If such a place exists.

But warriors need to believe in something beyond themselves, whether it be country, flag, unit, comrades, or Valhalla.

Neeley had told Roland of these creatures, the kraken.

He was elated to finally meet one.

Roland jabbed the point of his sword directly into the mouth end of a tentacle, right between the teeth, as it came straight for him. The sword went in and then farther in, the teeth snapping down on the steel, getting closer and closer to his hand, finally stopping at the cross-shaped haft before the tentacle pulled back, dripping gore.

Ragnarok was everywhere, swinging his massive axe and yelling orders. "Arrows! Spears! Into the water!" He was pointing over the starboard side with his axe, the head dripping gore.

Roland dropped his sword and grabbed a nearby spear. He jumped to the side next to Ragnarok and looked down. Just below the surface, in a swirl of blood, was a large eye peering up at him, part of a deeper, darker shadow from which the tentacles lashed up.

One of the tentacles darted toward Roland but never made it as Ragnarok swung his axe and severed it with one blow.

With all his strength, Roland thrust down with the spear, almost following it overboard, releasing it at the last second. The tip hit the eye dead center.

There was a flurry of tentacles and then nothing as the creature dove.

For a moment, all was still, the surface of the water settling down to a dead calm.

"Bowmen." Ragnarok was pointing with the tip end of his axe.

To the starboard side, floating in the air, was a ghostly figure about fifty feet away.

This Roland had seen before. "A Valkyrie."

Ragnarok spared him a glance. "You've met such before?"

"I have."

"Since you are here, that means we can defeat it." Ragnarok said it as a statement and Roland didn't have the heart to tell him it had taken a 40 mm grenade and a lot of bullets to do that.

Blood-red hair flowed over a smooth face with two red bulbs for eyes. Roland knew there was a human inside that articulated, white armor suit. A human from where and when he had no clue.

The twang of bowstrings was the only sound. The arrows hit and bounced harmlessly off the armor.

Tam Nok called out. "You cannot hurt it with your arrows."

"Stop!" Ragnarok called out.

Roland went to the Viking's side and they stared at the creature as Tam Nok joined them.

"It sent the kraken," Tam Nok said.

"Why doesn't it attack?" Ragnarok asked.

There was no answer.

The Valkyrie remained still for a long minute, and then the creature slowly faded away, floating backward into a fog bank.

"Someone knows you're coming," Ragnarok said to Roland. "Other than me and her."

"Why would it retreat?" Roland asked. "We have no weapon to stop it."

Ragnarok hefted his battle-axe and kissed the gore-covered head. "I can hurt it with Skullcrusher."

Roland had seen 5.56 mm rounds bounce off the Valkyries' armor. While he respected Ragnarok's power, he had a feeling the white armor could withstand the axe. "This doesn't make sense."

Ragnarok slapped Roland on the back. Not softly. "You hurt its pet with your mighty spear thrust. It is probably going off to sulk. You are a worthy warrior." He walked off, issuing orders for the boat to get underway. The crew was tossing severed pieces and parts of the kraken overboard.

Tam Nok put her hand on Roland's chest. "You have the heart of a warrior." She tapped the side of her head with her other hand. "I have the Sight. Together we can do what has to be done. It is the way it should be, seer and soldier as one."

"Except you can't see the goal of my journey," Roland muttered.

"We'll know it when we see it," Tam Nok said.

"I do not think you will be able to control Ragnarok and his men."

"They are transportation," Tam Nok said. "Nothing more."

The vagaries of the variables, Roland thought, a rather profound thought at that. He didn't like it. Roland was well trained and experienced in combat, which is controlled chaos, but he usually had a good idea of his mission and who the enemy was.

Whatever happened when they reached England wasn't going to be pretty.

It is 999 AD. In China, Bao Zheng is born and would become renowned for his honesty and fairness to the point where he would be woven into Chinese legend. Saint Adelaide, the second wife of the Holy Roman Emperor Otto the Great, and then regent of the Empire for her grandson from 991 to 995, passes away just before the turn of the millennia, which she had believed would bring the Second Coming. Panic over the end of the millennia has many flocking to monasteries and churches, turning over all their worldly goods in exchange for the blessing of eternal life.

Some things change; some don't.

And here, on a Viking longship, Roland was facing creatures of legend while on a mission whose objective he wasn't exactly certain of. But he had a shield and a sword and he was in the company of fierce warriors in the midst of a battle.

Roland was at home.

And there was a seer. With the Sight. Who couldn't see what he needed.

Roland shrugged. *This was going to be all right,* he thought as he hooked his shield over the bulwark and put the sword down at his feet.

He grabbed his oar and put his back into it.

Los Angeles, California, 1969. 29 October

Scout wasn't there, and then she was there, but she'd sort of always been there. It was the best way to explain how she arrived, becoming part of her current time and place without fanfare or excitement. She was in the bubble of this day, not before, and hopefully she wouldn't be here afterward.

Scout lifted her head and felt the drool parting from the side of her mouth and the page of the open textbook. She could tell it was a textbook because the pages were of good-quality paper and had no smell at all. She blinked, focusing, and figured it was a physics book from the confusing equations that covered the open page. Something Doc or Ivar might scrawl on a whiteboard. And actually understand. She flipped it shut and the title confirmed the subject.

She was sitting at a desk. A rather neat desk, one her mother would be proud of. She glanced out the open window and realized it was morning, the sun slanting across the UCLA campus. Something about the fact it was morning worried her for a moment, as if she should have been up earlier, but she shunted it aside.

The vagaries of the variables as Dane was so fond of saying.

She had time to do whatever it was she had to do. Or more accurately to make sure what was supposed to happen happened.

Whatever.

From the attire of the people meandering about with their wide-bottomed jeans and with patches on said jeans, such as Snoopy or that guy with the big nose who wanted you to just keep on truckin', she figured they'd gotten the time right.

It is 1969, California.

The weather was nice, but Scout had never been to California, so she assumed it was always nice. They made songs about that, especially in this era. Were the Beach Boys hitting it big now, she wondered, conjuring up the only old California band she could think of? Then she realized she'd never heard of the Beach Boys back in her old life, so that must have been something they downloaded. With a rush, the information tumbled through her brain: *Formed in 1961; Hawthorne, California; three brothers, Brian, Dennis, Carl Wilson, cousin Mike Love, and friend Al Jardine.*

Scout rolled her eyes as she stopped the cascade of thoughts. Now she was truly a nerd. A walking Wikipedia. What every young woman aspires to.

She even had the frakking songs in her brain, so she shut that down right away. No "Good Vibrations" echoing through her gray matter.

But . . .

It was a pretty good tune, she allowed.

She was alone in the room, but there were two beds. Twins. They were plain; just sheets and blankets because it was decades before helicopter moms hovered in and outfitted college beds with dust ruffles, duvet covers, and twenty matching pillows. Scout thought how the pillow business in 1969 had no idea how bright their future was and briefly considered whether there was a way she could invest in the market.

But that would be breaking the rules and the Administrator had been quite explicit about not breaking the rules.

Good luck with that, Scout thought.

Shouldn't have brought the Nightstalkers in if he wanted rule followers.

Shifting her focus, Scout caught her reflection in the mirror and grimaced. Her hair was brown, very brown, with no colored streaks, because the hair-streaking business was still in the future. She had a part in the middle. Most unattractive and nondescript. But one did have to fit in. Her thin little peasant top revealed she was braless, but her breasts were small, so no issue there.

So. She was a feminist. Victoria's Secret was still a few decades down the road too and maybe braless was the way to go until someone thought up a pretty bra. She checked the waistband of her low-riding jeans and sighed. Yep. Cotton bikini panties. Gross, but thongs were as far off as pretty bras. And thus is the place of underwear in history, she thought.

The sacrifices she made for her duty.

The pants were a bit loose and she noticed the insanely wide leather belt lying on the desktop next to the textbook. Certainly not a coincidence, she knew right away. She checked the jeans and the loops were big enough to accommodate the belt, as the one she'd been issued was also wide. By its look, the belt on the desk was hand tooled. There were a few marijuana leaves carved in it, dyed an atrocious green. She picked it up and noted a name etched into the inside: Luke, and then some hieroglyphics.

Which her mind automatically translated.

WELCOME TO THE REVOLUTION

Funny guy, this Luke. But the hieroglyphics indicated he was her contact.

So where the frak was he?

Someone had made the belt; her first order of business would be to find him, then find Luke.

What a strange era when belts were the cutting edge of individuality, but hair was long and straight and plain.

No wonder there was so much turmoil going on with the kids here and now. They had few resources to makes themselves special, so they used the time to read stuff and make their minds unique, rather than bowing to social media, which hadn't been invented yet.

Yet.

Which reminded her.

Scout sighed. Duty waited.

Watching the students going back and forth across campus, she pondered their situation. They all wanted to be different from the Establishment. That was a word that really wasn't bandied about in her time. She wondered what had happened to it? Too many letters? MSM, perhaps in her time? Main Stream Media. The idea was the same.

The Man.

She searched and found a drawer stuffed with cheap cosmetics. She accessed the data that had been downloaded into her brain and carefully made up her eyes to match the time. Gross. Baby-blue eye shadow wasn't a good match with dull brown hair and no hair products. Her mother would be appalled, and that made Scout feel slightly better about the look.

Prepared to sally forth, Scout checked herself once more in the mirror. She didn't like what she saw, so she figured she was ready.

It is 1969. Muammar Gaddafi stages a coup and comes to power in Libya. The "Miracle Mets" win the World Series. Wal-Mart incorporates. The Boeing 747 makes its first passenger flight. Charles Manson and his followers murder Sharon Tate and others. Dwight D. Eisenhower passes away. Yasser Arafat is elected leader of the PLO. Hurricane Camille, a Category 5, makes landfall along the Mississippi Coast, killing 248 people. Rupert Murdoch purchases Britain's largest Sunday paper. *Midnight Cowboy*, rated

X, is released. The first ATM in the United States is installed. Two Black Panthers are shot dead in their sleep by police officers. *Sesame Street* is broadcast for the first time.

Some things change; some don't.

As she went toward the door of the small room, it also occurred to Scout that this was the era of free love, which Scout doubted was ever free.

But still. She was only here for a day and then she would be gone.

Scout had a strange feeling. It took her a moment to recognize it: excitement. This could be interesting.

She was sure her mother wouldn't approve of the feeling or the thought.

London, England, 1618. 29 October

Mac wasn't there, and then he was there, but he'd sort of always been there. It was the best way to explain how he arrived, becoming part of his current time and place without fanfare or excitement among those around him. He was in the bubble of this day, not before, and hopefully he wouldn't be here afterward.

"Let them at least comb it, if they are to have it!"

Mac saw the reason for the man next to him crying out, although it took him a second to process what it meant based on the data that had been downloaded to him. On the stone walkway, surrounded by guards with pikes, an old man was being escorted back to his prison in the Westminster Gatehouse, his white hair unkempt and in disarray. The sky was dark, not long after midnight, and torches lined the walkway. Despite the hour, a small crowd had gathered and the originator of the complaint was standing next to Mac.

The prisoner was about six feet with soft brown eyes. He was worn and tired, and his face twitched as he tried to smile at the outburst. But there was also a surprising confidence about him given his dire circumstances.

The prisoner was brought to a halt on a small dais.

"Beeston," the prisoner called out to the man who had protested, "do you know of any plaster to set a man's head on again when it is off?" The man's voice was small, a surprise given his stature and his reputation.

Some in the crowd laughed and the condemned man smiled.

Gallows humor, Mac thought. Except the man wasn't destined for the gallows, but rather the chopping block not long after daybreak, scant hours away.

The Clerk of the Crown stepped up next to the prisoner along with the Lord Chief Justice. The Clerk held up a scroll and read from it: "Sir Walter Raleigh has been a statesman, and a man who in regard to his parts and quality is to be pitied. He has been a star at which the world has gazed; but stars may fall when they trouble the sphere wherein they abide. It is, therefore, His Majesty's pleasure to call for execution of the former judgment, and I now require order for the same."

The crowd murmured, but Mac couldn't tell whether it was with approval or dismay. Mac was dressed in the Elizabethan attire of the time and continued to feel quite awkward. His hand drifted down to a rapier stuck in his belt, the only thing he approved of in the outfit. He remembered dressing like this in high school, when he was in the drama club. His father had given him unbearable grief about the "girlie" costume. And Mac's fledgling acting career had ended right there.

Who knows? In another timeline he could have been a movie star. He was very good at pretending. He had the looks. But the drive had been sucked out of him that moment his father belittled him. Replaced with a different drive to prove his worth, a drive which had propelled him into the Army, into volunteering for Special Forces, to being drafted into and then accepting assignment with the Nightstalkers.

And now here he was.

"Raise your right hand," the Clerk of the Crown ordered.

Sir Walter Raleigh did so.

"Do you have anything to say as to why execution should not be awarded against you?"

Mac thought Raleigh looked sick. His white hair was unkempt, his visage haggard. A red flush was in his face. He spoke, his voice low and harsh. "As concerning the judgment, which is so long past, I think His Majesty, as well as others, have been of the opinion that in my former trial I received but hard measure."

The information tumbled through Mac's brain, even as he marveled that he was here, in London, staring at a man he'd read about in history books: After Queen Elizabeth died in 1603, Raleigh's enemies, and there were many, had him arrested and imprisoned in the Tower of London. He was tried for treason, convicted, and sentenced to death.

But he was not executed for a variety of reasons.

So Raleigh remained on the Elizabethan-age equivalent of death row for thirteen years, writing his first volume of *The History of the World.*

Some make the most of their time.

Strangely, he was released by King James in 1616 and led an expedition to South America in search of the famed City of El Dorado and its gold. In ill health and advanced years, Raleigh remained in Trinidad while his son led an expedition into the interior of South America.

His son was killed, no gold was found, and his forces attacked a Spanish fort, thereby violating a treaty and almost causing war between the two empires.

What Mac found amazing was that despite the failure, the political blundering by attacking the Spanish, and living under a death sentence, Raleigh actually returned to England, where he was promptly arrested and thrown back into prison, with the sentence reinstated at the Spanish ambassador's insistence.

Was it pride? Was it ego? Was it a sense of duty? Sense of loyalty? Family? Why would a man who had just failed return to a death sentence?

Mac stared at the man on the dais, trying to reconcile him with the dashing explorer and Elizabethan courtier. Perhaps all the years imprisoned in the Tower had broken something in Raleigh?

But strangely, he didn't look broken to Mac. Physically he was beaten down, but there was a glittering look in his eyes that didn't match the despair a condemned man in his last night should be showing.

It is 1618. Osman II deposes his uncle, Mustafa I, as Ottoman Emperor. An avalanche buries the town of Piuro in the Alps, killing over 2,000. Chief Powhatan (father of Pocahontas) dies. The first dredger is patented. The Ming Chinese embassy of the Wanli Emperor presents tea to the Russian Czar.

Some things change; some don't.

The Lord Chief Justice took a step forward. "Sir Walter Raleigh, you must remember yourself; you had an honorable trial, and so were justly convicted; and it were wisdom in you now to submit yourself.

"I pray you attend what I shall say unto you. I am here called to grant execution upon the judgment given you fifteen years since; all which time you have been as a dead man in the law, and might at any minute have been cut off, but the King in mercy spared you. You might think it heavy if this were done in cold blood, to call you to execution; but it is not so, for new offenses have stirred up His Majesty's justice, to remember to revive what the law had formerly cast upon you. I know you have been valiant and wise, and I doubt not but you retain both these virtues, for now you shall have occasion to use them. Your Faith has heretofore been questioned, but I am resolved you are a good Christian, for your book, which is an admirable work, does testify as much. I would give you counsel, but I know you can apply unto yourself far better than I am able to give you."

Raleigh's head drooped down, the messy hair falling over his face and mostly hiding it. But Mac caught the hint of a smile on Raleigh's face through the hair.

The Lord Chief Justice continued. "Fear not death too much, nor fear death too little; not too much, lest you fail in your hopes; not too little, lest you die presumptuously. And here I must conclude with my prayers to God for it, and that he would have mercy on your soul." He paused, and then announced: "Execution is granted and will be carried later today."

As the guards stepped up next to Raleigh to escort him away, he lifted his head and looked at the man next to Mac. "Will you be present at the show later this morning, Lord Beeston?"

"I hope so," Beeston said. "If I can find a place in the crowd."

Raleigh smiled. "I do not know what you may do for a place. You must make what shift you can. But for my part, *I* am sure of having a place."

The guy had guts, Mac had to grant him that.

And with that, Raleigh was hustled away.

Beeston edged close by Mac's side and spoke in a low voice. "You are here to help save him. Say the word is yes. I will lend my sword to yours, as will those who have gathered. Surely history cannot allow such a man to suffer this fate. It is not in the prophecy."

It was also not stated as a question to Mac.

Mac looked at the old man, well dressed for the time period, sporting a wig that didn't quite hide his baldness. He had a wicked rapier scar slashing across his left cheek, a piece of nose missing, and a gash ending above the right side of his mouth. The wound had not healed well. And his eyes glittered, in which Mac recognized the confidence of a fellow warrior.

Nope, Mac thought, *I'm not here to save him.*

"I'm just a visitor," Mac said.

"From time, not another place, am I correct?"

Well that didn't take long, Mac thought. "What do you mean?"

"I was told you'd be right here, right now," Beeston said. "It's part of the prophecy."

"All right," Mac allowed. "Yes. The prophecy."

"Come with me," Beeston ordered.

So his contact thought he was here to save Raleigh, because the contact didn't know the future, while Mac knew the past.

But then the question for Mac was: Why *was* he here?

And what prophecy was Beeston talking about?

Andes Mountains, Argentina, 1972. 29 October

Moms wasn't there, and then she was there, but she'd sort of always been there. It was the best way to explain how she arrived, becoming part of her current time and place without fanfare or excitement. She was in the bubble of this day, not before, and hopefully she wouldn't be here afterward.

Luckily, Moms's instincts were faster than her conscious thought.

Something was behind her, something dangerous and maleficent. As quickly as she sensed this, she whirled about, bringing the silenced M14 rifle to bear, but the thing was too close and too big. The bulky suppressor on the end of the barrel hit the creature's side, and then the rifle was torn from her grasp.

In the darkness, through falling snow, all she could see was a large hulking figure, hairy. And teeth, glinting in the starlight. Large teeth, fangs, mouth opened wide. Moms tried to back up, feet pushing in knee-deep snow. She felt trapped in slow motion as the beast closed on her, blocking out the stars.

Moms's hand was scrambling for the pistol on her right thigh, the other hand held up in a vain, instinctual attempt to stop the assault. She couldn't get the pistol, her gloved hand fumbling with the release. So she grabbed the haft of a machete, Nada's old machete, and drew it.

The beast growled, a deep guttural noise, spraying Moms with saliva.

Beyond that was a noise Moms recognized: the chugging

sound of a suppressed weapon firing. Letting out a cry of pain, the beast wheeled away from Moms to face its attacker.

Moms lay on her back, still trying to understand, but her training prompted her into action. She got to her knees, holding up the machete and then preparing to swing it. The creature was over seven feet tall and broad in the chest. She slashed at its back, the razor-sharp blade slicing through fur and into flesh.

Between her machete and the shooter, the creature had enough. With an outraged roar it dashed off into the falling snow, irritated but not fatally wounded by the bullets and blade.

Moms slumped back. She sheathed the machete and picked up the M14. She had no idea from which direction the shots had come, so she quartered the vicinity, rifle tight to her shoulder.

She caught a flash of something out of the corner of her eye, higher and to the north. She froze. She didn't stare directly at the location, but rather used the off-center part of her retina, more sensitive to light.

A flicker of movement, so quick one could imagine it wasn't real. It was real.

Someone else was out there—the shooter.

Moms's gloved finger was over the trigger, but she didn't fire

The shooter rose up out of the snow and began moving toward her. Like her, the shooter was covered in white camouflage, a hood draped down over the face.

Moms aimed center of mass at the approaching figure.

The figure stopped, slung a rifle, and raised both empty hands. Moms slid her finger off the trigger, but kept the rifle aimed.

"Come forward," Moms called out.

The man came toward Moms. "Welcome, my friend," he said with an accent.

"Who are you?" she asked.

"A friend. My name is Pablo Correa." He was carrying a large backpack and a rifle was slung over one shoulder. Moms recognized it as an FN FAL with a bulky suppressor on the end: an excellent weapon. "We need to get to shelter. We will not survive the night exposed like this. It will get colder as the sky is clear. It is already well below zero Fahrenheit."

"I can handle the cold," Moms said while also accepting that he was right.

Correa pulled down his hood. His skin was dark, his features sculptured. His moustache was tinged with ice, but his smile was striking, revealing perfect white teeth. However, there was a gauntness to his face, the cheekbones a bit too pronounced, that whispered of a recent illness or difficult time.

Correa shook his head. "The cold is bad, that is true. But there are other dangers as you have just seen." He pointed at the blood trail heading away in the direction the beast had gone. There were deep tracks in the snow, easy to follow, but slowly being filled in by the descending snow.

Moms had done a lot of hunting in her time, but she'd never seen a track like this. Large, over six inches wide by sixteen inches long. Almost human shaped, but different. "What made that? What did we shoot?" Moms asked.

"A monster," Correa said. "We did not kill it, as you could tell. It has gone off to nurse its wounds. It has had many names, in many lands. Yeti in the Himalayas. Abominable Snowman. Sasquatch. Bigfoot. Ts'emekwes among the Native Americans of the Pacific Northwest. Here in the Amazon and Andes it has been called Mono Grande, or Large Monkey." He shrugged. "I prefer Yeti. Much simpler." He slid the FN FAL rifle onto his shoulder.

He coughed, hard, for several moments, turning partly away from Moms and bending over.

"Are you all right?"

"A touch of the flu," Correa said, straightening up. "Nothing to worry about."

Moms didn't care for the cold. Early in her career she'd served in a Special-Ops unit that was oriented toward Winter Warfare training. That meant she was prepared, which was both a good thing and a bad thing. It was good in that she knew what she was doing here at 13,000 feet in the Andes in the middle of the fall.

It was bad in that she'd learn to hate being cold.

"Let me get oriented," Moms said.

Correa smiled. "I know where we are, but do as you wish."

It was nighttime, GPS was just being tested at White Sands using ground-based pseudo-satellites, and Moms had to go back to her early training. She took her compass out, unfolded the map, pulled a poncho over her head, and knelt in the two-foot deep snow. She flicked on the red lens flashlight, oriented the compass, and stared at the map for almost twenty seconds. The poncho rustled and there was Correa right next to her, looking down at the map. Moms's mind transferred the contour lines drawn on the map into what they looked like in the real world. She turned off the light, removed the poncho, and looked about in the starlight.

The peaks all around made it easy to get an approximate fix on her location.

"Oriented?" Correa asked.

"Yes."

"Want me to double-check? Two is always better than one."

Moms knew her objective was just over the ridgeline to the west. A ridgeline that was only three hundred feet higher than her current location, the problem being that a three-hundred-foot climb in snow and cold and thin air was a lot, lot harder than it appeared.

Then again, those on the other side were in considerably worse circumstances.

Moms couldn't tell if Correa was questioning her orienteering ability or backing her up. She knelt once more, opening the map under the poncho and turning on the light. "We're here," she declared as she pointed to a spot on the map.

Correa nodded. "Yes. Exactly."

It is 1972. The first handheld scientific calculator is introduced. President Bhutto announces Pakistan will develop a nuclear weapons program. Nixon orders Haiphong Harbor to be mined. The first financial derivatives exchange, the International Monetary Market, opens. Franco Harris makes the "immaculate reception." The first and second Watergate break-ins fail; they're caught on the third. George Carlin is arrested for obscenity for presenting his "Seven Words You Can Never Say on Television" gig. Kissinger announces "peace is at hand" in Vietnam. The concept of recombinant DNA is announced and tested. Genocide begins in Burundi with hundreds of thousands of Hutus killed; twenty-two years later the Tutsis would return the favor.

Some things change; some don't.

"The objective is over that ridge," Moms said as they got to their feet and she stuffed the poncho into her ruck.

"Yes. It is. But we can wait until daylight. Unless whatever it is you must do, must be done now?"

"We can wait until daylight," Moms said, because she really had no idea what it was she was supposed to do, but given there was going to be an avalanche the next evening, she thought it best not to move precipitously. The terrain was as dangerous as the weather. The presence of the Yeti, though, indicated she was in the right place. The Shadow was up to something.

Correa pointed and Moms suddenly noticed a large man-made shape resting in the snow about fifty yards away.

"Come." Correa led the way. Moms quickly followed, her rifle at the ready. As they got closer, Moms realized what they were heading toward: the severed tail section of an airplane. Correa made his way into the shelter of the debris and pulled off his pack.

"We wait for dawn," he said. "It is too cold and too dangerous to move at night. If any of those over there"—he nodded toward the ridge and what lay beyond—"are still alive, they would not venture out at night as they have not the proper clothing or gear to deal with the cold."

Moms had no argument with the plan to wait.

"I will take first watch," Correa said. He pulled a blanket out of his pack. "Use this."

"Let me take first watch," Moms said. "Looks like you need some rest." They both sat down with their back against the inner bulkhead of the plane, facing the outside through the severed section. Correa was close by her side.

Correa chuckled. "As you wish." He pulled another blanket out and handed it to Moms. "Let me know if you see the Yeti, eh?"

"You'll be the first to know."

Correa wrapped his blanket around his shoulder and then he leaned in close, pressing himself against her.

"Excuse me," Moms said, surprised.

"Warmth," Correa said, flashing his beguiling smile. "Surely in your missions you have done such? It is part of survival training. And if the monster grabs you, it will awaken me."

Moms had to smile at that. "Then you just have to run faster than me," she said.

But his answer was serious. "I will not run."

"I will not either," Moms said.

"I can tell."

"Who are you?" Moms asked.

"I am Time Patrol, of course," Correa said. "Surely you were briefed you would be met?"

"I was told it was likely someone would meet me. How did you know to be here?"

He chuckled. "My entire life has led up to this place and this moment."

That startled Moms, who knew this was just a twenty-four hour-mission for her, but this man whom she had just met had waited for this for years.

Correa continued. "I was born and grew up in Argentina. I served for a decade in *Agrupación de Comandos Anfibios*, the APCA. Amphibious Commandos Group. Weapons were my specialty."

Moms had no doubt of that as she took in the modified FN FAL and the Browning Hi Power 9 mm pistol with silencer in a specially designed holster. A bulge on his harness on the right side held something.

"What's that?" Moms asked.

"Three FMK-1 mines," he replied. "We don't know what we will meet up here." He changed the subject. "I was recruited into the Patrol five years ago. I was never called to action. Until now.

"South America is my area of operations. I have filed reports, but this is the first time I have met someone traveling back on a mission." He paused for a moment. "I would like to know of the future, of course. What you know to your time, whenever it is. But it is forbidden. We of the Patrol cannot know further than our present. Very frustrating, but it is the rule." He stopped to cough, a deep rattling sound that worried Moms. He nodded toward the west. "I would like to know what will happen to them. The disappearance of the plane was in the news for many days, but now no one, except the families, speak of it. They are assumed dead. Since you are here, I assume they are not all dead?"

"They are not," Moms said. "Eighteen are dead. Twenty-seven are alive."

"Ah. It is tragic some died but also good that some survived." He looked about the tail section. "Amazing that anyone could have survived if this got ripped from the plane and landed here. I spotted wreckage farther back along the flight path: one of the wings. The searchers were looking in the wrong area. I was surprised when I received the coordinates this far east and north. The pilots must have turned too soon into the mountains, missing the pass."

Moms knew exactly why Uruguayan Flight 571 had crashed and why the searchers had been looking in the wrong area: The pilots had been flying on dead reckoning from Uruguay to Santiago, Chile. They'd been forced to stop in Argentina because of inclement weather. With the Andes Mountains between their stop and their destination, and a limited ceiling for the aircraft, the plane had to take a route flying through Planchon Pass in the mountains, rather than over the top.

Unfortunately, heavy cloud cover required the pilots to rely on dead reckoning, to first fly south to the pass and then west through it based purely on flight time. But they'd failed to take into account a strong headwind as they flew to and through the pass. Figuring they were almost through the mountains, the pilots called into the airport in Chile, announcing they were beginning their descent through the pass. Unfortunately they had taken the turn and begun the descent too soon. Thus they weren't in the pass and they weren't in Chile when they dropped altitude.

The plane hit a mountain peak at 13,800 feet, ripping off the right wing, which flew back and severed the tail section of the plane.

Which Moms was now sitting in with Correa.

Then the left wing was torn off, leaving the remaining fuselage hurtling through the air. It crashed on a downward slope just over the ridgeline to the west of Moms's position, sliding and coming to rest in a snow bank. By some miracle, most of those on board survived.

Correa spoke through the information she'd been downloaded with. "They must be suffering. The survivors have been down there for eighteen days."

Moms knew the survivors had begun eating their dead a week ago. She didn't think that was something she should share at the moment. "They are."

"At least let me know if they survive?"

"If all goes as it should, many will live," Moms hedged.

"So the beast is here so that all does not go as it should," Correa said.

"Apparently."

"Why?" Correa wondered out loud. "Why would the Shadow care about these rugby players? Does one of them go on to achieve great things in history?" He waved a hand before Moms could answer. "I know you cannot tell me. But it is frustrating not knowing." He sighed. "When dawn comes, we must protect the survivors from the beast," Correa said, as if he were discussing a matter of no consequence. "I think that should achieve the goal of keeping things as they should be."

Moms wasn't so certain of that. "There is something I can tell you. About what happens this evening. There will be an avalanche. It will sweep over the plane and bury those inside. It will kill eight of the survivors. The rest will be trapped inside for three days before managing to dig out."

Correa considered that. "These mountains are very dangerous. There are over a quarter million avalanches of various sizes along the range every winter." He looked out at the dark night, the air filled with snowflakes lazily drifting down. "This is the third straight day of snow. The surface pack is heavy. Ripe for an avalanche." He shook his head. "I do not believe we can stop an avalanche. Unless the beast is here to cause it."

Moms considered that. "The avalanche is part of history. So it happens. And, in fact, it is the event that spurs the survivors to—" She paused, realizing she was going past the twenty-four-hour window she could speak of.

Correa seemed to understand that. "Then it must be about the beast. It will do something that changes things."

"Yes," Moms said. "Most likely."

"It cannot just be coincidence the beast is here on the day the avalanche will occur," Correa said.

"I agree."

"Then we kill it before it attacks the survivors." Correa pulled the blanket up around his chin and leaned over, melding his body into Moms's.

She didn't protest.

His voice was barely a whisper. "You have not told me your name, my friend."

"I'm called Moms on my team."

"Ah. Madre. It is a strange name to be given by your team."

"It is a strange team."

"There is a sadness about you," Correa said. "A pain."

"I recently lost a good friend," Moms said.

"Ah." Correa was silent for a moment. "I too lost someone recently. My lover."

"I'm sorry," Moms said.

"Death is part of the cycle," Correa said. "We move on to a better place after this life, do we not?"

But it wasn't really a question and not something Moms felt like delving into.

Correa patted her on the back. "You are a good person. I can tell." And then he fell silent.

So Moms sat in the remnants of a plane, staring out, looking for a monster, with a handsome Argentinean man leaning against her, his warmth sinking through the blankets. She tried to remember the last time she'd been next to a person and felt their warmth. And she couldn't.

Her mission had just begun, and already Moms had battled a creature of legend.

Nothing but good times ahead.

Not.

Eglin Air Force Base, Florida, 1980. 29 October

Eagle wasn't there, and then he was there, but he'd sort of always been there. It was the best way to explain how he arrived, becoming part of his current time and place without fanfare or excitement among those around him. He was in the bubble of this day, not before, and hopefully he wouldn't be here afterward.

"It's hard to remember your mission was to drain the swamp

when you're ass deep in alligators," Eagle muttered as he pushed through the knee-deep cold water and boot-sucking muck.

"Shut your trap, Ranger," a dark figure ordered in a Southern drawl.

Eagle focused on two little spots of luminescence, cat eyes sewn to the back of the patrol cap on the man in front of him. Eagle lifted one foot out of the mud and pressed forward. He had no idea where in the patrol formation he was, what his position was, or what the mission was.

He would, no doubt, fail this patrol.

Not that he cared, since he wouldn't be around for the end of it anyway.

But Eagle still had some professional pride. He'd earned his Ranger tab a long time ago, which was actually years in the future and . . .

Eagle shut down those confusing thoughts.

A tall, slender black man, Eagle's head was completely bald underneath his patrol cap. The left side of his head was etched with burn scar tissue, the gift of an IED in Iraq almost a decade ago.

One thing he knew for sure: He was too old for this crap. Ranger School was for the young and dumb and hardcore. Eagle liked to think of himself as older, smarter, and more laid-back.

Those who knew him would say he had the first two of three right, but he might give Edith Frobish a run for the money in terms of uptightness.

He wondered when the next headcount came down the line whether he would be an extra man, or if he was already factored in somehow? How the hell did this whole time travel thing work?

The Administrator had been light on some of the details, but very positive Eagle would be assimilated in with no trouble. In fact, there was supposed to be someone here from the Time Patrol to help. Eagle suspected Dane was light on details because there was a lot the Administrator didn't quite know himself.

The Ranger patrol was deep in the Florida swamp, somewhere on the Eglin Air Force Base in the panhandle. (Where, exactly, Eagle had no idea, another no-no for a Ranger student.) It was after midnight, and Eagle had just under twenty-four hours to accomplish his mission, the details of which were also rather vague, other than, apparently, making sure a plane crashed. Being a pilot, Eagle was bothered by this.

A lot.

Eagle lifted his foot up once more and was surprised to strike dry land. A hummock in the middle of the swamp, a haven of higher ground.

And their next patrol base.

Which meant—"Headcount." The word was whispered by the cat eyes in front of Eagle, who dutifully passed it to the silhouette behind him. Knowing he had to make a decision in mere seconds, Eagle debated whether he should add his number to the count that would come back up the line, or to keep himself out of it.

He was here, so when the man behind whispered "Seven," Eagle passed forward "Eight."

Someone, most likely the assistant patrol leader, came by, put his hand on Eagle's shoulder, and pushed him in a direction. "You're there. Cover between there and there." Eagle could barely make out the hand waving in the darkness, but he sunk down and took up a position, resting his M16 on top of his rucksack and scanning the assigned field of fire.

Ranger School.

Again. Eagle sighed.

This was going to suck.

The big figure who'd told him to shut up came over and knelt next to him in the dark. "I'm Master Sergeant Hammersmith. The next patrol is y'alls." The accent was deep South, something even years in the Army traveling around the world can't wash out.

Great, Eagle thought. He didn't even know exactly where they were.

"Get your poncho out," Hammersmith ordered.

Eagle took it out and Hammersmith pulled it over both of them. Then he turned on a red lens flashlight. In the glow, Eagle could see he was a bull of a man, with a red face and the veins of a drinker splayed across his nose. A drunken redneck Ranger Instructor, Eagle thought.

Great. Could it get any better?

Hammersmith opened up a map. "Y'all don't know where we are, do you?"

Eagle opened his mouth, but before he could respond, Hammersmith pointed at the map with a twig held between dirty fingers. "We be right here, son," he said, alluding to a spot in the big splotch of green that was the Eglin Air Force Base reservation in the Florida panhandle. The terrain was almost completely flat. Eagle remembered that during this phase of Ranger School, the last navigation was primarily by compass azimuth and pace count.

No GPS. It would be a decade before that was initially used by the military in the First Gulf War.

Eagle bristled at the "son," but it was better than "boy." He tried to remember what his pace count was, but it had been a while. He pulled out his compass and put it on the map, but right away knew something was wrong.

"Yeah," Hammersmith said, noting the arrow spinning about uncertainly, never settling into north. "That's been going on for a couple of hours. Not good."

"You ever seen this before?" Eagle asked as he considered possibilities.

"No," Hammersmith answered succinctly.

"Magnet nearby?" Eagle asked.

"No." Hammersmith seemed pretty certain. "Something weird is going on in the swamp. I assume it has something to do with your arrival. Forget about that for now. We got to move using pace count and what few terrain features we got. Plus I've been crisscrossing this area for years so I know it well. Good news is, direction we want to go in, is mostly dry, 'cept for a few stream crossings."

Hammersmith moved the twig, sliding it across the map. The direct path crossed a couple of streams, which Eagle knew indicated they were going to get wet. It was about forty-five degrees and near the end of October, so that wasn't going to be fun.

"You got Bob Sikes Road as your left limit," Hammersmith said. "Means we gotta get down in this crud. We loop this way,"—he moved the edge of the twig to the right and down—"we only gotta cross one stream. They come together here. I know a spot. Kinda easy crossing but poor fields of fire." He moved on. The twig stopped at an airfield set among the green. Two long runways met at an angle with a connecting taxiway near their bases. "Wagner Field."

Eagle took a hard look at Hammersmith. "How do—"

"Lots of history at that there airfield," Hammersmith told Eagle, while pointing with the end of a twig at the triangle of runways on the map. "March of '42, ole Doolittle hisself brought his raiders there. Trained them to take off in a short distance, just like they was gonna do the next month off the *Hornet* when they bombed Japan. Can still see tire marks where they burned rubber on the tarmac, cranking those old birds to full power, then releasing the brakes. Those marks have lasted longer than the men who made them.

"Then right after the Big War, they tested some flying bombs they copied off the German V-1, launching them in this field, here, off the airstrip. Abandoned now, but some rusting launchers are still there. Use them as objectives sometimes for the students. Those old-timers used Nazi scientists for that 'cause after the war, the Russkies were the enemy. Kinda strange ain't it, how yesterday's enemy is today's buddy, eh?" He didn't wait for an answer and Eagle began to suspect there was more to Hammersmith than his first impression. "Airfield been abandoned for a long time though." He looked up at Eagle. "Until lately. Been off-limits for a bit."

"So," Eagle finally said, "you're my contact."

"Yeah. Surprised, ain't you, son? Takes all kinds to keep the timeline ticking. I ain't gonna ask you when you come from. I don't want to know dick about the future. That would fuck with my head and my head's already kinda fucked up. I done two tours in 'Nam and sometimes I don't think so straight. And I know you're here only for twenty-four hours, so let's not be dicking around. Let's get this done. I don't suppose you know what this is about?"

"You know what's happening at Wagner Field?"

"Yeah. They're testing a modified C-130 for short landings and takeoffs. Almost Doolittle like, which I kind of find interesting. I gotta assume it's got something to do with the cluster fuck in the desert back in April. Know some fellows from the Battalion who were in on that. So maybe we're going to be trying again? And you're here to make sure that happens."

The last sentence was said not as a question, and that was enough warning for Eagle to keep the details of today's history from Hammersmith.

"Sort of," Eagle said.

"Fuck me to tears," Hammersmith said, and Eagle could only think of Nada saying the same thing, so many times. The Ranger Instructor was no fool.

"We gotta stop it, don't we?"

Okay, Eagle had seriously underestimated the Time Patrol agent. "Yes."

Hammersmith was silent for several long seconds. "Then that's the mission." A soldier accepting his duty. "Do we have to kill any of our own?"

"No." *Hope not*, Eagle amended silently.

"All right." Hammersmith nodded. "I can live with that. Time to get real." Hammersmith shrugged off his rucksack and opened it. He dumped a sack on the ground. "5.56. Live ammo. Take the damn blank adapter off your weapon and lock and load. I'll be your assistant patrol leader and I'll navigate for you. The rest of the men have live ammo in their rucks and I've already passed the word to load up." He slapped his own rucksack. "We got one M60 with eight hundred rounds of 7.62, claymores, some LAWs, grenades, pistol ammo. One of the fellas got an M21 if we need to pop someone at distance. Oh yeah, two M203s with fifteen HE rounds each." He held up a shotgun with a short box magazine. "And I have my Lola. SPAS-12 shotgun, loaded with slugs."

Eagle processed the inventory: Claymores were anti-personnel mines; LAWs were light-anti-tank weapons; an M21 was a sniper rifle. Live ammunition. The M60 was a medium machine gun, good firepower. The M203s were M16s with a 40 mm grenade launcher slung under the barrel. And there was Lola, a semi-automatic shotgun.

So they were prepared for battle.

It is 1980. OPEC raises the price of oil by 10 percent. A record number of viewers tune in to find out who shot J. R. Ewing. The Polish government recognizes Solidarity. An Australian baby disappears from a campsite near Ayers Rock, reportedly taken by a dingo. Richard Pryor is badly burned trying to freebase cocaine. Mobster (and Goodfella) Henry Hill is arrested for drug possession. An inmate convicted of murder in 1911 is released from prison after 68 years and 245 days. Tito dies. The US government bails out Chrysler.

Some things change; some don't.

Eagle was starting to feel better about this mission, but Hammersmith put an end to that flicker of optimism. "We might not have to kill any of our own, but that don't mean this is going to be a cakewalk. I been in these swamps for years, sonny. Grew up down here. Walked many a patrol so I can get us the airfield. But things ain't right." He nodded out toward the dark swamp. "There's something out there. Something that don't want us getting to that airfield. Something bad, real bad. Evil-like. And it's between us and the airfield and whatever it is you gotta do." He paused. "I don't suppose you can tell me what it is *exactly* you gotta do?"

"No, Master Sergeant."

Hammersmith sighed. "Figured." They were still for a moment. "Can you tell me this at least, for my peace of mind since I'm putting my life, and the lives of my men here, in your hands. Are they capable hands? Can you give me an idea of your background? I assume this ain't your first shit in the woods?"

"I graduated Ranger School," Eagle said. "And I've been deployed four times in two different conflicts that—well, let's say that are coming down the road. Served in the first Ranger

Battalion in Special Forces and then I served in a classified unit I can't tell you about, but it dealt with evil-like stuff. Stuff most people don't think exists. Stuff that goes bump in the night. We were, are, the force that protects the world from that evil."

Hammersmith's white teeth shone in the red light as he smiled. "Well, damn, sir. Sounds like you're just the man to lead this here patrol."

He turned off the flashlight. They emerged from underneath the poncho and stood up.

Hammersmith became formal. "Let me know when you want to move out, sir."

Eagle took a deep breath.

This was going to suck worse than doing Ranger School again.

Manhattan, New York, 1929. 29 October

Ivar wasn't there, and then he was there, but he'd sort of always been there. It was the best way to explain how he arrived, becoming part of his current time and place without fanfare or excitement. He was in the bubble of this day, not before, and hopefully he wouldn't be here afterward.

Today was a day of reckoning and the world was never, ever, going to be the same.

One way or the other.

But, Ivar mused as he walked down Wall Street, just after midnight, in the dark on October 29, 1929, was that a good thing or a bad thing?

As a Nightstalker he'd sympathized with Doc's concern about the rest of the team's *shoot and kill first, understand later* philosophy.

Not very scientific and a bit presumptuous.

Having experienced multiple Ivars during the *Fun in North Carolina*, he'd found himself having arguments inside his own brain and with echoes of other Ivar brains, which doesn't make much sense to outsiders.

You had to be there.

He'd never told anyone, especially Frasier, the Nightstalker shrink, about the anomaly, because he had a feeling a padded room somewhere deep under Area 51 would be his immediate destination. Perhaps followed by his brain being removed and studied.

The Nightstalkers were nice people and all, but those they worked for and with, not so much. Ruthlessness was an integral part of that world. Ivar didn't know it, but he was about to step into another world just as ruthless, if not more so.

They'd been wrong about the Rifts. Ivar wasn't surprised no one discussed that fact, because the Rifts were no longer a problem. But the Nightstalkers had always treated the Fireflies that came through the Rifts as the enemy, when in fact it was now apparent that whatever was on the other side of the Rifts simply wanted to make sure no more were opened from our end into their timeline. Especially since the first one we opened back in 1947 sent the Demon Core—a subcritical mass of plutonium—to the other side.

Not the best way to make an introduction to another timeline.

Now they were trusting this guy Dane, the Administrator, and his statement that our timeline was threatened by another timeline trying to adjust history, making ripples leading to a shift, perhaps leading to a time tsunami.

But what if the changes were for the better?

That was an issue Dane had shot down at the first mention, not allowing discussion or debate, which meant the Time Patrol wasn't much different than the Nightstalkers.

Of course, trained as a physicist, Ivar knew any significant timeline change, aka a tsunami, would probably lead to him, and everyone else, snapping out of existence. Then again, there were other possibilities, but . . .

Ivar refocused on his here and now, because even he remembered the various Nada Yadas and one had something to do with "theory later, staying alive now." A parallel to "shoot first, inquire later."

It was early in the morning and the streets were pretty much deserted. It was surprisingly dark for downtown Manhattan, but Ivar had to remind himself of the year; thus the bright lights of Manhattan weren't so bright. Ivar paused as a couple of shadowy figures appeared down the street, walking through a fog toward him.

Discretion being the better part of valor in Ivar's opinion, he moved to the other side of the cobblestone road. The two men paid him no mind, obviously intoxicated and leaning on each other as they wove their way to whatever destination they sought.

Ivar slid into a recessed shop doorway. There were bars on the door and windows; some things never change in New York. Ivar pulled the pocket watch out of his vest and angled it toward a flickering gas lamp so he could check the time. Twenty-five minutes after midnight. He stepped out onto the street and continued on his way. He saw a large statue of George Washington in front of an imposing building. That oriented Ivar as information poured into his brain, most of which he knew would give Eagle a hard-on but momentarily confused him: While the Stock Exchange was diagonally across from the statue on the other side of Wall and Broad Streets, the space behind the sculpture was where the original Federal Hall, built in 1700 as City Hall, later became the seat of the new government of the United States. George Washington was inaugurated on the steps of the old building. Congress passed the Bill of Rights there. When the original building was torn down in 1812, the statue of Washington was located approximately where the first president had been sworn in.

And just nine years ago from this time, a bomb inside a horse-drawn carriage exploded right across the street, killing thirty-eight people, the worst act of terrorism in the United States up to that point.

Ivar sighed.

Some things never change. Carriage bomb, car bomb, terrorism.

And Wall Street somehow being involved.

Wall Street: No one knows exactly how it got its name, the best theory being that the Dutch, the first Europeans to settle in lower Manhattan, built an earthen wall along the north part of their settlement, *de Waal Straat*. This was to protect them from attacks by Native Americans.

Apparently the twenty-four-dollar payout for the land to the Natives wasn't enough to keep the peace.

In 1685, Wall Street was laid out by surveyors along the path of the original stockade as a larger stockade was built a bit farther north. The street ran from Pearl Street, which was the shoreline back then, across an old Indian path, Broadway, to the other shoreline at Trinity Place.

From the beginning, Wall Street was a place of commerce, and not the most pleasant kind. Slaves were brought there to be rented out by their owners for the day or week. In 1711, New York City made Wall Street the city's official slave market for Africans and Indians.

The information didn't seem pertinent to the current mission, but Ivar thought it was. He had no particular affinity for the place or its business, and today was going to go down in history as Black Tuesday, tumbling the country, and indeed the world, into the Great Depression.

Which would only be ended by World War II.

So was his mission a good thing or a bad thing?

And what exactly was his mission?

It is 1929. Mother Teresa arrives in Calcutta to begin her work among India's poorest. The St. Valentine Day massacre in Chicago kills seven. Grand Teton National Park is established by President Calvin Coolidge. Herbert Hoover then becomes president. And the first telephone is installed at the White House. The yo-yo is introduced. The New York Yankees become the first team to put numbers on their uniforms. Vatican City becomes a sovereign state. The USSR breaks diplomatic relations with China. President Hoover proposes the Kellogg-Briand Pact, which renounces war. The first US roller coaster is built. Lieutenant James Doolittle flies over Mitchell Field in NY in the first all-instrument flight. The Peking Man skull is found.

Some things change; some don't.

More than the others who were sent back, Ivar was really bothered by all the practical things about time travel. He'd always been a fan of science fiction, even though as a scientist he knew most of it was widely impractical, especially time travel. Well, that's what he *had* thought. But now it was like watching that reality show about Big Foot where they never really showed Big Foot, but suddenly, one day, they did. Surprise, surprise.

Wall Street was quiet now, but it wouldn't be later. Ivar looked at the pavement and thought of people jumping.

Bad thought.

He started to whistle "Winchester Cathedral," and then wondered what the heck that was all about?

Ivar was startled as a man darted out from an alley and ran into him. He felt wetness on his face and realized it was blood as the stranger collapsed to the ground. There was blood everywhere and Ivar's instinct was to flee, but his Special-Ops training upon "joining" the Nightstalkers allowed him at least to stand his ground for a moment.

"Are you him?" the man gasped.

Ivar knelt, trying to find the source of the blood, but it was everywhere and he hadn't taken the emergency medical training as seriously as he should have. Then his hand sunk into the guy's stomach, intestines like soft, warm snakes, and Ivar realized the man had been gutted. And there was a gurgling noise and Ivar knew the guy had been stabbed several times, including at least once in the lung as the sound indicated a sucking chest wound.

So some of the training had stuck.

Are you him? Ivar thought. What kind of question was that?

The stranger held out a canvas bag. It was smeared with blood, but Ivar automatically took it. *Might be a bomb,* he heard Nada warning, but Nada wasn't here. Wasn't around in the then (or was it now?) either.

"What is it?" Ivar asked.

The man was looking over his shoulder. "Run. Run. They're coming."

"Who's coming?"

"Them."

"I'll help you."

The man winced in pain. "The mission is more important. Go!"

Ivar looked past the man and saw no one, but he had no doubt that whoever had wielded the blade would be following the blood trail.

Every instinct he had pressed Ivar to run away and leave the man as requested.

Ivar ripped off his overcoat and tied the arms tightly around the stranger's chest and stomach, partially staunching the flow of blood.

"Come on."

There was no protest. Ivar wrapped his arm around the man's shoulder and headed off. Past the statue of George Washington, marking his inauguration at this very spot where slaves had been bought, sold, and rented. He turned into a dark alley, searching for a door or window.

The world was indeed never, ever, going to be the same.

The Pentagon

Follow the money. It applies to conspiracies, crimes, elections, the mob, damn near everything. Follow the money and you get to the truth.

Which is why Neeley was on the lowest level of the Pentagon, a level that few knew existed. She imagined if those building this place during World War II had been as ruthless as the Egyptian pharaohs, they'd have killed all the workers involved and buried their bodies in the concrete foundation of the five-sided building.

But it had been easier just to fool people with compartmentalization and complicated building plans.

Besides, who cared? The country was in the midst of World War II and there were more important things to consider. By now, most of those involved were dead.

Except Foreman.

The corridor was empty as Neeley strode down it. She turned one of the five gentle angles and walked up to an old man sitting behind a desk. He peered at her over his reading glasses.

"Good day, young woman?" Sentry asked.

In one hand he held a crossword puzzle. The other was under the desktop and Neeley knew he could blow her to pieces with a twitch of a finger.

"Good day," Neeley said. "Hannah sent me. I need to speak with Mrs. Sanchez."

"How is Hannah doing?" the old man asked. "It was a pleasant surprise to see her last week."

"She's doing well and sends her best," Neeley said.

Sentry smiled. "Her best is better than most people's. And her worst, of course, is much worse." He glanced at a screen. "You're not armed. I appreciate that." The hand under the desk moved a few inches and he hit a different button. A door swung open behind him, revealing a telephone-booth-sized room. Neeley walked around his desk and got into the small booth. She sat down and the door swung shut behind her. With a slight jolt, the booth began moving. Sideways. Neeley always found this network of rails underneath the Pentagon slightly disconcerting. She'd never told Hannah, or anyone, but it gave her a bit of motion sickness.

A few shifts this way and that, and then another jolt indicated that she was coming to a halt. The door opened to an open space and then a chest-high counter. Like the motor vehicle bureau. At least she didn't have to take a number and fill out forms.

Neeley walked up to the counter. The older woman on the other side regarded her approach with a slight degree of trepidation. Even when they clearly knew they'd done nothing wrong, there was always that slight jolt of guilt all but psychopaths felt.

A visit from a Cellar operative tended to bring out that reaction from those government employees who knew of the covert group. Mrs. Sanchez was the comptroller for the Black Budget, which meant she knew how to follow money that even Congress, which allocated it, didn't know how to track.

Mrs. Sanchez wore a jean skirt and vest over a white blouse. She had flowing white hair, dark skin, and an aged but still beautiful angular face. She'd made the area on the other side of the counter her own, as much as one could, buried underground. Colorful Navajo rugs decorated the walls along with etchings of the desert.

"May I help you?"

"Foreman," Neeley said. "What's his budget?" Neeley noted that Mrs. Sanchez's daughter, who usually worked with her, wasn't back there at the other desk. It was normally the two of them.

"One hundred forty-six million, two hundred and twelve thousand, five hundred and forty-five dollars." She hadn't consulted a computer. Or a ledger. Just her phenomenal capacity for retaining numbers.

"Breakdown?" Neeley asked. She knew she was being harsh, but she was unsettled because Hannah was unsettled. It also disturbed her even further to realize how much she relied on her old friend to be her emotional anchor.

"He doesn't supply one." Mrs. Sanchez hurried to explain. "That's not that unusual. Several organizations are not required to supply one. Like the Cellar."

One sentence too many, an indication of Mrs. Sanchez's nervousness, but Neeley let it slide.

"Who does he report to?"

"As far as I know, no one," Mrs. Sanchez said. "Years ago he occasionally had to appear before various classified sub-committees of Congress, but it's been decades. I think—" She paused.

"Go ahead," Neeley prompted.

"I think he's outlasted all of them. Very few people even know he's still around."

Mrs. Sanchez was too nervous. Neeley knew there was an appropriate level of angst to be experienced having a Cellar operative show up in your office, but there was something off about the old woman. Neeley looked past her and noted there was a half-eaten sandwich on both desks. Her daughter had been here. And left, quickly out the back.

Most likely upon being warned by Sentry that Hannah was on her way.

Overreaction.

Which indicated something was amiss. There wasn't the reek that the truly guilty (those who weren't psychopaths) gave off. And the psychopaths could be spotted by the complete lack of *anything*. Neeley had met more than enough of those in her time, since the covert world seemed to attract them. They were useful in certain jobs, but not always controllable.

Years ago, Neeley had worried for a while if she were a psychopath, given her past and her current occupation. But when she'd mentioned it to Frasier, the shrink for the Nightstalkers, he'd assured her she most certainly was not.

When she'd asked why, the response was simple: A psychopath would never ask if they were one.

"What do you know about Foreman?" Neeley asked Mrs. Sanchez.

"He asks for odd currencies sometimes," Sanchez said. "Old currencies."

That made sense, given the Time Patrol. "Anything recently?"

"Yes. He asked for as many $10,000 bills that I could gather. They're very rare. Printed only between 1928 and 1934. Then taken out of circulation a long time ago."

"How many did you get him?"

"Only one hundred and eighteen. He was very upset I couldn't find more."

"When did he ask for them?"

"Last week."

Something, but not much, Neeley thought. And not enough to explain the undercurrent she was picking up. "What else?"

Mrs. Sanchez's eyes did that up and right shift, so quickly most people would have missed it. Neeley wasn't most people. It meant Sanchez was accessing the right side of her brain. The side that made up stories. Left side was memory.

Big difference between the two.

"Nothing," Mrs. Sanchez said.

A lie, and it meant she'd tried to think of a story to tell Neeley, but then given up.

"What else?" Neeley repeated.

Slight flicker of eyes up and left. "I don't like him," Mrs. Sanchez said.

Neeley almost smiled. It always amazed her how often someone was sabotaged simply by the fact they had an abrasive personality. Exchanges and conversations that most times would be ignored or overlooked grated on people. And if it happened enough, those people began to foster resentment. And resentment could lead in a lot of directions.

"What did you do?" Neeley prompted.

"I started checking into him," Mrs. Sanchez said. "I went to the Vault."

Neeley knew about the Vault. The paper records of the covert world that never, ever would be digitized.

"And?"

"I found something that didn't make sense," Mrs. Sanchez said. She shook her head. "Let me back up. Why I went to the Vault. The payouts to Mr. Foreman from the Black Budget are scheduled. Routine. Like most, I assume he relies on them to keep his organization, whatever it is, going. But during government shutdowns, that routine is upset. I get complaints from every organization. They believe they are exempt from such a shutdown. But they aren't. Everyone complains."

"Except Foreman," Neeley completed.

"Correct."

"So he doesn't worry about the money or need it?"

"I assumed he had his own source of funds."

"So you went to the Vault."

"Yes. I found some records. Things most people wouldn't understand. But Foreman does have another source of income. Revenue generated from stockholdings. Not as unusual as most would think. Lots of agencies use the market to launder money. But his dated back. All the way back."

"To when?"

"Nineteen twenty-nine. And they're worth a lot."

"How much?" Neeley asked.

"As near as I could tell, and the records were incomplete, his organization is worth almost two billion dollars in various stocks."

"Bought in 1929?" Neeley confirmed.

"Yes."

Neeley now had two pieces. How they fit, she had no idea. Ten-thousand-dollar bills. And a lot of stock. But gluing them together with the Time Patrol wasn't hard.

"So you gave him—" Neeley started to do the math, but Mrs. Sanchez was much more skilled in this.

"One million, one hundred and eighty thousand dollars in ten-thousand-dollar bills."

Foreman had his own agenda. What it was, Neeley had no idea, but she knew where she needed to go next.

Off the East Coast of England, 999 A D. 29 October

With the disappearance of the Valkyrie, the wind had picked up. Roland and the rest were able to lock down their oars and let the wind take the ship west. The Nightstalker had immediately stretched himself out on the bench and fallen asleep, another hard-learned lesson for warriors: sleep when you can.

He woke when the lookout, perched on a narrow wooden platform near the top of the sail, cried out: "Sail!" He pointed directly forward.

Roland hopped to his feet, picked up his sword (he was thinking he needed to name it, and was considering christening it "Neeley," but he wasn't sure whether she would be honored or insulted if he did so—women, hard to figure), and walked forward to join Ragnarok in the bow.

Roland could see nothing on the relatively flat sea, but the lookout had a height advantage on him.

"There," Ragnarok pointed and Roland squinted. There was the slightest smudge on the horizon.

"A small boat," Ragnarok said, and Roland could still only make out a speck. But it was coming closer.

"Enemy?" Roland asked for lack of anything better as he began to make out a shape. Tam Nok had joined them.

"Ahh," Ragnarok said in disgust. "Not an enemy. See the sail? Three black lines straight up and down?"

Roland could not. "Yes."

"Lika-Loddin. It is bad fortune to cross paths with that ghoul."

"Does it work for the Shadow?" Roland asked.

"He works for himself," Ragnarok said. "But since he's in front of us, we might as well speak with him. He knows more than most what happens on the sea."

"Only him on that?" Roland asked, impressed someone would be brave enough to venture out in such a small vessel.

"He can handle the sail. If there is no wind, he sits and waits for it. He has great patience. And he is an expert sailor, I will give him that."

Roland could clearly see the other vessel now. It was a much smaller version of the longship he was on. Instead of shields on the sides of the vessel, there were several long bundles wrapped in heavy canvas and secured with thick ropes.

A man was in the rear, a hand on the tiller. As he got closer, he locked the tiller down and got to his feet, lowering the sail. He was tall, about Roland's height. He wore leather pants and a long-sleeved leather shirt, both stained black.

"What cargo does he carry?" Tam Nok asked.

Ragnarok spit over the side. "Bodies. He is also known as Corpse-Loddin. He travels the northern seas, recovering the bodies of men lost during the winter or in raids. He is coming back from his first journey of the season. He sells the bodies back to their families so that the departed might move on to the next life in the correct manner."

Ragnarok raised a hand in greeting and the two vessels met with a slight bump. Loddin threw a rope up and one of the Vikings secured the smaller vessel. The man who plied his trade in corpses scrambled up the side.

"Ragnarok Bloodhand." Loddin's voice was hoarse, a man not used to speaking to others, spending most of his time alone on the ocean. Loddin put his hand out and Ragnarok grasped his forearm and they formally greeted each other.

"Lika-Loddin, greetings," Ragnarok replied. "One hopes you are not carrying any relative of mine."

"I am not." He looked past Ragnarok and took in the crew. Then he was staring at Roland and then Tam Nok.

"Are there any supplies you need?" Ragnarok asked.

"Who is she?" Loddin bluntly asked.

"A Disir," Ragnarok replied.

"Ah," Loddin said. "Interesting."

"How so?" Ragnarok asked.

"Strange things are afoot," Loddin said. "Berserkers are not far away."

"How far?" Ragnarok asked. "What direction?"

Loddin nodded his head from the direction he'd come and in which they were heading. "They are an hour ahead of you."

"Ahh," Ragnarok said. "They will sack and pillage the monastery before us."

Loddin shook his head. "I do not think that is their goal."

"What is it then?" Tam Nok asked.

"I think they seek the Standing Stones," Loddin said.

"What Standing Stones?" Tam Nok asked.

"You will see them just past the beach," Loddin said. "A circle of stones. Similar circles are here and there among the islands. Strange places," he added, with a glance at Tam Nok. "It must have something to do with the darkness."

Roland decided to enter the conversation. "What darkness?"

Loddin looked at him. "I do not know you. What is your family?" He smiled, revealing rotting teeth. "In case I come across you in the course of business."

"His family is far from here," Tam Nok said.

"As is yours, I am sure," Loddin said. He nodded over his shoulder. "There was a fog bank. A most unusual one near the shore. Near the stones. A black fog. I've seen the like before. I always steer clear."

"A gate," Roland said, before he realized he wasn't supposed to say that.

"Yes," Tam Nok confirmed, which helped Roland feel better.

"A gate," Loddin said. "Curious. To where?"

"No one is sure," Tam Nok said.

Ragnarok was a little bit behind and focused on what he did understand. "How many berserker ships?"

"One," Loddin replied.

"Crew?"

Loddin looked around. "Roughly the same as what you have."

"Who are these berserkers?" Roland asked.

Ragnarok shook his head in disgust. "They are Vikings with no home. Who live for war for no cause beyond the fighting and the payment they receive. They have no honor. They wear wolf skins, if they wear anything at all. Some fight naked. Their shields are painted with blood. One will throw himself onto a shield wall, knowing he will die, to break it for the others."

Tam Nok cut to the key issue. "Why are they here? Going to the same place?"

Loddin shrugged. "That is your problem. How would I know their intentions?"

"Whose banner were they rowing under?" Ragnarok asked.

"The black."

Roland could tell the Viking didn't like the answer. "What does that mean?"

"They are serving no one," Ragnarok said. "They are rogue."

Loddin seemed bored with it all. "I would like some salt. And fresh water."

Ragnarok waved a hand and one of his men went to get the supplies. "Will you be returning home?"

Loddin looked at Ragnarok as if he were crazy. "Of course not. I anticipate an increase in business very shortly."

Los Angeles, California, 1969. 29 October

Scout felt comfortable because she fit right in. All the girls were slender. Everyone was slender. Food was still food in 1969 and people metabolized all of it just getting through their day. She paused and accessed the font of mostly useless information that had been downloaded into her brain and pulled out one amazing tidbit: Doritos hadn't even been invented yet! She couldn't imagine Edith Frobish including that in the download, so someone in that big Possibility Palace had a slightly warped sense of what was important and what wasn't.

Scout knew her mother would like it here, then realized her mother *had* liked it here. Well not here, here. But this time. Roughly. Okay, probably a little bit later. It occurred to Scout that she couldn't picture her mother as a college student. She'd always been her mother. Had her mother partied? Hung out? Made out? Dropped out?

Whatever.

People looked fit, but the clothes were awful. And some of the girls more generously endowed than Scout were going to rue giving up much needed support for their delicate breast tissue. She wondered if her mother had had sizable breasts once upon a time before she dieted and exercised herself into a stick?

Then she wondered why she was wondering about her mother. She was sure Frasier, the Nightstalker shrink, could figure that one out, but like Nada, she sure wasn't going to let him into her brain, and that thought stopped her in her tracks as she remembered Nada and that he was gone. Into the past and into death. Long buried in Arlington. Or yet to be buried at Arlington. Yet to die.

Where was Nada in 1969? Scout wondered, realizing she didn't know how old he was, or had been.

Her head hurt and with great force of will she turned her thoughts away from the sadness of remembering her friend.

Scout continued across the expanse of grass, noting that these college kids seemed more mature in some way than her compatriots. Of course they had a war going on, but her generation had a war going on. However, this generation also had a thing called the draft.

Yeah, that could make a difference, Scout thought. *A big one.*

Scout paused in the shade of a tree on the surprisingly warm late October day and her brain looped back to clothes and accouterments. What a sad way to protest the establishment by ruining one's breasts. A mundane thought of no real consequence, but it was all rather overwhelming. Rifts, a zombie, Fireflies . . . whatever. Those she had faced and dealt with.

But she was alone and she was in a different time. She wasn't sure which was more troubling. She missed Nada more than she could acknowledge without becoming a blubbering mass of protoplasm. And to actually be in the past, before her birth . . . there was something fundamentally disturbing about it. So she was focusing back on the mundane to ground herself.

In the here. And, more importantly, the now.

Another observation. No backpacks. How odd. Surely there were backpacks somewhere in 1969, or was that solely the province of soldiers—*The Things They Carried*? Everyone was carrying stuff in their hands. Who would be the first to start putting their stuff into a pack they slung over their shoulder and carried on their back? Seemed a no-brainer, especially since the girls had long bags made of cloth or macramé hanging on one shoulder. But the concept of taking that strap and simply putting it over the head to the other side hadn't seemed to occur to anyone.

Or had it, but no one did it because no one did it?

Except mailmen. Oh, Scout immediately realized. How sexist. But in this day and age it was mailmen. And stewardesses, not flight attendants—*Coffee, Tea or Me*? Scout knew that despite all the information downloaded into her brain, it didn't change who she was, and it was going to be hard to keep the gender thing straight because that specific revolution was bubbling and fomenting in 1969 but not yet ascendant. Everything was still male unless specified not male.

Scout moved out from under the shade of the tree, heading toward a street that marked the edge of campus where there were lots of students, non-students, and small storefronts. The sort of place one could pick up information. And find a belt maker.

But the hair thing really bothered her. Lots of lank hair and split ends.

It surprised and depressed her to suddenly realize she was a lot more like her mother than she'd ever imagined. She had to cut the people here some slack because there were probably no shampoos to close the pores of the hair follicles.

She passed by some long-haired guy (badly needing a washing) who stuck out a mimeographed piece of paper. She automatically took it, realizing that was wrong. Nada wouldn't have approved. What if the Shadow had put poison on it? But damn, Nada was dead, and he had indeed been a bit paranoid, and damn she missed him so bad sometimes she thought her chest would explode and her heart would be spread out all over this beautiful lawn here in beautiful sunny California in a thousand little pieces.

Mission.

Scout glanced down at the paper. A protest against the war in Vietnam.

This generation's war. Her generation had inherited the Global War on Terrorism where the enemy was . . . well, who the hell was the enemy? And how had some people in a country most Americans had never heard become the enemy back here and now?

Scout wanted to turn back to the long-haired, smelly guy and tell him: *Hey, dude, you did stop that. Good job. Keep it up. The people we're killing will be selling America furniture inside of a generation. And consider a bath?* Not like her generation was going to stop the War on Terrorism.

What a future to look forward to: perpetual war.

Couldn't we do better? Scout wondered.

Scout stuffed the piece of paper in her own patchwork big bag hanging on one shoulder, and resisted the temptation to slip the bag over her head to the other shoulder and carry it in a more comfortable way. Frak knows how that would change history and cause a ripple to cause a shift to cause a tsunami. Because of the bag on the wrong shoulder the timeline was lost!

Besides, it would be hard to start a trend here in 1969 without social media. 2014, sure. But not now. She imagined trends had to start now by people actually interacting with people, not with a machine in between the people.

Wow! Scout came to an abrupt halt as she realized what was really, really different. No cell phones. No laptops. People were actually talking to each other. Looking each other in the eye. No one was head down, tuned out, checking their e-mail. No one had their hand to the side of their head, ignoring the person they were next to in order to talk to someone they weren't next to. People were reading books, not computer screens.

Surreal.

She was here to save the Internet, but was the Internet really a good thing?

Scout stepped over the grass onto the sidewalk and left UCLA proper. Across the street was a head shop, what would be called a "medicinal marijuana store" in her time and sold cookies and would even be legal in some states, but in 1969 it sold everything *but* the weed. She was sure it was a place she could find information.

In a corner there was a guy hammering out leather covers for bongs.

No weed for open sale but they sold bongs. *What the frak else would someone do with a bong other than smoke weed,* Scout wondered? *They couldn't do backpacks, but they had excellent bongs?*

The guy was thin, like pretty much everyone else, and had no bulky muscles. No universal gyms. Heck, Nike hadn't even invented a shoe yet, so running really was running, like from danger or to get somewhere faster. Scout was sure there were waffle makers around. Someone would just have to connect the dots. In Oregon. Oh yeah, even that was in the download. Still a year out from borrowing the wife's waffle iron.

Scout checked out the guy working the leather. He had long hair that was too curly for his face. He had scruffy facial hair indicating an inadequate razor, not an attempt at style.

So that market, along with pillows, hair color, and some others, was still wide open.

He looked up and saw her and smiled.

With teeth that hadn't been whitened or perfectly straightened. Scout remembered all that time wearing braces and putting those stupid, tiny rubber bands in and being miserable. But his teeth were pretty good, the result of genes, not cosmetic dentists. It occurred to Scout that things here and now relied more on what you were born with rather than what you could buy to change what you were born with, and she wanted to think about that, but he was talking.

"Like the belt?" Scout was still thinking about her orthodontist who probably owned black leather and whips, and had a dungeon in his house for his weekend relaxing, so he kept speaking. "Did I sell that to you? I'd have remembered a groovy chick like you."

Did he just say "groovy"? And "chick"? Was he Austin Powers?

He stood up. "I'm John. I made the belt. You like it? What's your name?"

She finally pulled herself into the moment. "Scout."

"Far out, man! *To Kill a Mockingbird.*"

Okay, kinda cute and he'd read a book. Or seen the movie she immediately knew, as the data dumped into her consciousness: book published 1960; movie 1962. Atticus Finch, aka Gregory Peck, standing tall in the face of racism, stupidity, and more.

"It was a gift," Scout said. "I'm looking for the person you made it for."

He cocked his head, puzzled. "You don't know who gave it to you?"

"It was, uh, given to me by a secret admirer, you know? Anonymously." Oh yeah, she thought. Anonymous. Hacking stuff. She could stop them in their tracks today, eh? "Do you remember who you made it for?"

"Oh, sure, I made that for Luke. Put his name on the inside." He reached for her waist in a way that would get him pepper-sprayed in Scout's time.

"I saw the name," she said. She twisted the belt so he could see the inside. "What's this stuff?" She pointed at the hieroglyphics.

John frowned. "I burned the name, but not that other stuff. What's that, some sort of art?"

So Luke put it there for her to see, which is what she'd figured from the start.

"Where's Luke at?"

He gave her an odd look and Scout regretted dangling the preposition. People weren't texting or using emoticons yet. They still tried to speak proper English. Or was it a stupid question?

"So where would I find Luke?"

Argh, Scout thought. Still a coordinate conjunction and not some strung-out interjection. How the frak did she know all this grammar stuff she wondered? She suspected Edith had added that in. She looked like the type of person that might throw some extra education into the download. Poor Roland, Scout thought. His brain was probably exploding.

"Luke's a brainiac," John said. "He'll be in the library most likely." He smiled. "Plus he does a little dealing there. So people usually know where to find him. You know. Everyone goes to the library."

A library as a social hub? Made sense in this time of no laptops, cell phones, Wi-Fi, and info-dumping brain machines.

She smiled at him. "Thanks," she said, while thinking that if he was still alive in her time (not drafted and becoming fodder, not smashed in a car accident, whatever), that he was probably some neatly barbered, silver-haired guy checking his texts.

"How about a bong?" he asked. "We could check one out together."

She saw Wall Street in his future, perfect salesman.

"I don't smoke."

He did that head-cocking thing, confused. Oh, yeah, smoking now meant cigarettes, not pot. And she realized a lot of people she'd passed coming across campus had been smoking. A totally different world despite the Surgeon General warning first issued three years earlier.

While her mission was the computer network, still in its infancy, there was much else that would change. Cigarettes would go the way of the snuffboxes before them. *Actually, why smoke when you could get coffee on every corner and pop an Adderall,* Scout thought. Then she realized she'd seen no green mermaid signs on this street.

1969 was going to be hard to negotiate, free love or not, Scout realized.

"What do you do?" John asked, pulling her out of her Starbucks reverie.

I work for the Time Patrol, Scout was tempted to reply, just to see his reaction. "I'm a student."

"Far out." As if almost everyone who walked in here wasn't.

"So where's the library?" Scout asked, realizing that was a really poor segue.

But John didn't seem to pick up on a student not knowing where the library was to be the slightest bit odd. Probably too much hitting on the bong. He walked over to the front of the store and pointed. "Powell Library. They have a bunch of smaller ones on campus. But he'd be in the main one. There. That building. But why don't you just hang out here for a while?"

"Thank you," Scout said. "Maybe I'll be back," saying the last three words in her best Arnold, which earned her a confused look from John. Ahead of his time. Literally. He probably thought she was a nut.

But wait, Arnold *was* here. Not here, here. But in California, arriving a year ago and training in Venice Beach. Twenty-one years old. For some reason the thought of a twenty-one-year-old Arnold Schwarzenegger gave her the creeps.

She paused at the door, realizing she'd forgotten one key piece. "Uh, what does Luke look like?"

Reefer dude smiled. "He's fine as wine, or so all the chicks tell me. But just ask the desk to page him. You know."

"Thanks."

And with that, Scout left reefer madness behind. She tried to remember the last time she'd been inside a library. She walked up a broad pathway to an old building that was actually pretty neat looking while data scrolled through her brain. Most of it useless, but she knew Nada would tell her the key was hidden somewhere in the details: UCLA Library among the top ten academic research libraries in the country. A frak-load of books, in the millions. It is a United Nations Depository Library . . . which meant what? She had no idea and shut down the info that wanted to dump into her consciousness about that.

She felt pretty good that she was learning to control this.

She smiled as she saw the inscription above the entrance: LIBRARY.

Wow. Deep. Above that, engraved in the stone, were two people reading facing an owl in the center. So, like wisdom or something? Scout thought, shutting off the info that wanted to tell her the history of the engraving, the library, the owl, and stone working.

She entered a cool, large foyer. There was that hush, sort of like being in a church. The reverence for the book—or more likely bitchy librarians who shushed anyone who was too loud.

Scout walked up to a large desk. It was manned by half a dozen people, all female (duh), and ranging in age from some obvious students to the professional matriarchs with their permanent scowls who'd probably get along fabulously with Edith Frobish.

She went to one of the students.

"May I help you?"

The girl had black-framed glasses, hair that made Scout's look absolutely cutting edge, and a complete lack of makeup. Scout didn't see much excitement in this girl's future.

"I'm looking for Luke."

The girl's pale face flushed red as if Scout had just asked to see the secret porn stash. The spectacled student glanced nervously left and then right. "Are you a pig?"

A moment of offense, until she understood the context. Then Scout almost laughed, but kept it in. "Nope. Friend." She slid the belt around and turned it so the girl could see the name. "He sent me this and I wanted to thank him."

"So he's around your pants," the girl said, "but did he get in them?"

It was almost a challenge, as if the girl had some proprietary interest in Luke. Hmm, give her a few more points than initial assessment.

"I just want to talk to him."

"He's got a study room. One four two."

"Right," Scout said. "I think I'll go study."

She felt the girl's eyes on her back until she got out of view. It didn't take long to find the study room. The door was open and Scout walked in and hit the brakes. She was staring into the bluest eyes she'd ever seen, beneath a mop of blond hair that urged her to run her fingers through it. Luke stood, revealing a tall, lean, totally ripped surfer dude. He smiled at her, showing his pearly whites.

"Welcome to California. I'm Luke."

Scout could only nod in return as she tried to collect her thoughts, her pulse, and her mission.

Luke reached out and ran a finger along the top of the belt, which meant the top of her pants, which meant below her peasant top, which meant his finger so lightly grazed the thin line of exposed skin. A tingle ran from the skin into Scout's stomach.

Scout couldn't stop staring at him. He was really beautiful in a way guys weren't any more in her time. His long unkempt hair had natural blond highlights that could only come from a lot of time in the sun. One of his teeth wasn't quite straight and that tiny flaw made everything else just perfect. The body underneath the T-shirt with the big-footed guy who's gonna *"Keep on Truckin'"* and the jeans that flared with a little bit of a bell at the bottom wasn't the result of a gym, but rather a very active lifestyle. She'd never thought of that before, but working specific muscle groups in a specific workout routine wasn't the same as just overall using the entire body. He was fit from the core outward and now she realized that she was staring.

But he was staring right back, his eyes roaming her body without a shred of discretion or modesty.

This might be a fine assignment after all.

"You're a surfer?" she asked, for lack of jumping right in and asking how the Shadow was going to try and destroy the startup of the Internet this evening. It was obvious he was: the hair, the mark on the ankle from the board's leash, and the tanned feet inside the worn leather sandals, which indicated he was on the board longer than he was in the water.

Scout was liking this way too much.

Which brought a little tingling sensation deep in some primordial part of her brain.

Which she scrunched down right away.

He even had a small smiley face tattooed on the arch of his foot. When did the smiley face become a thing? And the answer was there: 1963.

"Hey. I'm up here."

He probably thinks I have a foot fetish, Scout thought. "I like your ink," she said, lifting her gaze to meet those adorable eyes once more.

He looked puzzled.

Oops, not slang yet. "The tattoo."

He smiled. "You seem to like a lot more than that."

Whoa, Scout thought. Was everyone so forward in this summer of love? Well, fall actually since it was October. It was the time of the pill and the only possible negative of casual sex was pregnancy and thus the pill.

My, oh my, Scout thought, *this must have been a wonderful time.*

Except Scout wasn't on the pill, she suddenly realized.

And why was she realizing that? And why should she care? And why didn't anyone think of that and prepare her? Who knows what sacrifices she might have to make for the mission?

"Hey," Luke said. "I got something you might really like. Let's go out back."

"Sure," Scout said before even thinking about it.

Nada would have been very unhappy.

But, hey, one has to perform sacrifices in the name of duty. Take risks.

He led the way through a labyrinth of corridors in the library with a surety that indicated this wasn't his first time going out back. He pushed open a fire escape door that had no alarms on it and they stepped into an alley. Apparently the whole "garbage is a bad thing" hadn't quite made it here and now. Scout's nostrils were assaulted by smells that didn't seem to bother Luke, or which he easily ignored. Scout made a mental note that if she ever went back to the Middle Ages, she'd better be prepared for the smell. She knew Roland was in a pretty smelly time, but she doubted the big guy even noticed.

Luke looked, if it were possible, even better in the sun. He sat down on a crate and tapped it, inviting her to join him. From inside a pocket he pulled out a joint.

"I guess it's nine o'clock somewhere," Scout said, earning her another quizzical look.

"That from your time?" Luke asked, the first blatant indication he was Time Patrol. He fired up the roach, took a long hit, and extended it to her.

"I can't tell you," Scout said, feeling proud she was sticking with Dane's rules.

She almost passed on the weed because she could hear the stems burning and it was the worst-smelling pot ever. But he seemed to like it.

"It's good stuff," he insisted, still holding the roach toward her.

You have no idea what good stuff is, Scout thought. Her time had gotten some things better, but what was science for if not to improve the quality of the marijuana?

She took a hit and forced herself not to sputter and cough and prove herself an amateur. But the word "harsh" must have been invented for this crap. Her eyes watered and she exhaled much too quickly because it felt like she'd inhaled a smoking piece of newspaper rolled into another piece of newspaper.

She handed it back and she could tell by the look on his face he thought she was a novice, and that was okay. But he was nice enough not to pass it back, sucking at it until all that was left was a tiny nub. Then he brought out a pair of clips to hold until there literally was just about nothing left.

Efficient at least. Waste not, want not.

It was done, with just the lingering odor of the roach mixed with the lingering odor of all the other obnoxious stuff in the alley. Scout thought she smelled some benzene and that would make sense; not outlawed in California yet. Luke didn't seem to be too high and she wasn't surprised since the amount of THC in whatever it was he'd just smoked probably wasn't much. Which explained John and his handmade bongs.

"I like you," Luke said in the manner of extremely good-looking people who think their compliments are a favor they're doing you.

"I like you too," Scout said, even though she hardly knew him, other than he was a drug dealer and a member of the Time Patrol.

She wondered about the recruitment arm of the Patrol, but then realized she was here, so she'd passed whatever low bar one had to crawl under to get in. There was something about Luke, an aura that was very, very attractive.

The things she did for a mission. Sometimes you have to sacrifice in the line of duty. But it occurred to her she was a bit more baked from just that one puff than she'd thought. Some slow-acting stuff.

"All right then," Luke said. "There's a talk early this evening at the computer lab. The geeks will be there. I don't know what you're here for, but I was told it had something to do with the computers? This ARPANET thing they're working on in conjunction with Stanford?"

"Uh, right."

"Yeah. Figured. They're doing stuff for the military. I heard it's to build a way to maintain communications after a nuclear war. But what would be the point of that? We'd all be dead. And you're here from the future so I figure we've dodged that fate so far."

He hopped off the crate. "So. Nothing going on for a while. Meet me at Boelter Hall at five. See what's happening. There's a lecture being presented by one of the geeks in the project. Figure if the bad guys are going to try something, it will be then or later. We take care of business. Then we can go have some real fun."

Scout felt a little quiver at the thought of real fun. "Okay, let's do that."

"Wear something cute," he added with a wink.

And the quiver froze. Don't do that, she thought, and for a moment his hair just looked messy and the alley really did smell bad. And she already thought she *was* wearing something that could at least be defined as cute.

"All right then," Luke said. "See you then. Have a nice day!"

And then he was gone into the building, leaving Scout in the garbage-strewn alley. She waited for a few moments, and then followed him into the library. Not to follow him, but because she had to look some things up, because the almighty download hadn't downloaded everything. Edith wasn't on target as much as she probably thought she was.

And since Scout didn't have her iPhone, her iPad, her laptop (and even if she did there was no Internet—yet), and thus no Wikipedia, she was going to have to do this the old-fashioned way: books.

London, England, 1618. 29 October

Mac followed Beeston through the streets around Westminster. The 29th of October, the feast of Saints Simon and Jude, was also to be the annual Sir Mayor's Show. So despite being very early in the day, there were a number of people out and about.

Everyone smelled either awful or they were drenched with perfume, with the majority leaning toward the former. Mac couldn't tell which was worse. He'd have to remember this for his next mission; the wrong smell could give one away. Seems to have been an oversight in Dane's planning, although Roland had smelled a bit rank during the pre-op briefing. But Mac knew that was sort of standard for Roland even when he wasn't time traveling or dressed like a Viking.

This mission was odd for Mac, and not just the smell, and the time travel, which he supposed would make it odd for anyone, but because the goal wasn't clearly stated, and neither were the parameters. He was used to Nightstalker missions where they went in fast and hard with things often uncertain, but they'd always had their three Cs: Containment, Concealment, and Control. Which usually meant Roland leading the way, guns blazing, and they pretty much destroyed whatever possible threat there was.

First, Mac didn't have a gun to blaze, just this thin-ass rapier on his belt, which he wasn't exactly trained on. Second, he didn't know who the enemy was. Third, the only thing he really knew was that history said Raleigh was to get his head chopped off later this morning.

But he had no clue what he was supposed to do or even who the enemy was other than some group called the Shadow.

That train of thought gave Mac a moment of pause as he followed Beeston into a pub. Did Raleigh have to be beheaded or simply be dead by the end of the day? Could method of death affect history?

The smell was worse inside, which Mac didn't think was possible. The noise inside the pub was also overwhelming, so one had to shout to be heard. Beeston elbowed his way through wall-to-wall people, all here, Mac supposed, to see the big event later in the morning. The endless human fascination with death, especially when it wasn't your own, ruled once again. Rarely do people get a chance to see death occur on schedule. And a beheading— Mac remembered that tons of people had scoured the Internet to try to find the videos of hostages beheaded in the Middle East, unwittingly lending power and motivation to the terrorists who posted them.

"Here," Beeston said, indicating a heavy wooden door in a corner of the room. He swung it open and came to an abrupt halt as the point of a rapier came to rest underneath his chin. "Easy!"

The rapier was withdrawn from Beeston, who entered the room, but then it snapped back up, stopping underneath Mac's chin.

"Who be this?" the man holding the sword demanded, throwing the question toward Beeston, not Mac.

"A friend of the prophecy," Beeston said. The point was reluctantly withdrawn from Mac's neck and he slid inside, the heavy door swinging shut behind him with a solid thud, dropping the noise level appreciably. The room was narrow and smoke filled, which reminded Mac of another of Raleigh's claims to fame: introducing tobacco to England. From his download, Mac knew tobacco was already in other parts of Europe, so it wasn't that great a claim to infamy, but certainly Raleigh had played a role.

The room was narrow, barely big enough to contain the long wood table with benches on either side. The table had seen many knives scar its surface. It was also disgustingly dirty with what Mac swore were vomit stains mixed in with spilled ale, food remnants, and other nasty bits. There was a window at the far end of the room where one could barely see outside through the streaked panes of glass.

These people were literally breathing in disease, but Mac supposed when you lived in an age where disease killed often and swiftly, you just learned to make it part of your life. He was sure Doc would be appalled to see this. He was glad his shots were up to date, since he had to be ready to deploy anywhere in the world as a Nightstalker.

"Take a seat," Beeston said, indicating a spot at his side.

As he squeezed in, Beeston slid a mug of ale over in front of Mac. There were eight other men at the table, four on benches on each side.

"Our friends," Beeston said, indicating the other men. They all stared at Mac and one, a lean fellow with only one hand, spoke up.

"Who's he?"

"He's here to help," Beeston said. He leaned close to Mac and whispered in his ear. "They're not to know you're from the Patrol. But they're with us in the prophecy. All came to London in the past few days. This is the first time we've been all together. Some I know from past service, but others are new." As if that explained everything.

"He got a name?" One-Hand asked.

"I've got one," Mac replied. "But maybe sharing names is not the most prudent course of action?"

"Good point," another one of the men acknowledged. "It's likely to be bloody work today. And if we fail, it's not just the head chopped, it's drawn and quartered for high treason. There's not much I fear, but I won't be going that way. I'd rather take my own blade."

Mac's download filled in the details. The sentence for high treason: being tied to a ladder or panel, pulled to the place of execution, and hanged. To a point just short of death. Unhanged. Then emasculated, disemboweled, and finally beheaded. Dying somewhere in that process, the sooner the better for the victim, the later for the executioner. Then the body was quartered—cut into four pieces, which were sent out to four corners of England to be disposed of.

Gotta love humanity, Mac thought.

At least they didn't do it to women. They just got burned at the stake.

Really gotta love humanity.

"Do you have a plan?" Mac asked since they all seemed more clued in than he was.

The conspirators exchanged glances, and then Beeston spoke. "It's simple. Since we know not how exactly the prophecy will be fulfilled, we must get as close to Sir Raleigh as possible and then be prepared to help him get away. The prophecy will keep him from the axe, but then we must get him from England."

Someone needed to fill him in on the prophecy.

"So we just wait?" Mac asked.

Beeston nodded. "We have time before they bring Sir Raleigh out for the trip to the block. Since we know he will not end up as they desire, we must help him."

"Let's drink then," One-Hand advised, the most sensible thing Mac had heard since arriving. Of course, it was obvious they'd all already been drinking, to judge by the number of mugs scattered around the table and the slurring of the words. If Raleigh was counting on this group of conspirators to free him, he'd better be preparing to meet his maker.

One-Hand dipped his mug into a wooden bucket at his end of the trestle and Mac realized that was the source of the ale sitting in front of him. He looked at the motley crew gathered at the table and was pretty sure there was some bad stuff to be transmitted via mug, via bucket, via ale. They were sharing more than high treason.

Mac sighed as he lifted his mug. It was true: The less you knew, the easier life was. And, he supposed, the more fun you could have as he quaffed a good portion of the ale, quite aware it wasn't even dawn yet. Well, five o'clock somewhere, but he had a feeling these people had no qualms about what time of day they drank.

He finished off the mug and passed it down the table. It was strange to realize how limited he was by fear when it came to his own life. Looking around he saw a bunch of people who'd probably never heard the phrase "live hard, play hard," but they embodied it. He supposed when you lived in an age where the plague could sweep through and wipe out a goodly percentage of folk, you didn't worry too much about the future.

And it's not like they had television or radio or the Internet or soccer games or any of that to entertain themselves on the odd half hour they got off from backbreaking work. They had drink and—that's when Mac noticed another thing. There were only men in this room, and his gaydar was ringing off the charts.

There was always sex.

Mac glanced down the table and there was a handsome young man staring back at him. And not in the manner of One-Hand, who looked like he'd stab Mac as soon as he'd fight alongside him.

"Did they announce the execution for certain?" One-Hand asked Beeston.

"Aye."

Surprisingly, One-Hand smiled. "Fools. Raleigh won't be taken by no king's axe for treason."

Another one laughed. "The prophecy says that be so straight on."

Everyone turned back to their ale and whatever they were talking about before with whomever, which meant there were about six conversations in the room with eight people because some were talking at the same time to each other.

Mac was rather amazed they all hadn't been gathered up and had their heads chopped off already if this was the way they ran things. They still didn't know his name but were willing to so easily accept him into this room just on Beeston's word.

" 'Scuse me," Mac said to Beeston, who looked slightly startled as Mac left his side and went around the table to shove himself on the bench on the other end.

"No name, eh?" the young man asked. "I'm Henry."

"I'm Mac."

"Odd name, that."

"Short for something."

"Odd accent too," Henry said. "Never heard the like."

"I come from far away."

"I suppose."

Henry's face wasn't so attractive up close as it was pockmarked from acne and had rarely known soap.

"Why does everyone think Raleigh is going to get away?" Mac asked.

"The prophecy," Henry said, giving Mac an odd look.

"I've been in prison a long time," Mac lied.

"Then how do you now Beeston? Or Beeston know you? Or you know to be here?"

"Long story," Mac said, which he supposed was a partial truth. And at least this guy was still suspicious while the rest just seemed to be relying on some prophecy to take care of business for them.

Henry leaned closer and Mac wasn't surprised when he felt Henry's hand on his thigh, but he was a bit repelled by the breath, although he tried not to show it, maintaining his position. Impolite to lean back when asking for secrets.

The things he had to do in the name of duty.

Henry was so obviously suspicious that Mac wished he could play poker with him, 'cause he was all tells. So Mac slid forward a little on the bench, allowing Henry's hand to ride farther up his thigh.

He'd seen other drunken men outside being a little more brazen on the way in although no one was actually humping on the bar. It seemed combining impending death with alcohol was an aphrodisiac; but in a pub where women weren't allowed, the options were limited. Strange to be in a society that was so close-minded on so many things (to the point where they'd burn you at the stake over slight variations in essentially the same religious beliefs) but tolerant of other things. And yet they all smelled like muddied barnyard chickens. Mac wondered what this place would look like under a black light and shuddered. Henry took that as enticement, the hand going even farther up.

"So the prophecy?" Mac asked.

"Only those who served close by Lord Raleigh are privileged to know of it," Henry said.

Max took a guess, given how young this guy was and that Raleigh had been in the Tower for a long time with only one trip out. "You went to the New World with him?"

Henry nodded. "I saw his son die. It was a terrible thing. But the prophecy only protects the Lord, not his family."

Mac noted that Beeston was staring hard at the two of them. But beyond Henry, Mac was picking up snippets of the other men at the table talking, catching up, or telling stories to newfound comrades. There seemed to be a theme—that Raleigh was the benefactor of some sort of prophecy and was sort of bulletproof, or, in this case, head-losing-proof.

"So," Mac said, deciding he didn't have much to lose and the clock was ticking as Henry fondled him, "what's this prophecy?"

"Ah. I don't know all of it. Not sure anyone but the Lord himself knows all, but I do know of the three promises he received from the angel."

"Oh yeah," Mac said. "The angel. Heard of that," Mac lied.

Beeston came around the table and slid in next to Mac, pressing him up against Henry even tighter. Things were getting weird, for sure.

Henry glanced worriedly at Beeston, but the nominal leader of this ragtag group nodded. "Tell him, Henry, what you know of the prophecy."

Henry's hand had gone limp at Beeston's arrival, which meant he feared the other man more than he was horny. "The key part is the three promises the angel made to Lord Raleigh."

"And they are?" Mac prompted.

"'Thou will never die at sea; thou will never die on field of battle; and thou will never lose thy head from treason's fee.'"

Who would cross the Bridge of Death must answer me these questions three, ere the side he see. Mac couldn't help the thought that popped into his head: Eagle reciting that in the team room more times than he cared to remember, from the Bridgekeeper in *Monty Python and the Holy Grail.*

"An angel told him that?" Mac asked.

"Indeed."

Beeston patted Mac on the back. "Just you wait. You'll see us ride off with our Lord, clear and free."

That was oddly phrased, Mac thought.

The door started to open and the man closest to it was on his feet in a flash, rapier out. At least someone wasn't totally soused.

A man shrouded in a cloak, his face hidden beneath a drooping hood, slipped in, the door easing shut behind him. He didn't seem fazed at all about the rapier at his neck. He pointed toward Beeston, and then crooked his finger.

Beeston forced his way around the table, pushed the rapier away, and leaned in close. The two men whispered fiercely while everyone else in the room fell silent. After a minute the cloaked man disappeared.

Beeston turned to face the room. "Lord Raleigh wishes to meet with me. I've been granted a few moments with him at Gatehouse Prison." He smiled. "I am sure it will be about future plans."

The men pounded the table with their fists.

"My friend,"—Beeston indicated Mac—"you are to come with me. Lord Raleigh wishes to meet you."

Grateful to escape the under-table groping and curious to meet the great man face to face, Mac quickly left the room with Beeston.

Andes Mountains, Argentina, 1972. 29 October

Moms saw the Yeti an hour into her guard shift. To the north, about four hundred yards away, a large bulky figure was briefly silhouetted along a ridgeline. She brought the M14 up, wishing she had a night vision scope, wishing she weren't so cold, wishing that she didn't wish.

It was moving northwest, occasionally bending over, as if sniffing. It didn't appear as if Correa's rounds or her machete cut had done any significant damage. As it came down off the ridge-line, it disappeared, melding into the dark background of the terrain. She nudged Correa.

He was awake in an instant, making her wonder if he'd ever been asleep.

"Yes?"

"Yeti," Moms said.

"Coming this way?"

"Not yet. Moving that way." She pointed.

"Not toward the wreckage," Correa said. "So that is good."

"It looked like it was bending over and sniffing. Didn't look wounded."

"It might not be," Correa said, and Moms understood right away that she'd made an assumption; one Nada would have chided her for. Correa said the obvious. "Might be a second one." He was silent for a few moments. "The beast must know where the wreckage is. So, like us, it is waiting. Scouting the area."

"If Yeti are the only things to come through the gate from the Shadow," Moms said, "they might be here to stop us."

Correa chuckled. "Stop us from doing what? We are not certain why *we* are here. No. They have a plan. And you are right; there might be something, or someone, else who came through. We must be on guard."

"How do you know of this monster?" Moms asked. She was still keeping watch, quartering the area around them.

Correa looked surprised at her question. "It is part of the lore of the Time Patrol. Many legends and myths throughout history have their basis in reality. We too often dismiss such things because they are beyond our ability to comprehend their existence. For most, our mind is limited to our world, our time. In the Patrol, we know there is so much more.

"When gates are opened on our planet, in our timeline, strange things come through. Most regular people dismiss these sightings because they are very rare and the"—he seemed to search for a word—"presence of the species is not enough to make it believable that they are sustainable. But that is because they *are not* sustained on our planet. Furthermore, some of these creatures seem so strange that they could not have developed naturally. And that is correct; they did not."

Moms had seen, and battled, many strange things in her time in the Nightstalkers. "Will our guns take it down if we put enough rounds into it?"

"I hope so," Correa said. "I have seen the like once before, but did not engage it. The Shadow uses genetically engineered creatures to do its bidding."

"Like the kraken," Moms said, remembering what Neeley had reported encountering en route to the Bermuda Triangle gate. "One of my team ran into one near the Bermuda Triangle."

"I have heard of that creature, but have not seen it," Correa said. "A perversion of science, taking various species and merging them to build monsters."

"We took physics and perverted the power of the atom into a weapon," Moms noted.

Correa smiled. "You see the world in a curious way. I find it amazing that the human race has made it this far. I take that as an encouraging sign. And given you are here, from some time in my future, it seems we last a bit longer than 1980." He paused. "Do you know why you are here?"

"Not quite," Moms said.

He nodded toward the west. "They are suffering over there. The search was called off over a week ago. Are we to just stay here and allow them to die? You must be here for a reason."

"I know how it's supposed to turn out," she said. She was uncertain what to tell him, knowing the rule, but realizing he needed hope. "After the avalanche, three more die from hunger and exposure. But two of them make a trek to Chile and get rescue."

"To Chile?" Correa shook his head. "That makes no sense. They are closer to civilization going east, toward Argentina."

"They don't know where they are," Moms said. "The pilot, before he died, told them the wrong position. They think they are in Chile."

Correa pondered that. "But in history, your history, they went west and eventually found rescue?"

"Yes."

"We could make it easier for them by letting them know where they are." He pointed east. "There is an abandoned hotel just thirty kilometers in that direction. Would that be so bad to let them know? Would it change the timeline?"

When Moms said nothing, he sighed. "We must let things be what they will be. But the beast is not what should be, so we will deal with that."

"How long will it take us to make it up to that ridgeline where we can view the crash site?" Moms asked.

"Four or five hours," Correa said. "It does not look far, but moving uphill in this snow is very difficult."

That agreed with what Moms had estimated. "We should start moving soon. Our movement will keep us warm."

Correa looked up at the dark sky. "We leave in one hour. You get some sleep. I will keep watch."

Moms put her rifle outside the blanket, resting it on the side of the plane so it wouldn't warm up and "sweat" and then freeze up later.

She closed her eyes, but sleep would not come.

Correa must have sensed this. "Do they find this? The tail section?"

"Yes."

"Hmm." He reached into his pack and pulled out a small box. "Chocolate. May I leave it here?"

Moms knew the answer right away, but it confused her. The survivors had indeed found some chocolate in the tail section, coming upon it when they were searching for a way out of the mountains. If that was Correa's chocolate, they'd violated the rules. But it had been found.

Moms surrendered to empathy and gave up on trying to solve the puzzle of time. "Yes."

Eglin Air Force Base, Florida, 1980. 29 October

The patrol was gathered round Eagle. Ten men plus Eagle and Hammersmith. They were just silhouettes in the dark but they exuded an aura that Eagle was used to from his time in Special Operations and then the Nightstalkers.

They were not students. Eagle knew professional, combat-tested soldiers when he was around them. How and why Hammersmith had formed this patrol, Eagle had no idea and he supposed it didn't matter. They were here and now and had a job to do. But, and it was a "but" he couldn't quite define, something was off about these guys. A strange vibe.

Eagle barely saw their silhouettes. One had the obvious bulk of the M60 machine gun.

"Master Sergeant Hammersmith," Eagle said, "you'll take point. You know the area and you know the objective."

"Roger," Hammersmith said. "They're running the last test flight later today. A dog and pony show."

"Sir?" one of the dark figures spoke up.

"Yes?" Eagle said.

"How do I get out of this chickenshit outfit?"

Before Eagle could reply, Hammersmith stepped in front of the man. "Caruso, we're in the Army. What you want, what I want, don't mean squat. We follow orders. We die following orders if that's what's required. The only way out of this outfit is to make it through today and do what you're ordered to do."

"Geez, Sarge," Caruso said. "I know that. Was just asking. We'll do whatever . . ." He paused and shifted to Eagle. "Sorry, sir, don't know what your rank or name is?"

Eagle reverted to his last official rank. "I'm not a sir. My rank is Master Sergeant. My name doesn't matter."

"Well, Top," Caruso said, using the familiar term for a master sergeant who was assigned as a first sergeant, "we're all yours."

One of the other men snickered and Hammersmith wheeled toward him. "Do you want to go back to where I found you, maggot?"

The figure straightened. "No, Sergeant."

Eagle had no idea what Hammersmith was referring to, and he was a bit surprised that Hammersmith would call one of his men a maggot. But that got a worrisome reference stirring in his brain.

"Listen," Eagle said, "I know this doesn't make sense. But it's what we have to do. It's important. Not just for us and those we know. But it's important for our children and our children's children. For the human race. It might not seem like it. It might seem like I'm overstating it. But trust me. I'm not." Eagle paused, waiting for a reaction. At least a chorus of "Hooahs!" which was Ranger for "Okeydokey."

Nothing.

Something was definitely off here. Eagle had served in many units over the years, but these men seemed more resigned than motivated. Hammersmith's words seem to have passed into the men, been absorbed, and ultimately meant little.

"We'll move out in five mikes," Eagle said. He tugged on Hammersmith's elbow and drew him away from the others. "What gives?"

Hammersmith spit. "I couldn't exactly pull a squad from the Ranger Battalion to do this. And, well, there were other considerations. So I got an authorization from someone in the Pentagon, someone high up, someone from the Patrol I guess, to pull together a squad. They're all good soldiers, or putting it more accurately, were good soldiers. All combat vets. Served in Vietnam."

Eagle was already ahead of this explanation. "*The Dirty Dozen.*"

"Counting you," Hammersmith said with a grin, "we got a dozen. I went to the big house at Leavenworth, some other places. All these fellows been locked up a long time."

"How much do they know?"

"They know they have to do whatever they're told to do," Hammersmith said, "or they go back to where I got 'em."

"What's the promise?" Eagle asked.

"Complete pardon." Hammersmith paused. "Listen. Doesn't matter what they did or were facing. Doesn't even matter we're dangling the carrot of freedom. They're here. They want to get out of whatever is coming alive, they have to fight."

Eagle knew there was a big difference between positive motivation and being forced to do something. "Gather the men."

The eleven clustered in close. Eagle mentally ran through a list of Nada Yadas, but couldn't find one that specifically applied. He channeled the spirit of the former team sergeant for the Night-stalkers.

But before he could get started, Caruso brought up one of the problems that had already occurred to Eagle.

"Sergeant Hammersmith," Caruso said, "what's to keep the ten of us from killing the two of you and escaping?"

"I don't die easy," Hammersmith said. "But the bigger problem you got, Caruso, is if I don't bring you back in tomorrow or account for you, then a special unit called the Cellar is coming after each and every one of you sons-a-beasts. You ain't never heard of the Cellar, have you?"

"I been in one," Caruso said, "for twelve years now."

"The Cellar will come after you," Hammersmith said, "and they will execute you on the spot. You won't be going back to your cell. You will die. And the Cellar, I am told, never fails. Do you all understand?"

A low chorus replied. "Yes, Sergeant."

Eagle stepped up. "Men, as Sergeant Hammersmith has told me and most of you are picking up, there's something out there between us and that airfield. Probably something, or some things, that, well, are beyond what you can imagine. Terrible things. I've faced some of them. Lost teammates to them. One or two of you might be thinking of taking off at the first sign of trouble. But I'm telling you: Your only hope to survive today is to fight through it as a team."

"Hey, Top," Caruso said, "you should see some of the things we've seen at Leavenworth. Anything is better than that."

Eagle knew Caruso was wrong, but he didn't think it prudent to correct him.

"Let's move out."

———

Manhattan, New York, 1929. 29 October

The guy was dead. Dead, dead, dead. Ivar had known the wounds were fatal, but he'd tried and there was comfort in that. He'd held the man's hand as the light faded from his eyes, and Ivar had to suppose that was better than dying alone in the dark in some rat-infested alley. Or in the middle of Wall Street.

Ivar was now alone in a dingy basement via an alley. He'd been able to make it only a hundred yards, carrying the man, before his energy gave out. He broke a window, pushed the man through, and then followed. It had been pitch black inside, but with dawn lighting up the smeared half-windows at street level, he could see his surroundings a bit better. Crates were haphazardly stacked throughout the room and there was a door at the far end from where Ivar sat with the body.

Reluctantly, because he knew nothing good could come of it, having been a Nightstalker long enough to understand that, Ivar opened the bloodstained canvas bag.

He stared at the contents for several moments, trying to comprehend what he was seeing.

Several thick wads of $10,000 bills. He hadn't even known—

The first $10,000 bill was printed just a year previously, in 1928, when the entire banknote system was overhauled. The actual notes were shrunk, an inch less in length and half an inch taken off in width. A $500 (William McKinley), $1,000 (Grover Cleveland), $5,000 (James Madison) and $10,000 bill (Salmon P. Chase) were circulated.

Who the hell was—

Sixth Chief Justice of the United States as well as Lincoln's Secretary of the Treasury, Governor of Ohio, and senator. And Chase Manhattan Bank was named in his honor.

Ivar wished he'd had access to this downloading when he was in grad school. Would have made things a lot easier.

A 10K bill. Hard to get change for that at Starbucks, except there were no Starbucks now and Ivar regretted that 'cause he could really use a mocha right now, since he was cold and tired and hungry and scared, mostly scared.

There was a note and, like opening the bag, Ivar really didn't want to read it. Someone had killed the guy lying over there, stone cold, and Ivar had no doubt it had to do with the money and whatever was in the note.

He unfolded the paper. Just a bunch of stocks and an amount listed next to them. And a long string of numbers; probably a bank account.

It didn't take a genius, or even Ivar, to figure out the intent.

Buy these today. On a day when everyone else was going to be dumping stock, some brokers right before they took a header out of a window.

Unsummoned, more data from the download dumped into his consciousness: Some *did* jump out of their windows but asphyxiation by gas was very popular; also stepping in front of a train. Some broker in Chicago would poison himself later in the day. Some financier in Boston would shoot himself at his country club, perhaps to make some sort of statement or to just get his money's worth in brain cleanup?

So Ivar began to count the $10,000 bills, and he was only up to five million with a couple of bundles left when the door was kicked in by two guys holding guns, M1911 semiautomatics about which Ivar's training and download informed him. The weapon was a single-action, semiautomatic, magazine-fed, recoil-operated pistol chambered for the .45 caliber round. Designed as a standard sidearm for the US military in 1911. (Duh.) It was developed because Army guys fighting Moro guerillas in the Philippines found their .38 pistols just didn't have the stopping power. A lot of the Moros tended to charge hopped up on drugs and adrenaline and could take a half dozen .38 hits and still split one's head open with a bolo.

Great, Ivar thought. He was going to die knowing the history of the type of gun that killed him.

Dead is dead.

"Hands up." One of the gunmen trained his weapon on Ivar and ordered the other: "Check the stiff, Jimmy."

Both men wore suits and fedoras, trying to look classy, but the scuffed up shoes Jimmy wore betrayed his real status: he was muscle.

The other guy, though, was something else. His clothes were several echelons above in cost and fashion. His shoes were brilliantly polished. He wore his suit like a man who'd murdered and stolen his way into his style with great effort, and it reflected that effort.

Jimmy kicked the body, apparently the extent of his medical training. "Dead, Mister Siegel."

Alarm bells were sounding in Ivar's head.

"Who are you?" Siegel asked, taking a step forward and sliding the gun into a shoulder holster. He spit on the body as he went past it, DNA testing at a crime scene not yet being an issue.

Ivar thought the prudent course of action at the moment was to say nothing.

Siegel apparently didn't agree. He pulled a switchblade out of a pocket and flicked it open. As he got closer, Ivar realized Siegel's fine suit was stained with a splatter of blood. And the blade was also covered in blood.

Siegel put the blade to Ivar's throat, hard enough that it cut into the skin but not seriously deep. Of course, for Ivar, any cut was way too deep.

"I hate asking something twice."

"My name is Ivar."

"Ivar what?" Siegel said. "You Russian?"

"I'm American."

"Right," Siegel said. "So am I. But I'm also a Jew. That bother you?"

"No, sir."

But Siegel was already looking past him at the money. "That's more than he stole from us."

"I don't know who he is," Ivar said. "He literally ran right into me. Asking me for help."

"So you took him here to this basement, let him die, and are now counting the money," Siegel said. "Didn't call the coppers or take him to a hospital. And you just met him?"

"I'm an opportunist," Ivar said.

Siegel laughed. "Yeah. I can see where one would figure this was a good opportunity. Unfortunately for you, it ain't. Jimmy," he ordered, "put it back in the sack. We're taking it and him to the Boss."

As he did so, Ivar slipped the list of stocks out of his hand and down his sleeve.

When Jimmy was done, Siegel nodded. "We're going for a ride."

Going for a ride with Bugsy Siegel to see the Boss. *That's not good*, Ivar thought.

He wished he were back on Wall Street.

Siegel and Jimmy shoved the Nightstalker into the back of a car. They flanked him, pressing against his body. Siegel had the satchel on his lap and Jimmy had his pistol jammed uncomfortably into Ivar's ribs. Some no-neck guy was at the wheel and started driving the moment the door was closed.

Ivar was now pondering the future of both the mission and his life. It had just occurred to him that if he died now, on this mission in the past, it probably meant that his future, back in the future, meant little to his timeline since he was so easily expendable, which was a terribly depressing thought. And the mission would probably be a failure too, he realized as an afterthought. At least his part.

Of course, Ivar knew, of the six sent back, he was the weak link and most likely to fail. Even Scout, young as she was, had more on the ball on an operation like this.

Another depressing thought.

Dying depressed. Geez, that made Ivar even more depressed.

The trip wasn't far. The car pulled into an alley. Ivar was led through a door into what in his time would be considered an extremely dirty and unhealthy kitchen. No one looked up from what they were doing, which indicated two armed men leading another bleeding man through was a rather common event. That gave Ivar a flicker of hope—they can't be killing that many people? Maybe they just wanted to talk?

Then his data dump depressed him: Murder Incorporated. But, wait, that wasn't formed until the thirties, so maybe . . .

They passed out of the kitchen, down a hall, and turned right. A clone of Jimmy—i.e., big, smashed nose, cheap suit, fedora, dull look in the eyes, and scuffed shoes—stood stoically in front of a metal door. Spotting the incoming party, he rapped on the door behind him twice. Ivar could hear dead bolts being pulled back, and the door swung open on hinges that needed some oil.

Jimmy shoved Ivar through the door.

The room was filled with smoke and hushed conversation. Red velvet meets dark wood. Along the wall were big men, more muscle, faces blank.

It wasn't hard to see the sun around which this entire operation revolved. At a round table in the center of the room were two men, well dressed like Siegel, faces guarded, not blank. They were obviously men who were rarely surprised and never frightened, which is one of the definitions of psychopath.

Ivar wished Eagle, or even Frasier, were here, because he had a very bad feeling about who he was seeing. Jimmy pushed Ivar forward, then paused at a predetermined position. Siegel put the satchel on the table.

There was obviously something going on, something big. Ivar wondered if it had anything to do with what was already happening nearby on Wall Street, since the opening bell had sounded not too long ago.

Then again, these were guys whose business was very different from that world financial center, although some might argue that their business was very similar to what Wall Street did. They just did it more bluntly.

Siegel took a seat at the table. He leaned over and whispered to the other two. The center guy nodded and indicated the satchel. Siegel dumped the contents.

That got everyone's attention.

"The guy?" the Boss asked.

"Dead," Siegel said. "We found *this* guy with the loot."

"And who's he?"

"Says his name is Ivar," Siegel said. "I figured I'd wait until we were back here before asking further."

Ivar noticed there was an empty chair at the table.

"You know who I am?" the Boss asked.

Ivar shook his head, although he had a very good idea.

"You know how to talk?"

"Yes," Ivar said.

"You know who these guys are?" the Boss indicated the men flanking him.

"Uh, he's Mister Siegel," Ivar said. "That's what he," indicating Jimmy, "called him."

Siegel laughed. "You got our loot and you don't know who my friends are?"

"It's a lot more than our loot, Benny," the Boss said. "A lot more." He ran a finger along his upper lip and contemplated the pile of bills. "My name's Meyer Lansky. Heard it?"

Ivar didn't even need to access the info dump. "Yes."

"Then you know who this other gentlemen is?"

"I suspect Mister Luciano?"

"Wrong," Lansky said, "which means you're either playing real stupid or you really don't know." He twitched his thumb toward the man on his left. "This is Frank Costello." Thumb to the handsome man to his right. "You've already met Mister Benjamin Siegel."

"Bugsy," Ivar said before he remembered an important scene early in the movie. He regretted the word immediately as Siegel rose out of his chair, pulling the knife, apparently his default mode to any slight, imagined or real.

"Easy, Benny," Lansky said. "There's a lot of money on the table and we don't know where it came from, other than our share. And the only two people I can think of who got cash like this and wouldn't run to the cops are Masseria and Maranzano, which really makes me wonder who this guy is. Don't it make you wonder, Benny?"

Siegel sat back down but didn't put the knife away. "Want me to ask him, less politely?"

Lansky didn't reply. He pointed at the empty seat. "So you know who our absent friend is, then?"

"Mister Luciano."

"Very good. You know what happened to Mister Luciano twelve days ago?"

Ivar accessed the dump, which he should have done earlier instead of focusing on Murder Incorporated. "Seventeenth of October. He got taken for a ride to Staten Island. Beaten badly. But he survived. Lucky Luciano." As soon as he said it, Ivar knew he'd made his second mistake and realized too much information could be a bad thing.

Lansky's face turned to stone and he spoke in a voice that cut through the room. "Everyone out."

The muscle left the room, leaving the brains, if one wanted to include Ivar in that number with Siegel, Costello, and Lansky. Right then, Ivar wasn't feeling too smart.

Siegel leaned close to Lansky. "How the hell does he know that? We was the only ones in the room."

The door slammed shut behind the last person. Leaving just the four of them.

"My friend, Mister Siegel, is correct," Lansky said. "Benny called Mister Luciano 'lucky' just two days ago, when we were all in his hospital room. You were not in that room. I'd have noticed. No one's ever called him that before. So how do *you* know about it?"

They're not paying me enough for this, Ivar thought, and then realized he really wasn't sure whether people in the Time Patrol got paid at all. Did he have health benefits? Because he had a feeling if he did make it back from this day, he might well need them. At the very least a Band-Aid for the cut on his neck. It was still trickling blood.

"Uh, well, I heard someone on the street call him that," Ivar tried. "You know. Surviving getting taken for a ride. And Staten Island. Really. People think he's lucky. So they say that."

"You're not funny," Lansky said. "Who do you work for?"

There was a knock, more of a muted thud really, on the steel door. Siegel got up, walking past Ivar as if he just wanted to reach out and rip his head off. He cracked open the door, there was a muted conversation, and then he came back to the table. He leaned over to Lansky and Costello, who had yet to say a word, and whispered something.

"Curious," Lansky said when Siegel was done.

Lansky looked back at Ivar. "Your dead partner worked for Masseria. Except he also worked for Maranzano, it turns out. Robbed both of them. And then robbed us. Slippery fellow to pull all that off in one day. He got off easy. You will not."

THE PRESENT; OUR TIMELINE

The Pentagon

Following the money hadn't been enough. It had only deepened the mystery.

Neeley rattled along the rails underneath the Pentagon. The booth came to a halt and the door slid open. Neeley knew there was an alert, an infrared sensor on the inside of the door leading to an office beyond the booth.

That was fine with her. She stepped into the office, tripping the alarm. She was in another windowless room, the same size as Mrs. Sanchez's. Except this was the one, of all the ones underneath the Pentagon, that had been inhabited by the same person the longest.

Neeley had read Doctor Golden's report on Foreman's office, so she wasn't surprised at the aluminum foil lining the walls.

She'd seen stranger things in people's offices over the years.

He was messy. Not a hoarder, or one wouldn't be able to move in the office, but he'd been around so long, he'd collected a lot of stuff. A lot of paper. Files were piled everywhere. She noted the map. She recognized the outline of the Bermuda Triangle, where she'd run into the kraken and then been sucked into the Space Between.

Here There Be Monsters Foreman had written.

Neeley believed that. Now.

She knew Foreman's supposed history. Ditched near the Devil's Sea off of Japan. Assigned to the unit that lost Flight 19 in the Bermuda Triangle. His interest in the strange. A real Fox Mulder.

Neeley circled the office. A poster had a saying from Shakespeare:

> *And all our yesterdays have lighted fools*
> *The way to dusty death!*

An MRI was pinned to it. Golden had reported that it indicated Foreman had a tumor in his brain and was not long for this world.

Neeley knew men like Foreman didn't fade away like old soldiers. She thought it amusing that old Douglas MacArthur had "faded away" by giving a speech about fading away that every single West Pointer afterward had to memorize.

Neeley went to the old, gray metal desk and sat behind it. She went through the drawers. There was a .45 pistol in one and she pulled it out. She pulled the slide back and it was loaded, so she placed it on the top of the desk.

She slid open a file drawer and scanned the labels.

One caught her interest immediately: *Operation Angkor (SR-71, Scorpion)*, and then scrawled in, almost as an afterthought: *Dane*.

Neeley opened the file. There was nothing inside. Whatever documents it had held were long gone, most likely shredded. But written in the same scrawl, on the inside cover, was: *Dane, KIA, 1968????*

Neeley looked at the crowded desktop. There was an open file on the right side. She looked at it. A photo of the Valkyrie suit captured in the Met was displayed. Then the gruesome pictures of the autopsy of the Russian Ratnik who'd been inside the suit. Detailed medical notes filled pages and pages.

Neeley considered that for several moments.

The door to the transportation system slid open and two guards armed with automatic weapons appeared, the result of the tripped alarm.

They trained their weapons on Neeley. She didn't bother to pick up the pistol. "I work for the Cellar," she said. "Call Sentry."

One of the men whispered into his throat mike. The reply was instantaneous and he reached out and tapped his partner on the shoulder and gave a hand signal. Both men lowered their weapons.

"Where's Foreman?"

The two exchanged glances. "We haven't tracked him in here for two days," one replied.

Neeley stood up. She walked past them and got into the booth, knowing what her next step was because she had a good feeling what Foreman's had been.

The East Coast of England, 999 AD. 29 October

They hit the beach in a thick fog.

An unnatural one as Corpse-Loddin had warned them.

Literally hit the beach. Ragnarok knew when they were getting close to shore. They all did. They heard the sound of the surf pounding on the shore, but it came up fast, appearing less than fifty feet in front of them, and then they were scraping up onto the pebbly beach.

Roland was impressed as the Vikings embarked tactically. Five bowmen stood in the prow of the ship, arrows notched. A dozen swordsmen slid over the side and ran in three groups of four into the fog, covering front and both flanks, similar to the way a danger area was crossed in Ranger School.

Ragnarok waited, Roland at his side.

Finally, one man from each of the three groups appeared, waving an all clear.

"Which way is the target?" Roland asked.

Ragnarok pointed to the right. "I would have preferred to go along the shore, but in this fog we could get hung up on a sand bar offshore. Then we would simply be a pile of shit for the English pigs to descend upon like flies. It has happened."

"And the Standing Stones?" Tam Nok asked.

"I know of no Standing Stones." Ragnarok was obviously irritated. "Loddin said they were over the dunes."

"The berserkers?" Roland was more interested in the warriors.

"Their ship will be on the beach wherever they landed," Ragnarok said. "Unless they put it back out to the sea for security." He'd gone from irritation to frustration. "If either of you would tell me what we must do, I can make a plan."

Tam Nok held up a hand while she closed her eyes. As the rest of Ragnarok's crew deployed, other than a handful to guard the ship, she turned slowly in a complete circle. She took a deep breath, and then opened her eyes. "The stones are there." She pointed inland, to the right.

"The monastery is there," Ragnarok countered, pointing inland but farther to the right. "That's where you told me we were to go. The men expect to plunder it."

"The stones first," Tam Nok said.

Ragnarok turned to Hrolf the Slayer. He signaled in the direction Tam Nok had indicated. Without hesitation, Hrolf issued orders and the party moved out.

Roland walked next to Ragnarok. Tam Nok at first walked behind them, but then she came up and walked at Roland's side.

"Do you have a weapon?" Roland asked, always the practical one.

Tam Nok tapped the side of her head. "Yes." She leaned closer. "And I have a dagger inside my robe."

Roland grunted, a response he'd learned a long time ago to give when he had no clue what to say.

He missed Neeley.

He missed Nada.

He missed his team.

Because even Roland sensed something wonky about Ragnarok. He glanced at Tam Nok and she looked back, inscrutable.

The fog was troublesome because it indicated trouble was nearby.

The Vikings and company clambered up through the dunes.

Right into the ambush set up by a contingent of berserkers.

Roland caught a glimpse of someone charging in from the right. He wheeled, sword at the ready, and caught a naked man wielding an axe on the point of his blade. Roland twisted the blade hard and instead of taking the impact of the charging berserker, he ripped through the man's spine and cut him in half, letting both parts fall to the ground and stepping over him to take on the wave of attackers that followed.

"Behind me," he yelled at Tam Nok as he clashed swords with a berserker wearing just a wolf-skin tunic. As the two were in stalemate for a moment, sword to sword, Roland took advantage of his opponent's obvious weak spot and kicked him in the scrotum.

Even a berserker could feel that.

As the man doubled over in pain, Roland decapitated him with one powerful stroke.

It was a good sword.

The ambush was over as quickly as it had started. The dozen berserkers were dead except for one who ran away into the mist. Two of Ragnarok's men were dead, one wounded.

Tam Nok went to the injured man to tend to the wound, but Ragnarok beat her to him and voided her mission by slitting the man's throat.

"We don't have time for wounded," Ragnarok said. "And they don't survive the journey back."

Tam Nok stared at him without expression. "Why would they attack like that?"

"I told you," Ragnarok said. "Berserkers make no sense. Under a standard, when they are paid, they follow some order. But on their own, when rogue, they are unpredictable."

But Roland knew there was a very valid military reason for such an attack if one was willing to take the losses: the lone survivor who'd run now knew the strength and capabilities of the Viking war party.

They moved through the dunes, wrapped in the unearthly mist.

Suddenly a tall stone, about two meters high, appeared out of the fog. And then others, each stone roughly shaped, placed in a circle. In the center was a three-meter-high stone, but it was angled almost forty-five degrees, pointing.

Ragnarok halted. "I sense something."

"I do too," Roland said. Not the feeling of unease that the mist was giving off, but something ancient and powerful.

Tam Nok was almost in a trance. "These are from the original people. Our ancestors. Who sailed the oceans in vessels we can only imagine. When there was a great land in the middle of the great sea to the south and west of here."

"I have heard of such a land," Ragnarok said. "Green Land. It is said—"

Tam Nok cut him off. "This land no longer exists. It was destroyed. But the survivors spread out across the Earth." She pointed. "These stones were placed here by those survivors." She walked forward, into the circle, until she was standing underneath the angled stone. She closed her eyes and remained perfectly still.

There was grumbling among the Vikings, who had not made this journey to stare at stones set in the ground.

"My men want to attack the monastery," Ragnarok said.

Roland shook his head. "We have a mission."

"And you need my men to do it," Ragnarok reminded him. "And the rest of the berserkers are around here somewhere. They did not come here for stones either. They are probably pillaging the monastery while she does . . . whatever it is she is doing."

"This is more important than that," Roland said. "You've been paid."

Ragnarok spit. "Not enough. I am taking my men. You can meet us at the monastery."

With that he signaled and the Vikings disappeared into the mist, heading north, leaving Roland alone with Tam Nok.

Los Angeles, California, 1969. 29 October

"What we're working on," the young man at the lectern said to the sparse crowd in the hall, "is a way to transmit data over a computer network. In basic terms, to enable different computers in different locations to speak to each other electronically."

Behind him, via overhead projector, was a very complex transparency with a bunch of boxes, lines drawn, and words too small for anyone to read.

A typical presentation by a scientist, Scout thought. She was dressed in an amazing soft suede leather halter top (courtesy of a purchase from Reefer Madness dude, who'd invited her to bong and bang, in that order, which she'd politely declined). She had low-riding jeans, held up by the Luke belt. She even had a Snoopy patch stitched on the bottom of the bells on her jeans. It would be considered a Halloween outfit in her time, but it was high fashion for 1969 for California. The shoes were platforms, which wouldn't seem so out of date in Scout's time, but she'd had a hard time walking across campus wearing them, since high heels had never made it into her hair-dying, rebellious attire growing up. Seems shoes didn't change that much. High and hard to walk in seemed to be a torture women inflicted on themselves no matter what the year. They'd be hard to run in, and she wondered if that was the purpose?

The lecturer plowed on, handling objections before they were raised. "While it is funded by the Department of Defense's ARPANET, which stands for Advanced Research Projects Agency Network, its application goes far beyond the military."

"Working for the man," someone called out two seats to the right of Scout, but was ignored.

Luke was still in the flat thong sandals but he'd changed into a billowy peasant shirt with intricate embroidered flowers. Not anything any guy would be caught in now or then she thought, but he pulled it off. She was thinking Jerry Seinfeld and puffy shirt, but that was a ways off in the future. She could smell that he'd washed his hair. Long flowing locks a bit frizzed from the lack of product or blow dryer. Scout decided most of her modern economy was comprised of grooming products. He was cleanly shaven because there was no razor that did half a shave, so it was either grizzly or smooth. Yep, men had few options in this time. He'd doused himself with something full of musk and it turned her stomach a bit. Musk and a feminine shirt—strange times indeed.

The lecturer, who'd introduced himself as Chuck Keane, shrugged. "The man has the funds for science to advance."

"And to build bombs," the same heckler called out, "that kill babies."

"This isn't a political debate," Keane said. "This is science. And the future. And the rumor that we're designing a network to survive a nuclear attack is flat-out wrong. The goal is to get people at distant sites to be able to work together on their research via their computers. And the reality is that ARPANET has been funding almost fifty percent of all computer science in the world.

"The problem right now is that different computers are incompatible and can't talk to each other. What we're building, have built, is a switch that goes between the computers. So each computer only has to be able to talk to the switch, not every other different computer."

They should have sent Ivar here, Scout thought. *Or Doc. Why me?*

"This all actually started about four years ago." Keane glanced at the heckler, before continuing. "A man named Bob Taylor, who worked for the Advanced Research Projects Agency, was in his office and he had three computer terminals. Three because he had to be able to communicate with three other remote computers. So to send the same message, he had to go to each machine and type in the same message. Which is certainly not efficient. He envisioned a network that would allow him to do that only once. That would connect all different computers."

Keane was getting into it now, even though his scant audience seemed rather bored. Scout supposed the students in the audience were here because their professor had ordered them to be. None were taking notes and most were barely paying attention.

"Taylor reached out to us here at UCLA. Interestingly, he also put out a contract to major corporations, such as IBM and ATT, inviting them to bid on it. None of them did."

"Why not?" Scout asked.

Keane seemed surprised anyone was interested, much less a woman. For the first time Scout realized she was the only female in the room. "Uh, well, they think the way to go is to build bigger and better mainframes. Where each computer can do all the work needed by itself with no need to communicate with another machine. Plus," he added, "I've seen memorandums from them back to Taylor, where they told him he was wasting his time. That this network couldn't be done." He paused to see if she had another question. When she didn't, he went on.

"We call the switch an IMP, or Information Message Processor. We built the first switch here at UCLA and the second one is at SRI—Stanford Research Institute. This all sounds simple, but inventing the IMP was just a start. We then had to build our own hardware to connect the IMP to the computer system. Just as they had to do at Stanford. I predict that's something that will get standardized in the future, where you can just plug a computer into it, but right now, well, we're doing what we can."

Scout thought of her laptop, iPad, and cell phone and realized she had no clue how they worked. Or how the technology that ran them had been developed. And then it hit her. She truly was at the genesis of a communication and technology revolution that was going to change the world. And no one other than this guy at the lectern seemed to have any clue about what was to come.

"How big is this IMP?" Scout asked.

"Uh, well, about the size of two big gym lockers."

Scout glanced to her right at Luke. He caught the glance, smiled, and put his hand on her thigh. Scout resisted the temptation to pull out the stiletto she'd also purchased and stab him in the arm with it.

"You understand what this geek is saying?" Scout whispered to him.

"Not a clue."

She looked back at Keane. "Why tonight? Why are you testing it tonight?"

Keane shrugged. "It's ready." He looked down at his notes. "And it's not just hardware. We also had to develop software that was compatible with our operating system in order to be able to transmit data. So far, all I've been able to do is transmit information back and forth to myself but—"

"Brilliant!" the heckler called out.

Done with the interruptions, Scout leaned across the empty seat separating her from the loud mouth. She hissed: "Shut up or I will rip your throat out."

The heckler was startled. He stared at her, started to say something, and then saw the look in her eyes and slumped down a little lower in his seat.

"—but now, with Stanford coming online, we can test it." Keane stumbled to a halt. "Uh . . . any questions?"

"Okay," one of the other dozen people in the room spoke up. "So you got a computer here. And a computer at Stanford. If it works, how many other computers can your system talk to?"

"Uh. Well. Just those two."

"Seriously?" the guy rolled his eyes. "How big is your computer?"

"You mean size-size or memory?" Keane asked.

"Both."

184

"The mainframe takes up an entire room downstairs and we need air conditioners running full-time when it's on. It's got a huge memory, almost four megabytes."

Scout tried to process that. Her iPhone had 64 gigabytes. She tried to do the math, once more thinking this was much more up Doc's alley. That meant her iPhone had sixteen thousand times the memory capacity of their room-sized computer. She guessed they had to start somewhere.

The heckler rallied some courage and asked a question, not looking at Scout. "How much does this computer cost?"

"Four million dollars," Keane replied.

A bit more than her iPhone had set her back.

"What a waste," the heckler said over his shoulder as he scurried out of the room and away from the Nightstalker.

No one else had a question and the sparse crowd drifted out. Keane disappeared through a door next to the lectern, leaving Scout sitting with Luke.

"So what's the plan?" Luke asked. "Think the bad guys are going to whack him?"

"How long have you been in the Patrol?" Scout asked.

"They recruited me a couple of years ago," Luke said.

"This your first mission?"

"Yeah."

"This is your time," Scout said. "Any suggestions? Have you picked up anything strange happening around here?"

"Other than your pretty face showing up?" Luke saw that his attempt at charm fell flat and that Scout was shifting into another mode, one he hadn't seen yet. He shifted accordingly. "I've run sweeps through this building daily. Making sure it hasn't been rigged with a bomb or poison gas; mainly checking for anything out of the ordinary. I think if someone wants to block this guy

Keane from doing this thing tonight, they either need to destroy the computer room or him, but I don't think the latter is the strongest possibility."

"Why not?"

"Because he's just a grad student. The professor who runs the lab will still be around as well as other grad students. Keane's a cog that can easily be replaced. The hardware, not so easily."

"So we need to hang around here and make sure no one messes with the hardware," Scout said.

"Bummer," Luke said. "There's a great party I wanted to take you to. We can still make it if this guy does his thing. Do you know what time he sends his message or whatever it is he's going to do?"

Scout stared at him. She wondered if this was how she'd appeared to the Nightstalkers when they first met her. Scattered and all over the place.

"They try for the first time at twenty-one thirty."

"Huh?"

"Nine thirty. They get two letters out and the computer at Stanford crashes. They reboot up there, then the first complete message is sent at twenty"—she paused—"ten thirty tonight."

"Do you think the problem might occur up at Stanford rather than here?" Luke asked, indicating he wasn't totally clueless. "Maybe we're in the wrong place?"

"We're in the right place," Scout said.

"How do you know?"

"Because I'm here."

Luke laughed and suddenly he was attractive to Scout again. "Then I guess we just hang around and make sure nothing bad happens here until that message is sent. If it's so important, I really don't see it. Although if this came out of the Pentagon, I don't care what that guy says, the military is going to weaponize it."

"Let's check the building," Scout said. "Thoroughly." She wished Mac were here. He'd know how to really look for a bomb. "Where's the lab?"

"I'll take us there." Luke led the way.

The building was a labyrinth, but as he had done in the library, Luke led her without hesitation. He stopped outside a door. "In there."

"There's no security in this building at all?" Scout asked.

"Nope."

Think like Mac. And remember your explosives training, Scout thought. "Does this have an outside wall?"

"Sure."

"Okay let's check above and below, just in case someone wants to use a shaped charge, then outside to make sure no one is targeting the outside."

"'Shaped charge'?" Luke asked as he led her to the staircase.

"A directional explosive," Scout said.

"Groovy," Luke said, and Scout felt that tingling sensation once more, much stronger. She was also much more certain of it, given what she'd just learned in the library.

The room above the computer lab and the one below were clear.

"Let's check outside," Scout said.

They exited the building. It was getting dark and the campus was much less crowded. They walked around the building, trying to approximate where the computer lab was. Scout walked between a pair of tall trees and pointed up. "There."

Luke nodded. "Most likely."

Behind the trees, the two were relatively isolated. Scout turned and looked in the opposite direction. "Bad field of fire for a rocket launcher." She accessed the download. "LAW or RPG-7."

"Where'd you learn all this stuff?" Luke asked, moving closer to her side.

"You know," she said, "you haven't asked me a single question about the future."

"I'm not supposed to."

Luke put a hand on her shoulder, drawing her closer to him. "Yes, but aren't you curious?"

"Would you tell me if I asked?" Drawing her around in front of him. Both hands were on her shoulders. She was looking up at him.

He was most definitely in her personal space. She stared into those incredibly blue eyes. He leaned into her and she could feel his hard body, *all* the hard parts. He kissed her and for a moment Scout was out of it, kissing him back.

Not a very long moment, but she knew Nada wouldn't have approved.

"Geek," Scout whispered as he briefly broke off the kiss.

"What?"

"It's not a very popular word in 1969."

"So?"

"And have a nice day really didn't become popular until the seventies."

Luke laughed. Damn he was good. "I'm ahead of my time."

He kissed her again, and this time she felt some tongue, and her body was feeling other things, but that irritating buzzing in her brain was getting louder and louder. His hands gently slid from behind her head and down her back, pulling her close.

When he broke this kiss off, Scout was momentarily breathless. Dane had not briefed her at all about this possibility. And Nada had never prepared her for it.

And it was the memory of Nada that steeled her as Luke leaned in once more, this time nuzzling her neck, his hands cupped behind her head, fingers entwined in her non-dyed hair.

His tongue gently curled around the base of her ear, a surprisingly wonderful feeling for so strange a place Scout thought, wishing she'd done more necking in high school.

It would have prepared her better for this, because her knees were weak and her will was bending, but she conjured up Nada and his Yada sayings, trying to find one that applied to this and then figured frak it, she had better start coming up with her own Nada Yadas.

"Your eyes," Scout whispered as his tongue worked its magic, sliding down to the little hollow in the front of her neck, his hands at the back of it. And she knew he was going to keep going down, and, well, damn the call of duty.

"Soft contact lenses weren't invented until 1971," Scout whispered.

And just as quickly those hands encircled her neck and he squeezed, hard.

Scout sensed movement nearby, behind Luke, but she was also experiencing a moment of real loss because she'd hoped he really did like her. He drew back, hands cutting off her flow of oxygen, and she could see the glint in those eyes, even through the contact lenses—bad mistake there, she thought—and it was pure business.

He was a killer. Scout knew not just because he was currently trying to kill her, but because she served with killers.

And now she became one as she expertly slid the stiletto under the sternum, angling it up to the heart just as she'd been taught, although she was sure her instructor would have preferred she'd gone for the brain through the eye, because that was instantaneous. This, not so quick.

Luke blinked in surprise. His hands were still tight, but Scout knew time was on her side. She twisted the blade, shredding his heart muscle, knowing he had about fifteen more seconds before he passed out. She had enough oxygen to last longer than that.

But then a pair of arms looped around Luke's neck, and did a quick twist. The sound of his neck snapping was surprisingly loud.

He dropped to the ground, taking Scout's stiletto with him, his hands pulling her partway down, and then letting go as he went limp.

Dead, dead, dead.

Scout looked up. A guy was standing there, dressed in black pants, black T-shirt, and with a calm look on his face. He had a few day's growth of beard and looked rough.

Not Lukish at all, but then again, Luke had just tried to kill her.

"Heart's not the best place to strike," the man said.

"I know," Scout said, a bit affronted. She leaned over and pulled her blade out of the body. She wiped it off on Luke's stupid shirt. "But he'd have let go of me soon enough. And died not long after."

"You slice the heart once the blade was in?" the man asked, as casually as if asking her opinion on the weather.

"Of course."

He seemed satisfied with that. "Amateurs pull the blade out. And the heart can temporarily seal itself. Long enough for the stabbee to kill the stabber."

"I'm not an amateur," Scout said, but it occurred to her she actually was when it came to killing. "And who are you?"

"Time Patrol," the man said. He kicked the body lightly. "He was pretending to be Patrol, wasn't he?"

"Yes." Scout was beginning to realize she'd just killed someone. For the first time. Well, mostly killed him, but Luke would have died anyway even if this guy hadn't come along. She felt surprisingly detached from the act, as if someone else, someone outside of herself, had actually done it. "Do you have a name?"

"Do you?"

"Scout."

He nodded. "Price."

She noticed a tattoo on his right bicep. It triggered something familiar in her brain, but she couldn't access it, so that meant it hadn't been downloaded into her, but was from her own memory. Her brain was processing things like the tattoo, avoiding the growing surge in her chest, as if some alien was trying to rip its way out to turn and scream at her: *You just killed someone!*

"I don't understand it," Scout said, but her eyes were forced on their own volition, and against her own, to look down on Luke's body. Inert. Dead, dead, dead. Those eyes, with their betraying contact lenses in them never again to see. Everything all done here, now.

"I don't either," Price said, "but—" He paused as Scout turned to the side and threw up.

She realized she was beginning to hyperventilate. Price stepped over Luke's body and put an arm around her shoulders. "Breathe slow. Deep breaths. Easy. Easy, Scout."

And there was something about him, something Nada-like, because she did as he said and got herself under control.

But then the strangest thing happened. Luke's body slowly collapsed in on itself, crumbling down to just a few specks of gray.

"What the frak?" Scout asked.

"An agent for the Shadow," Price said, reassuring arm still around her shoulder. "They disappear and go back to their time or their world or something. He wasn't of this world and this time, so once he loses his life force, that's that."

"How do you know?"

"I've killed their agents and their creatures before," Price said, as if this was a normal thing.

"Well, we don't have to worry about hiding the body," Scout said, straightening up.

Price pulled his hand back and nodded. "Exactly. One benefit."

"So what was his plan?" Scout said. Then she realized: "Oh, is my mission complete now? No bad guy anymore?"

"Not quite," Price said. "I've been tracking him for days."

"Days?" Scout said. There was a trembling in her chest and she wondered when that would go away, if it would ever go away? "What if he decided to do something a little more abrupt than choking me?"

"Then you'd be dead," Price said. "I couldn't interfere because I had to see it play out."

"Could have played out with me being dead."

"Could have," he agreed. "But it didn't. You did good, Scout."

"Then why aren't we done for the day?"

"We almost are," Price said. "I was wondering why he was hanging with you. Why he put that belt in the room. Just seemed odd to me he'd draw attention to himself, when his mission was that." He nodded toward the computer science building. "He has a device planted, by the way."

"Where?" Scout said.

"Air-conditioning unit servicing the computers. And not explosive, but poison gas. Primitive device, but it will get the job done." He looked at her. "Why is it so important to the Shadow that those scientists get stopped?"

"No clue," Scout lied. She realized the trembling in her chest was gone. She was focusing on the situation ahead, not the one behind. Not that she would ever leave behind what she had just done but . . .

Price stared at her with those eyes that had obviously seen a lot of death. "All right. Well, would you like to deactivate the bomb with me?"

"Certainly," Scout said. Not exactly a date, but . . .

Without another word, Price walked away and Scout hurried to follow. She spared one glance over her shoulder to the spot where Luke had died. Then she put that in a box and shut the lid.

"Here," Price said, pointing at a large bulky machine that was emitting a loud noise.

He didn't wait, but pulled out a Swiss army knife and unscrewed a panel. It took a few moments to get all the screws. He put the panel to the side, revealing the guts of the machine.

It was getting dark, but it was still light enough to see inside. Scout spotted the device right away. A canister hooked into a line. A battery was attached by wires to the canister. A simple egg timer was attached to it all.

It was ticking.

Without hesitation, Price slid the blade of the knife through a wire, and then removed the timer. "I'll have to clear all this out before scheduled maintenance, but it's good enough for now."

"That's it?" Scout asked. *Then why the heck did they need me here?*

"Yep," Price said as he put the panel back on and replaced

the screws. "Well, I hope so. But then I wonder why they sent you back if I could have handled it. So maybe this"—he pointed with the knife at the machine—"wasn't all there is to this day." He flipped the blade shut on the knife and put it back in a small sheath on his belt. "They tell you anything?"

"Just that I had to make sure that message goes out tonight on ARPANET."

"Interesting," Price said. "Why is that so important?" He held up a hand. "Yeah, yeah, I know. You can't tell me." He ran that hand over his beard stubble and Scout suddenly realized he was quite attractive, albeit in a much different way than Luke had been. She tried to pin it down, then had it: Luke was a boy trying to be a man. Price was a man. And he was dangerous. And he was capable. A winning combination in Scout's book.

"How old are you?" Scout asked.

"How old are you?" he shot back. "Twenty-four."

"You look older."

He nodded. "Two tours in Vietnam will do that to you."

"I've seen that tattoo somewhere," Scout said, pointing at his bicep.

"MACV-SOG," Price said. He didn't decipher the letters. "A Special-Ops unit that does a lot of dirty work in Vietnam and over the borders into neighboring countries where we aren't supposed to be killing people. But, of course, we are."

He began walking around the building toward one of the doors. "So let's go babysit some scientists and make sure they do whatever it is they're going to do, so you can go back to Dane and tell him mission accomplished."

That stopped Scout in her tracks. "How do you know about Dane?"

"That's probably where you saw this," he said, tapping his arm. "Dane was in MACV-SOG too. But he disappeared under very mysterious circumstances. He's running things, ain't he? Or involved somehow."

"I can't talk about that."

"Yeah, no problem," Price said. "That's what the last agent from the future told me, when I threw that tidbit out there. Just a fishing expedition and by not telling me, he was telling me." He held open the door for her and they entered the building.

London, England, 1618. 29 October

"Stone walls do not a prison make, nor iron bars a cage," Mac recited as he walked to Gatehouse Prison at Beeston's side.

"What was that?" Beeston asked.

"Nothing," Mac said. "Just something I read a long time ago." And hadn't been written yet, he realized. Richard Lovelace wouldn't pen "To Althea, From Prison" with that famous line for another twenty-four years while locked up in this same exact place. The info dump thing was a bit irritating if not monitored correctly, Mac realized. He wondered how Roland was dealing with it. He was probably coming off as pure genius among the Vikings. The thought made Mac smile.

Gatehouse Prison wasn't actually designed as a prison. It was what the first word indicated: the gatehouse to Westminster Abbey. It was first used by the Abbot to imprison subordinates and apparently that seemed like a good idea at the time, so more were locked up over the years. It was also closer to the place of execution, so there was that convenience.

As they passed the palace yard, the sound of men at work echoed off the stone walls of the palace on one side and Westminster Abbey on the other.

The scaffold for Raleigh's execution was being erected within hearing distance of the man's place of confinement. *A little dig perhaps?* Mac wondered.

A pair of guards briefly questioned Beeston, relieved him and Mac of their weapons, and then allowed them to pass inside.

They seemed pretty confident of their planned execution, as confident as Beeston and his cronies felt about the prophecy.

A guard shut the door behind them and they could hear the lock being turned, which gave a sense of at least some sort of prison. Mac's download was trying to dump information about Gatehouse Prison, Westminster Abbey, and Raleigh simultaneously, more than he cared to get, but he did find it interesting that Raleigh had actually conceived a son during his incarceration in the Tower during his previous time awaiting execution. For thirteen years.

Maybe that was part of their confidence? He'd been in a similar situation before?

"My Lord!" Beeston exclaimed, going to one knee.

Mac followed suit, but said nothing.

The man himself wore a black cloak, a plain white shirt underneath. He was seated in a high-backed chair, a goblet in his hand. He gestured wearily with one hand for them to rise. He was looking at Mac, ignoring Beeston for the moment, although it was to him he addressed his question: "Is this the one from the prophecy?"

"Yes, my Lord."

"Your name?" Raleigh asked.

"Mac."

"Short for something Scottish? MacGregor perhaps? But you do not have the accent of the barren north. No, no," Raleigh said, running a finger along his upper lip, over his mustache. "You are a strange one, but I had a feeling you would be strange, ever since the angel spoke of you."

"And what did this angel say about me, Lord?" Mac asked.

One eyebrow arced on Raleigh's face and he turned to Beeston. "He does not know the prophecy?"

"No, Lord," Beeston said. "He's been told the three promises but I believe he knows nothing more." He cast a sideways glance at Mac.

"Curious." Raleigh pondered this.

While he pondered, Mac wondered. Raleigh did not look like a man facing impending doom. In fact, he looked like someone very concerned about a future he wasn't supposed to have.

"Perhaps that's for the best," Raleigh finally said. It was as if Mac was no longer in the room as Raleigh addressed Beeston. "Are the men ready?"

"Yes, Lord."

"Horses ready?"

"Yes, Lord."

"And the French? Are they holding up their end?"

"I spoke with our French agent just prior to coming here. He assures me a ship will be waiting at"—Beeston paused and glanced at Mac—"at the designated place."

"Good. Good."

"May I ask something, Lord?" Mac said.

Raleigh inclined his head, indicating he might.

"Where does this prophecy take you in the long term?"

Raleigh smiled. "I will be remembered in history as a great man. A man who changed the destinies of empires."

Not if I have anything to do with it, Mac thought.

Raleigh gestured to the door with a flick of fingers, dismissing them. "You may go."

Mac was getting a little tired of all of this. Everyone seemed to think he was part of something that was going to keep Raleigh alive. Except no one seemed willing to let him in on the plan.

"Lord?"

Raleigh was surprised to be addressed by Mac once more. "What is it?"

"How am I part of your prophecy? We've never met. I am new to London, indeed England."

Raleigh smiled. "And you are new to our time, aren't you?"

Mac opened his mouth to say something, but he paused. WTF? How could Raleigh know that? Something was very, very wrong here. Had Beeston told Raleigh about the Patrol?

Mac switched gears. "Lord, may I ask something else?"

Raleigh was growing irritated. "Yes?"

"When did you meet this angel?"

"On board ship, returning from France after fighting for the Huguenots. I was on a small vessel and it was late at night. I was the only one awake. The angel came to me and gave me the prophecy. The three promises and more."

Great, thought Mac. A loony.

"Lord, if I—" Mac began, but Raleigh was done with him.

"Enough. We have much awaiting us."

Yeah, like getting your head chopped off, Mac thought as he left with Beeston.

"How the hell does he know I'm not of this time?" Mac demanded of Beeston as they got outside of Gatehouse Prison.

Ahead of them the scaffold was taking deadly shape. There was also a growing crowd. Spectators were filling the yard, searching for vantage points from which they could watch the execution. The space around the chopping block stage was the choice position. *Hoping for some arterial spray,* Mac thought. "What did you tell him?"

Beeston shook his head. "I told him nothing of the Patrol. You were part of the prophecy given him. A man to appear on a dangerous day. A day when his head was to be at risk, but the three promises would keep him safe. A man from a different time. You fit the description."

"Why do you believe him?" Mac asked Beeston. "He's obviously delusional."

Beeston shook his head. "I was with him in Ireland. He told me of the three promises late one night, over the campfire, a night before battle. As soldiers will talk on those nights when we know we are to visit death in the morning."

Been there, done that, Mac thought.

"I too thought he was deluded," Beeston said. "But that next day and at several other battles afterward, he fought like a mad man. Leading suicidal charges, yet surviving while those all around him were cut down. Perhaps it was luck. Mad luck. That happens.

"But add in his journeys to the New World. And his naval expeditions against the Spanish. The odds keep piling up. But what really made me start to believe was after Elizabeth passed. And he was convicted of high treason and locked in the Tower, awaiting execution. And it did not occur. Year after year. While court intrigue swirled about and many others lost their heads. He survived the Tower for thirteen years. And then he is released to mount another expedition!" Beeston shook his head. "Tell me, sir, can one account all that to luck?"

"But all because of an angel and a prophecy? How do you believe that?"

Beeston stared at Mac. "Did you believe in time travel?" Before Mac could reply, he continued. "Do you know *how* you travel in time? But you are here from some time in the future, aren't you? So you have to believe in it because of your experience. I am a man of faith, so I do believe in angels, and I do believe that Sir Raleigh was visited by one because I have been with him for many years and seen him survive things that only divine providence could have brought about." Beeston reached over and shook Mac. "We are to maintain the timeline, yes. And Raleigh is part of that." His eyes narrowed. "That is correct, isn't it? You are from the future. Raleigh is part of the future, is he not?"

Mac was bound by his own rules and said nothing.

Beeston headed out of the yard and Mac hustled to catch up. "You are letting your faith cloud my judgment," Mac argued and immediately realized that was the wrong approach.

Beeston wheeled about. "I believe in God, the Almighty. I have watched thousands die for their beliefs. Both Catholic and Protestant. I was with Raleigh in France, fighting for the Huguenots. And while the horrors turned some away from God, it did the opposite for me, as I saw people of good faith die on both sides. So I believe God is larger than our religions. Larger than the Time Patrol. Therefore the Time Patrol is one of God's agencies on Earth to do his bidding. Since God sent an angel to Raleigh, then I, for one, will do God's bidding."

Beeston was on a roll. "God has existed since eternity, while we are just specks in time, even if, like you, we can travel in time. Your life is finite. God is infinite. He is beyond our ken. Therefore for us to try to understand his plans, his thoughts, his actions, is a waste of time. But the most important thing I believe is God is of infinite goodness, justice, and truth. He is the supreme governor and judge of our world, and all worlds."

Mac missed Scout. He had a feeling she'd understand this bizzaro situation. It was as if—and then it hit Mac.

"Do you know all of this prophecy the angel gave Sir Raleigh?"

"I know what he has imparted to me," Beeston said.

"Did he tell you what this angel looked like?"

"He said it came down from Heaven out of the dark. It floated over his head while it spoke to him the holy words. Its skin was pure white, as an angel should be, but it had no wings. Strangely, it had long flowing red hair. And Sir Raleigh said the strangest aspect were its eyes, which were not eyes but burning red coals that he said peered into his soul."

A *frakking Valkyrie*, Mac thought, and it all snapped into place.

Andes Mountains, Argentina, 1972. 29 October

Dawn slowly illuminated Moms and Pablo Correa halfway up the ridgeline, pushing through snow that was getting deeper and deeper. They'd fallen into a pattern; the lead would take six steps, breaking trail through the snow, and then step to the side. The trail would then take the lead for six steps.

The terrain, while covered with snow, was also rocky. It was bare of any kind of growth, being above the tree line, a true high-altitude desert of snow.

As Moms passed Correa to take lead once more, he said: "If we are having this much trouble, imagine those poor people who are starving and not equipped for this. How can two of them make it to Chile?"

Moms spoke to Correa's back. "That's what makes this so important in a way. While everyone was appalled—" she stopped, realizing what she had been about to say.

"Appalled at what?" Correa asked. He stopped and looked over his shoulder. He had sunglasses on, protection against snow blindness as the sun rose behind them. Both of them had their rifles in hand.

"Last week," Moms said, "they had to resort to cannibalism. Eating their dead." She hurried on. "For a while, that made worldwide news and gave the survivors an unwanted and negative notoriety, but then the true story came out of how difficult it was for them to survive, and how heroic the journey of the two who got help was. And that has overshadowed the cannibalism, which was seen as a necessary evil."

"Cannibalism?" Correa pondered that for a moment. "Will God forgive them?"

That question surprised Moms. That someone in the Time Patrol would bring up God struck her as odd at the very least. "Why would God judge them for doing what they had to in order to live?"

Correa shrugged. "God has strange ways. More to say, the church has strange ways. I suppose they have done what they have to do to preserve life, and God must approve of that. The soul would be long gone from the dead and in a better place. What becomes of the flesh—" he shrugged.

With that he pressed forward into the now-waist-high snow.

Moms pondered his words for a few seconds and that probably saved both of them as a Yeti exploded up out of its hide site, buried in the snowdrift next to a boulder ten feet to their right.

Its long, fur-covered arms were outstretched and it would have gotten both of them if they'd been closer together, but as it was, it managed only to smack Correa a glancing blow, missing Moms by scant inches.

A glancing blow from such a powerful beast was enough to send Correa tumbling into the snow, his rifle flying out of his hands.

Moms fired the M14, impossible to miss at this distance. Her first round hit center of mass of the Yeti and caught its attention. It turned from going to finish off Correa to deal with the greater threat.

Moms backed up along the path they'd plowed in the snow, firing as quickly as she could pull the trigger.

The Yeti didn't seem to notice the 7.62 mm rounds that slammed into its large body. In daylight, Moms could see it clearly: tall, over seven feet, broad, covered in dirty white fur. A three-inch claws extended from each finger, and as it roared, it bared fangs dripping with saliva. Moms fired and took another step back.

Moms lifted the barrel of the M14. Her next round tore into the side of the beast's face, narrowly missing the eye, which she'd been aiming for.

It roared even louder and was on her, swatting the rifle out of her hand with one paw while the other reached for her neck.

Moms threw herself to the side, the claws snapping just short of her throat. She pulled Nada's machete out and swung it back and forth, trying to gain time and space. The Yeti wasn't deterred. It reached out and caught the machete in its paw, howling as the blade sliced deep into flesh.

As Moms tried to pull it back, the creature clamped its fingers, locking the blade down in its fist. It ripped the weapon from her hand and tossed it away.

Correa yelled something in Spanish, trying to catch the beast's attention as he got back on his feet, bringing his rifle to bear. It worked momentarily. The beast turned, giving Moms the chance to draw her pistol. She fired a head shot, the bullet tearing a divot in the Yeti's head, but failing to penetrate the thick skull.

But that brought its attention swinging back to her.

Which is what she wanted. She fired twice, as fast as she could, hundreds of hours in the Killing House at Fort Bragg having honed her skill with the pistol. The first round hit the Yeti's left eye, penetrating the soft flesh and plowing into the brain. The second round followed the same path. The creature stopped as if surprised, dropped to its knees, which meant it was now Moms's height. She double-tapped again, into the other eye. It toppled forward with a solid thump into the snow, facedown.

Moms stood over the Yeti and emptied her clip into the base of its skull.

Nada would have approved.

She automatically pulled out another magazine and reloaded.

"It is dead," Correa said.

"Just making sure," Moms said.

"Are you all right?" Correa asked her. "Injured?"

"I'm all right. You?"

"It was waiting for us," Correa said. "That means intelligence. That is not good." He was next to the body and leaned over. "This is not the one we met in the dark. There are no wounds from my weapon."

Moms heard him, but her focus was on Correa's back. Four parallel red lines were sliced through his camouflage, jacket, and shirt into raw flesh.

"You're wounded," Moms said.

"I am afraid so," Correa said.

"Take your jacket off," Moms ordered.

Correa didn't comply right away. "How bad is the bleeding?"

"I can't tell if you don't take the clothes off."

But before he could do anything, the Yeti's body began crumbing inward, as if some inner force was consuming it. Within seconds there was nothing left except the imprint in the snow where the creature had died.

"I suppose," Correa said, "that is also why these things are just legends."

"What happened to it?" Moms asked.

Correa shrugged, which brought a hiss of pain. "Back to its own world perhaps? Back to nothingness? I have read reports of this. When the life force is gone from a visitor to our timeline, their physical presence dissipates."

"Will this happen to me if I die here?" Moms asked.

"It is possible, but this is your timeline, if not your time. So perhaps that is different?"

One more tidbit Dane had neglected to include in his briefing, Moms thought. "Take your upper garments off," she ordered.

Correa sighed and removed his jacket, and then shirt, shivering in the freezing air. As he peeled off the ripped T-shirt, revealing his torso, Moms was startled by what she saw. His back was scarred with red blisters, the claw marks cutting through them and the skin.

"How is it?" Correa asked.

"Not too bad," Moms lied. "Do you have a first-aid kit?"

"In my pack. Top left."

Moms quickly pulled it out. She worked swiftly, the cold biting into them. Some antiseptic, and then the best bandage job she could do under the circumstances.

"How long have you had this flu?" Moms asked, as she worked.

Correa didn't reply. Moms finished as best she could.

"Done. You can get dressed."

"Thank you," Correa said, pulling on his shirt and jacket. He was shivering. "We need to move. It will warm me up."

Moms had her doubts about that, but didn't express them. She recovered Nada's machete and slid it back into the sheath. Then they resumed their way up toward the ridgeline, leaving behind the quickly filling imprint in the snow.

They pressed on, moving up to the ridgeline without further incident. At the crest they pulled off their packs and settled down to observe.

"It is amazing any survived," Correa said, peering through binoculars at the fuselage half-buried in the snow below them, about a half mile away. It was barely visible through the snow at that distance, which was still falling, but the downfall had tapered a little.

There was no sign of movement at the plane, the survivors all huddled inside. There was only the fuselage, battered and broken in several places. The metal tube was a quarter turned on its side. The top had been painted white (not very helpful for rescuers to spot) and the bottom half gray. Moms could read FUERZA AEREA URUG on the side, the rest of it torn off in the crash.

"The Valley of Tears," Moms said.

"What?"

"That is what this place will be called. Later."

"That would be an appropriate name," Correa said. The snow surged thicker and the plane faded from view. They were huddled behind a large outcropping of rock. They hadn't spotted any other Yeti, but with the snow flurries they had limited visibility.

"The body of Christ," Correa said.

Moms was startled. "What?"

"I have been thinking," Correa said, "about eating the dead. They are mostly Catholics down there. The Church believes in figuratively eating the body of Christ and drinking his blood. It is not a sin what they have had to do. God will forgive them. They are not cannibals. Cannibals kill and then eat. The dead were killed in the accident. They are doing what God would want them do to. Live."

"There is something else," Moms said.

Correa nodded. "I am sure there is."

"Eight of them die tonight in the avalanche. But in a way, hidden in there is a terrible blessing for the remaining survivors."

Correa grasped the implications right away. "Ah. You are right. That is a most terrible blessing. But it must be God's will also."

"Do you believe God exists across the timelines?" Moms asked.

"I believe I am not smart enough or aware enough to know."

Moms had been doing her own thinking, but not in a religious vein. "People give blood. Donate their organs. It is all about living."

Correa began coughing. Slowly, then more quickly and deeply. Moms reached across and held him. "Easy. Easy."

Gradually Correa's coughing slowed. He removed his hand from his mouth and smiled at Moms. "Thank you."

All Moms could see was the blood staining his teeth.

"Your lover," Moms said, "who you lost. What was his name?"

Correa cocked his head and stared at her. "What do you mean?"

"As long as someone remembers your name," Moms said, "you live on."

"His name was Jose." Correa smiled, once more revealing the blood on his teeth. "Such a common name. A boring name. But he was anything but boring. He brought me alive. He brought me out of darkness to my true self."

"And he died of the flu?" Moms asked.

"They call it the gay flu," Correa said. "The doctors—" he shook his head. "They are confused. And I do not think they care much. They sent Jose home the day he died, even though it was clear he was in very dire condition. They were afraid. I could see it in their eyes. They feared this flu, as they call it. People always fear what they cannot understand. And since it seems only we, the gay, are affected. So they blame us somehow."

Moms had recognized the Kaposi's sarcoma lesions on Correa's back when she dressed his wounds. She knew that meant he had gone from HIV-infected to full-blown AIDS.

"How much pain are you in?"

"It comes and goes," Correa evaded.

"Do you believe God loves you?" Moms asked.

"Some say what I am is a sin," Correa said. "The Catholic Church certainly. They say acts I have done are an abomination. But I do not believe love can ever be a sin."

"How long ago did Jose die?"

"Two months."

"Of this gay flu?"

"Yes. The doctors do not know what it is, and most do not care to know. He was turned away from several hospitals even before that last day. He died at home. A friend of ours, a nurse, helped. But there was nothing to be done." He looked over at her, snowflakes framing his face. "You know what this is, do you not?"

"Yes."

"I will die from it, won't I?"

"I'm not a doctor," Moms said, and immediately felt shame for the evasion. She knew Nada would not have approved. A tenet of the Nightstalkers had always been honesty. "It is most likely you will die. The disease will be called AIDS. Acquired Immune

Deficiency Syndrome. It will kill many people before it is gotten somewhat under control."

"Thank you," Correa said. He got to his feet. "We must get closer in order to see what is going on."

Eglin Air Force Base, Florida, 1980. 29 October

Dawn was breaking as they moved through standard-issue Florida swamp in fall, one each. Each kilometer covered looked exactly like the last kilometer, except things were a bit dryer. Eagle had no idea how Hammersmith was navigating without a compass, but he trusted the man.

He had to.

But he didn't trust anyone else in the squad. He could see them in the early morning light and it was a mixed bag. A couple were sullen, carrying their weapons loosely, barely looking out at their sector. Others were focused, in the here and now. He caught Caruso staring at him every once in a while and couldn't decide whether the man would as soon put a bullet in his back or was trying to figure out the angles of this strange mission.

Their uniforms were sterile, meaning there was no rank, no name tag, no unit patch. Nothing. Just OD green Vietnam-era jungle fatigues.

Eagle checked his compass one more time. Same result. Then he checked his watch. It had stopped running too.

At least they were at a slightly higher level and on dry ground. Which meant they'd gained a whopping two feet of elevation.

Hammersmith raised a fist and every member of the patrol

froze in place, even in midstride, foot hovering over the ground. Then Hammersmith put one finger up and crooked it, indicating for Eagle to come forward, and then with open palm toward the ground, indicated for everyone to get down.

A hasty perimeter was set up, every man alternating his weapon outward, trail man covering their track. Eagle hustled forward and lay down next to Hammersmith, who was peering ahead.

At what, Eagle had no idea as it looked the same as it had all along.

Eagle waited for Hammersmith to tell him why he'd stopped the patrol. He scanned the swamp, searching for anything out of the ordinary. Hammersmith tapped him on the shoulder and pointed. Twenty meters to their right front, a tree was splintered, as if something large had hit it and knocked it partly over.

"Probably tracks," Hammersmith whispered.

Which was an implied question. Check out what had done that, or keep moving forward?

Despite the lack of a working watch, Eagle knew they had some time. There were too many unknowns. He rolled half on his side and looked back. He spotted the Ranger with the M60 and indicated for him to come forward.

When the machine gunner arrived, Eagle indicated for him to set up to the right, and with his hand, indicated a field of fire. The gunner popped down the bipod, flipped up the butt plate, and settled in, gun at the ready, hundred-round belt in place.

Hammersmith took the action as assent and got up. He moved out, half bent over, toward the tree. Eagle put his rifle to his shoulder covering the other side of Hammersmith from the machine gun. The Ranger Instructor reached the tree and knelt. Eagle waited as Hammersmith examined the ground.

Hammersmith straightened and came back with a troubled look on his face. He slid down on the ground next to Eagle. "Tracks. Ones I ain't never seen before. Something big. With clawed feet."

"Cougar?" Eagle asked and regretted it as soon as he said it because Hammersmith had said he'd never seen these tracks before.

"Bigger than a cougar and heavier," Hammersmith said. He pointed to their right front. "Was heading that way. Which is the way we have to go."

Eagle cocked his head to the side and sniffed. "You smell that?"

Hammersmith's nostrils flared as he inhaled. "Oily. Ain't never smelled that before."

Eagle had. In the Space Between. "We're going to make contact soon."

"With what?" Hammersmith asked.

"Monsters," Eagle said.

Hammersmith didn't seem surprised. "I'll pass the word. Watch out for monsters." And so he did, whispering it to the machine gunner, who would relay it down the line.

No one seemed surprised.

Caruso chuckled. "Monsters? Top, you got any idea what it's like to be shut up in a max security, federal prison? With the worst of humanity? That's monsters."

"Let's move out," Eagle said.

Hammersmith took point and they moved forward. Visibility was about fifteen meters through the dense vegetation. But as they went northeast the smell got stronger.

Eagle made sure the patrol had a flanker out on each side. Working with such experienced soldiers was like driving a well-oiled racing car. Each man knew his place in the patrol and his job with-out having to be told, despite his lack of motivation.

Hammersmith held up his fist once more, freezing the patrol, but he didn't signal for everyone to get down. He was peering about, getting oriented as best he could without a compass. Eagle moved up next to him noting the angle of the sun. It was prob-ably about 9:00 a.m., which meant they had several hours to make it to the airfield.

Hammersmith seemed satisfied and began moving forward again, the muzzle of his M16 moving back and forth in concert with his gaze. Everyone's weapon was off safe and fingers were resting on the trigger guard, ready for action.

They all froze as an inhuman scream undulated through the swamp.

"Oh, yeah," Caruso muttered. "That's a monster."

Eagle looked at the squad and he noted that even those who'd been slack were now paying attention, eyes peering about, weap-ons at the ready.

Hammersmith pointed and Eagle saw that the ground dropped about two feet to a sluggish stream of dark water. It was only about four feet across, but for some reason that distance seemed significant to Eagle. The water didn't look more than thigh deep. The scream had come from the other side.

And the far side was obscured by a wall of unnatural mist, yellowish-gray with darker streaks. It went up as high as they could see and ran along the far edge of the stream. Eagle turned and signaled for the patrol to come on line, maximizing their potential firepower.

"What do you think?" Eagle asked Hammersmith.

The sergeant first class shrugged. "The airfield is that way." He looked left and right. "I'm gonna assume that this extends either way. We're going to have to go through to get to the objective."

"Water seems to be a barrier," Eagle observed.

"Or maybe it's just using the water as its boundary," Hammersmith said.

"All right. Doesn't matter." Eagle signaled for them to move out. He stepped down into the stream and was across in three steps, up the slight bank on the far side and into the mist.

Eagle shivered. The temperature had just made an abrupt drop of at least ten degrees. The air felt like it was crawling across his exposed skin.

"Tighten up," Eagle said to the soldiers on either side of him, and the word was passed down. He had Hammersmith to his left and the M60 gunner to his right. He could barely see the man past them on either side.

"Contact right!" someone yelled from that direction, and then there was the sound of an M16 firing on full automatic, which indicated either poor fire discipline or something very bad.

"Hold!" Eagle ordered the rest. He grabbed a strap on the M60 gunner's load-bearing equipment and pulled him along the line.

The firing ceased and a scream undulated through the swamp. Eagle collided with one of the patrol members running away from the firing.

"It got him!" the man yelled. He ran past Eagle and right into Hammersmith, who turned him around.

Eagle stopped, the M60 gunner next to him.

Something came flying out of the mist and slammed into a tree, slowly sliding down—the flanker, without his head, his sternum sliced wide open, leaving a bloody smear as it plopped onto the ground.

Eagle had his M16 to his shoulder.

Something was moving in the mist in front of them, something big.

And definitely not human.

"Fire," Eagle ordered as he pulled his own trigger, aiming at whatever it was.

The M60 gunner expertly fired twelve to fifteen round bursts, every fifth round a red tracer, burning through the mist.

There was another scream, not human, and the thing bounded out of the mist, almost on top of Eagle and the machine gunner. As he flipped his M16 to full auto and emptied it, Eagle had one quick impression of the beast: body of a lion, head of a serpent, and tail of a scorpion.

That tail flicked forward and impaled the M60 gunner.

The head struck at Eagle, jaws open wide, fangs dripping venom.

And a blast right next to his head set Eagle's ears ringing as Hammersmith fired Lola. The first slug went right into the thing's mouth and stopped its forward momentum less than a foot from Eagle's face. Hammersmith jammed the muzzle of his shotgun into the creature's mouth and emptied the six rounds in the magazine as fast as he could pull the trigger, following the path of the first. The huge rounds blew the back of the skull off.

It dropped to the ground.

Hammersmith cursed and dropped the shotgun, the end of the barrel sizzling as if it had been sprayed with acid.

The scorpion tail was still twitching, moving the gunner about, so Hammersmith drew a machete and, with one swipe, severed it from the body.

"What the hell is that?" Caruso was now with them, along with the other surviving members of the squad.

"Perimeter," Eagle ordered. "Caruso, take the 60, orient that way." Eagle pointed in the direction the beast had come from. There was no hesitation as the survivors deployed in a tight circle around Eagle, Hammersmith, and the two bodies. Caruso flipped down the bipod legs and bellied down to the ground. He loaded a fresh belt of one hundred rounds into the gun, and then put the butt plate on his shoulder.

"Yeah," Hammersmith said. "That's a monster." He picked up Lola and checked it. "Damn." He reached into his pack and pulled out a spare barrel, quickly changing the acid-eaten one out. "Magazine is still good," he noted as he clicked the new barrel into place. He sounded more upset about the shotgun than the two casualties.

The Ranger Instructor reloaded Lola.

Then Eagle and Hammersmith stood perfectly still for several moments, side by side, listening. Dead silence.

"Whoa," Caruso said, as the creature crumbled in on itself until there was nothing left. "What was that?"

"It went back to . . ." Eagle began, but realized the truth would make no sense. "Its organic structure couldn't survive once it was dead."

"Yeah," Caruso said. "Right."

"You ever see that before in your journeys?" Hammersmith asked.

"No."

"Know what it was?"

"A chimera," Eagle said.

"A what?"

"Greek mythology," Eagle said. "The original was a fire-breathing beast that was a mixture of lion, goat, and a snake's tail. But almost every country has a beast that's a hybrid of various animals. The Chinese have the Pixiu; the Persians the Simurgh; the Jewish people have the Ziz; the Japanese the Nue. None of them are exactly this mixture, but legend tends to have some basis in truth."

"Think there's more?" Hammersmith asked, ignoring the history of the chimera and focusing on the immediate issue.

"Probably," Eagle said. "I don't believe this is the extent of what is between us and the airfield." He turned to Hammersmith. "How much farther?"

"Four klicks."

Eagle looked up, into the indeterminate mist, trying to figure where the sun was. "Any idea what time it is?"

"Nope."

"Then let's move out."

Manhattan, New York, 1929. 29 October

Ivar was bound to a stout wooden chair. Blood trickled down his face from a half-dozen cuts. Nothing major, just the kind that hurt like hell and were going to look bad if he didn't get to a plastic surgeon soon. But Ivar figured it was more likely he was going to meet an undertaker than a doctor before the day was out.

Siegel seemed happier, having blooded his knife several times. Lansky not so much.

"You don't seem to know much of anything," Lansky said. He turned to Siegel and whispered something to him.

Which wasn't true, Ivar knew. He knew lots, he just didn't know anything about how the guy he'd just met had gotten all this money. Heck, he could tell Lansky who was gonna win the World Series; then he realized that was just past, the Philadelphia Athletics beating the Chicago Cubs in five games. Well, 1930 World Series then! After all, Lansky's mentor, Arnold Rothstein, had put the fix in on the 1919 Series. Then again, Rothstein was dead, gunned down over a gambling debt the previous year.

Ivar had plenty of information and if Siegel kept it up, he was afraid he was going to sing like the proverbial canary.

There'd been a couple more hushed conversations at the door while Siegel used his knife.

Costello had counted the money while all this was going on. Lansky seemed almost distracted, thumbing through the bills after Costello counted them.

It took a while.

Costello spoke for the first time. "We got fourteen million here. In cash."

"I don't believe in coincidences," Lansky said, looking up from the bills in his hand. "You show up with fourteen million in cash on a day when pretty much every person with any money is having the bottom fall out. Wall Street is going crazy. Notes are being called. And you're sitting here with a boatload of cash. Not a coincidence."

Siegel walked over. He flipped open his knife and slashed down Ivar's left arm, opening up the shirt and a very neat wound.

Again, not too deep, but enough to hurt like hell and bleed.

"What's this?" Siegel picked up the piece of paper. He opened it, not understanding what he was seeing. He brought it to Lansky, who understood what he was reading immediately. He cocked his head and stared at Ivar, but it was obvious he was thinking. Hard.

"Benny. Frank. Would you let me speak to our friend alone for a little while?"

It was a real question, indicating power was shared, especially with Lucky Luciano being AWOL.

"Okay," Costello said.

"You sure, Meyer?" Siegel asked. "He ain't been too talkative."

"I think I can have a conversation with him," Lansky said.

"Okay, Meyer," Siegel allowed.

The two gangsters left the room.

Lansky picked up his chair and brought it over, turned its back to Ivar, and then straddled it. He tapped his upper lip for several moments.

"Don't lie to me, Ivar," Lansky said. "You will not leave this room alive if you do. And I know when people lie to me. And, before you die here, in this place, I will allow Bugsy, as you foolishly called him, free rein to inflict as much pain as he can. And he can deliver a lot of pain. It might take several days before you die."

That gave Ivar both a sense of dread and hope. The pain, not too happy about. But if it was going to take several days, he'd be out of here at midnight tonight. Good news wrapped in painful news.

Lansky looked at the list. "Some of these stocks I recognize. Others. No. But here . . ." He tapped something at the bottom. "This is a bank account number. Whose is it? Masseria? Maranzano?"

"I don't know," Ivar said. "Really, I just ran into that guy. He'd already been stabbed."

"But you had this," Lansky said, waving the piece of paper. "So you recognized what was on it. And you were counting the money. Nothing you did indicates this all just happened and was a surprise to you. You expected to meet someone on Wall Street, didn't you?"

The accuracy of that assessment startled Ivar. Then he realized he was dealing with the man who would become known as the mob's accountant. Who would survive for decades when almost everyone around him was murdered or sent to prison; who would not only open a Swiss bank account to avoid Al Capone's fate, but then *buy* a Swiss bank. This was a man who could unravel and understand complex situations quickly.

His life depended on it every second of every day.

Ivar doubted, though, that Lansky would understand time travel.

Then again?

"Someone has to place these trades," Lansky continued. "We're getting reports. It's very bad on Wall Street. Been bad for a while. The market was down thirteen percent yesterday. Margin calls went out. And today, it's looking the same, except the volume is unprecedented."

Ivar knew that not only was the volume of trading unprecedented, but it wouldn't be matched for over forty years. The market wouldn't recover to the peak closing of early September until 1954.

Lansky shook the paper once more. "I had my man check. Some of these stocks are air pockets. Do you know what that is?"

Ivar was sure that was in his download somewhere, but he shook his head, because every minute Lansky spoke was another minute Bugsy Siegel wasn't in the room with his knife.

"Stocks for sale that no one is buying no matter what the price is," Lansky explained. "People don't even want them for free. No one can get any credit, never mind margin." He looked over his shoulder at the $10,000 bills piled on the table. "But cash. Today, someone with that much cash could buy a portfolio that would be"—Lansky smiled—"unprecedented."

Ivar had begun figuring that out as soon as he opened the satchel, but it had taken him a little longer than Lansky to see the long play involved. And what Lansky didn't know was that those stocks were probably picked by someone from the future knowing what the stocks' futures were.

Lansky, of course, went right to that next. "The problem is, if no one is buying a stock, how do we know it doesn't end up being just a piece of worthless paper? And you're spending real wealth, cash, for that paper?"

Lansky drummed his fingers on the back of his chair. "Lucky, as you called him, is in court today. They're trying to indict him for getting picked up and beaten to a pulp, which would be funny, except the cops are serious. But who beat him up? My money is on Masseria hiring the muscle. Frank thinks it's the cops, even though he pays off the cops. He says other people pay off the cops, which, then, leads us back to Masseria."

Ivar listened, hoping this would continue for a while.

"This money is an enigma," Lansky said. "You know what an enigma is, right?"

Ivar nodded.

"Yeah. You strike me as the smart type," Lansky said. "School smart. Streets, maybe not so much or you'd be in my chair and I'd be in yours. Anyways, two million of this money is ours. Stolen four days ago. Had to be an inside job, except Benny hasn't been able to figure out who. Which is odd, because Benny's pretty good at getting information, as you, my friend, are becoming keenly aware. It's like someone knew the combination of our safe. Knew everything they needed to know to walk right in and walk right out with our money.

"We're assuming that the rest of the money was stolen from either or both Maranzano and Masseria, since they're the only ones who'd have such cash around." He reached over to the table and grabbed a bill.

"You got a broker?" Lansky suddenly asked.

Ivar was startled. "What?"

"Someone to make the trades?" Lansky asked.

"Uh, no."

"By the way, you know the name of your dead buddy?"

"As I told Mister Siegel," Ivar said, "I just met him."

Lansky smiled. "You know, I kind of believe you. We did some further checking. He is, was, actually, a bag man for Joe Kennedy, although he pretended to work for both Masseria and Maranzano. A real slippery character. You know who Joe Kennedy is, right?"

"Yes."

"Kennedy worked on Wall Street a while. Made a killing, pun intended, my friend. He was there in '20, right there on the corner, when the bomb went off. Strange coincidence." Lansky smiled. "You know my theory on coincidences, eh?"

Ivar was beginning to understand. Lansky wasn't telling Ivar all this. He was reminding himself, putting pieces of conversation out there, and sorting them verbally.

"He started his own firm. Did well in the bull market. I keep telling these lugs we can make more on the market than on booze, but what's the fun in that? Strange, though. This year, Kennedy's been shorting the market. And making a killing. Him, J. P. Morgan, some of the others, it's like they got secret information. Making deals that make no sense at the time, but turn out rich. I don't think those guys are hurting today, like everyone else."

Lansky sighed. "And you know what's strange. Couple of months ago, Kennedy began pulling out of the market. As if he knew what's going on was gonna happen. Weird thing that. He's sold almost everything." Lansky held up the $10,000 bill. "About ten million worth is what I'm told. Not all of that ten was his; he's got partners, some we know about. Some we don't, although he's had some dealing with the Outfit in Chicago. And, of course, he's got the Boston Irish. They're some tough fellows. But he's worth about two million at least.

"So," Lansky said, "I know two million of this is ours. But about the rest, I think some of it might have been stolen from others. I think a good chunk is from Mister Joseph Kennedy and crew. Why this fellow or whoever he works for needed more, I don't know. But greedy people, tend to be, how shall I say, greedy? An event like this crash, who knows where it will end? Who knows whether something like it will ever happen again? So maybe today, today is a very unique day. A unique opportunity. And they all wanted in on it?"

Lansky snapped the bill and peered at it. "So. What to do? What to do." The first was a question, the second a statement.

Lansky pointed with one finger at Ivar. "Do you work for Kennedy?"

"No, sir."

"But you don't work for Masseria or Maranzano either. And I got a feeling you might well die under Benny's knife before telling. But let me tell you what could happen. The possibilities here."

Ivar stiffened at that word.

"If I tell Bugsy," Lansky smiled, "and I will tell him using that name, which is guaranteed to get the man's blood up, that Kennedy stole from us, you know what's gonna happen?" He didn't wait for an answer. "Benny will visit Mister Kennedy and he will no longer grace this earthly coil with his presence."

Ivar was shaking his head before Lansky was done.

Lansky smiled triumphantly. "Ah, something you care about! You don't work for Joe Kennedy, but he's important to you. Why?"

Ivar knew he couldn't answer that.

Lansky waited, but when nothing was forthcoming, he continued.

"I got someone checking out this bank account here," Lansky said, indicating the piece of paper. "If it turns out to be in Kennedy's name, then he is a dead man. There is no question of that. It's a matter of precedent. We cannot be stolen from."

Ivar's mind was racing ahead, downloading the Kennedy family history. Joseph Kennedy, Jr., was alive right now. Born in 1915. But he would die in World War II. John Fitzgerald Kennedy was the next, born 1917, which meant he was twelve years old now. Living somewhere close by as his father still worked on Wall Street. That sent a chill down Ivar's spine.

How would it affect JFK if his father was murdered by the mob when he wasn't even yet a teenager? And if he lost the money and the mob connections that influenced JFK's career later in life? Those wouldn't exist. It was as if Ivar could feel the future change as a subway rattled nearby.

"But we have a much, much bigger problem here, my friend," Lansky said. He snapped the bill he'd taken off the table in front of Ivar. "I don't think Kennedy and his friends took ten million out of the stock market. And even with the money from the two from us, they got some of this elsewhere. Perhaps Masseria and Maranzano, but we've heard nothing. And how would they get this list?" He held up the sheet in his other hand. He pressed the sheet and the bill together. "This stinks. It makes no sense. No, this is much, much bigger."

Lansky sighed deeply and put the list back on the table. He held the $10,000 bill right in front of Ivar's face, less than a foot away. "Tell me, my friend, what our other problem is. The really, really big problem."

Ivar had no clue what Lansky meant.

"Look at it," Lansky ordered.

Ivar stared at the image of a balding Salmon P. Chase. Then the rest of the note. And there it was, underneath the crest of the right side of Chase's image.

Washington, DC
Series of 1930

THE POSSIBILITY PALACE, HEADQUARTERS, TIME PATROL

When: Can't Tell You. Where: Can't Tell You.

"You're as good as we've ever had," Dane said to Doc. "You worked on the Rifts, which are a form of gate. And—"

Doc cut him off. "We have no idea how the Rifts really work."

"Bull," Dane said. "We opened the Rifts into that other world, where the Fireflies were. And whatever else. The first one was opened a long time ago, in your time, back in 1947 at Area 51. You, as a member of the Nightstalkers, were able to close those Rifts."

Doc and Dane were walking along the balcony overlooking the Possibility Palace. The other members of the Nightstalkers were gone, zapped through a gate to accomplish their mission. Doc felt rather exposed without his team to back him up, a rather unique feeling, especially as he often looked down on the way the Nightstalkers handled missions.

Dane continued. "We're fighting a defensive battle against the Shadow. Always have been. Always will be unless we change something. We've never taken the fight to the Shadow because we don't know where or when it is."

"As it doesn't know where and when we are," Doc threw in, indicating the facility they were in. "Nor do I," he added.

Dane ignored that. "A defensive strategy has one inevitable outcome. Defeat. What we would like to do is shut the gates. All of them."

Doc considered that, with what little information he had. "That would end time travel wouldn't it?"

"Most likely," Dane said.

"And implode the Space Between."

"Probably."

"What about the people there?" Doc asked.

"This is a war," Dane said. "There are always casualties in war."

Doc paused and turned to face the gaping hole in the ground. He put his hands on the railing. "Let me ask you something first."

"What?"

"How do they get back?" Doc asked. "Everyone is always keen on infiltration, but what about exfiltration? You simply told them that when the twenty-four hours runs out wherever and whenever they are, they come back, sort of like Cinderella."

"That's exactly the problem," Dane said. "We don't know 'how' they get back. We just know they get 'snatched' back by the HUB." He pointed at a door, one of many doors. "They'll be back in that room pretty much at the same time. A few seconds difference here or there."

"You don't know how your own stuff works," Doc said, his point made. "How do you expect me to figure out something that's bigger than that? The entire theory of the gates and time travel and parallel worlds?"

"Think about it," Dane said. "This all"—he waved his hands to take in the Possibility Palace—"dates back to Atlantis. It wasn't as big at first. Just some survivors. But it's grown over the years. We've picked up bits and pieces of stuff, like the block/download device. Usually via the Space Between. Now that our timeline has a Valkyrie suit and it's being examined at the labs at Area 51, we'll pick up more technology. But we're chasing the monster's tail instead of the monster. The key question is: When was this monster born?"

"The first split," Doc said. "The first timeline that was tsunamied off."

"Exactly," Dane said. "We don't know when that was, but our best guess was just after Atlantis was destroyed. Because the tale of that destruction is the one constant in every timeline."

"You're missing something," Doc said. "If the Shadow destroyed Atlantis, then there was already another timeline *before* Atlantis."

"That's true," Dane allowed.

"The earlier question that we need to answer," Doc said, "is where did Atlantis come from? In 10,000 BC, it's estimated there were between two and ten million people. Hunter-gatherers. No cities. Not even villages. They kept on the move. Yet at the same time, you're saying there was this great civilization in the middle of the Atlantic Ocean. It makes no sense. For the rest of the world it would be almost two thousand years before true agriculture begins in the Fertile Crescent. That's what we consider the beginning of civilization. So you're telling us that before all the rest of mankind had civilization, there *was* civilization. How?"

"Your numbers are a bit off," Dane said, "but overall, you're correct." He sighed. "The Ones Before."

"The who?"

"The Ones Before," Dane said. "They're the enemy of the Shadow. But we have fewer clues about who they are than what the Shadow is."

"So the Ones Before are pre-Atlantis?" Doc asked.

Dane shrugged. "One would have to assume so."

"And the Ones Before built Atlantis? Founded it?"

"Perhaps." Dane turned to Doc. "That's why we need you, Doc. You *do* have the most current knowledge of physics. We want you to take a look at the original documents we have from Atlantis. Read them. Study them. Maybe you'll see something we haven't seen yet. Some clue to how all this came about. How it works. Because if we can understand that, maybe we can shut all of this down. And mankind can develop on its own, in each timeline, without interference."

"I can try," Doc said.

"Good." Dane turned around and pointed at another door. "Everything is in there."

The East Coast of England, 999 AD. 29 October

Tam Nok opened her eyes after a few more minutes. She didn't appear surprised to see Roland standing there alone. She signaled for him to come to her. He walked over. There were markings on the stone faded by time, a form of the hieroglyphics that they were using at the Possibility Palace but too faint to read.

"Do you feel it?" Tam Nok asked.

"I feel something," Roland allowed, mainly pissed at Ragnarok for abandoning them.

Tam Nok reached up and placed her hands on either side of Roland's head. "Clear your mind. See the possibilities."

Roland immediately knew the crack Mac would make about that, which indicated Mac didn't know Roland as well as he thought he did.

For a moment there was pure white in Roland's mind. Then flames. He saw a battle, Vikings versus berserkers, and caught in the middle the people who lived outside the monastery and those inside, the monks, dying without fighting back. There were also nuns, and the vision zoomed in on one young woman, at the end of her teens, her hair shorn tight, wearing a plain brown dress. She was cowering in the corner of the chapel, a cross held in front of her as a form of protection.

A figure was approaching her, but Roland couldn't see who it was. The figure was all black, a silhouette moving with purpose and rage. A hand knocked the cross aside. Her dress was torn. She screamed.

The vision blinked black, and then showed the same young woman, lying on a straw bed in a hut. A midwife was between her legs and a baby was brought forth and—

A young boy, sitting in a room, a monk, switch in hand, looming over him, teaching, making him read scrolls and—

A warrior teaching the boy swordsmanship, a whip at the ready to correct any mistake, and—

The boy, now in his midteens, strapping, powerful, but without the full muscle adulthood would bring, wearing armor, riding into battle and—

The man riding out of battle, blood and gore-covered, obviously reveling in the combat and—

The man wearing fine armor, standing behind a pulpit, exhorting a crowd of soldiers and priests and monks and nuns and—

The man wearing a crown, now an emperor, of what wasn't clear, but there were armies following him and—

Ships sailing from England, filled with soldiers, but also with priests among them, priests wearing a strange emblem around their necks: a silver cross inside an iron circle with an iron slash across the top of it all and—

Ships landing; slaughter; conversion forced upon those who surrendered and—

Roland staggered back as Tam Nok pulled her hands away.
"What was that?" Roland demanded.

"That is a possibility that springs forth from this very evening," Tam Nok said, "if it is not stopped."

Roland, as usual, had a simple solution. "Then let's stop it."

Los Angeles, California, 1969. 29 October

Three hours later, watching through two tiny boreholes that Price had drilled in the wall between the room they were hiding in and the computer lab, they watched as Keane sat down at his keyboard. There was someone else in the room with him.

Price and Scout were shoulder to shoulder, each with their own hole, watching and listening.

Keane had a telephone headset on and was talking to someone at Stanford.

He pecked at the keyboard once. "Okay, I typed in 'L.' You got that?"

Apparently the answer was positive, because Keane tapped a single key. "Got 'O'?"

Keane was nodding and they could tell he was getting excited. He typed a single key. "Got the 'G'?" His excitement disappeared quickly. "What? What? All right, get back to me when you're back up." Keane cursed and turned to the other guy in the room. "His system has crashed."

"Crap," the other guy said, checking his watch.

"The buffer," Keane said, staring at his own computer screen. "What?"

"He's got a one-character buffer up there on his IMP. But look." He pointed at his screen. "Our computer anticipated the 'I' and 'N,' figuring I was typing 'LOGIN.' Sent them at the same time. Overwhelmed the buffer."

The other guy yawned. "Well, it's going to take at least an hour to get back up at Stanford. I have to be in the lab first thing in the morning. You can do this later if you want."

"Good night," Keane said, hardly aware the other guy was leaving.

Scout leaned back from the peephole and looked at Price. She leaned in, putting her mouth close to his ear. "The full message gets sent at twenty-two thirty," she whispered.

Price nodded, checking his watch. He signaled a small circle with one finger, indicating he was going to do a sweep, and Scout nodded. She went back to peering through the peephole.

This was really, really boring, she thought.

And then she continued thinking, trying to take a Nada perspective on this mission, because it wasn't adding up. Why did Luke even bother coming after her? Was he afraid she'd stop him?

Price was gone quite a while and Scout still hadn't untangled this clusterfrak. But she figured maybe she didn't need to understand as long as nothing went wrong in the next fifteen minutes. Finally the door to the room creaked open and Price was back. He gave her a thumbs-up and took his place next to her.

Keane was pacing back and forth, leashed by the cord to his headset. He was worse than a kid in the backseat on a long trip: Are we there yet? "Are you up yet?" he asked Stanford for the umpteenth time over the phone.

Scout checked her watch: 22:25.

Not long now.

She shifted slightly and her shoulder touched Price's.

That tingle was back. Scout closed her eyes, wondering why she was getting all excited about some dork typing onto a keyboard. But with her eyes closed she saw it in her mind's eye: Keane gasping, clawing at his eyes, at his throat. Collapsing on the floor. Then a figure wearing a gas mask entering the room. Placing a package on the computer. Walking out.

And the whole vision disappeared in a large explosion.

Scout was faster by less than a second, stabbing the stiletto into Price's side as his own knife came toward her throat. She jerked back and the blade nicked her cheek rather than her carotid artery.

The tip of her stiletto came to rest in Price's heart.

That stone-cold killer look in his eyes flickered, replaced by confusion. But Scout was moving, all that training in the sand pits at Camp Mackall, all those screaming Green Beret instructors coming through in an automatic movement as she used her non-knife arm to clamp down on Price's knife arm, locking it in place. Then she twisted, hearing the crack of the bone, and his knife fell to the floor.

She still had the stiletto deep in his chest.

But she hadn't shredded his heart yet.

"What did you do to the Time Patrol agent?" she asked.

Price was staring at her, disbelief clouding his eyes.

"Did you kill him?"

Price nodded, a slip up, not professional at all, but it's not every day you know you're going to be dead in a minute or so. Quicker if Scout shredded. Right now, the blade was actually helping to keep him alive, partly sealing the hole it had made.

"A double blind," Scout said, awareness settling over her with absolute certainty. "Luke's role was to die. To have me trust you. But he didn't know he was the bait, did he." She didn't say it as a question.

Price finally spoke. "We knew the first one to come for you wouldn't stand a chance since you have the Sight."

The frakking Sight. She wished someone would explain it to her. Sin Fen had said something . . .

Then she had the next inevitable realization. Price was playing for time, even with her blade in his heart. "Nice try," Scout said and she jerked the handle of the stiletto, killing him. She ripped the Swiss army knife out of the sheath on his belt. She was out of the room, running toward the outer door well before his body disintegrated.

She checked her watch: 22:28.

She took a deep breath as she reached the air-conditioning unit, and then rapidly unscrewed the cover using Price's knife. She put the cover to the side and stared at the canister, and the wires. The timer had to have been a distraction. A show to make her believe Price had disabled the device.

Where was Mac when you needed him?

She remembered the somber-looking staff sergeant who'd spent six days with her on the demolitions range. Only her, his only student. He was a grizzled Green Beret, one who'd seen more IEDs than almost anyone. He'd treated her as an equal, a true professional. Never asked her who she worked for. Where she came from. Where she was going. He'd shown her as much as he could in that time, focusing more on understanding the system of explosives and detonators and the mind-set of those who put them together.

He told her that the bottom line was a good tech could always make the device almost impossible to disarm. And that the blue wire, green wire movie BS only worked if you'd been watching the person building the device. Or if you had the time to fiddle with it.

She didn't have the time to fiddle with it.

In that case, his last words echoed in her head: What do you do when your computer seizes up? Unplug the frakker.

She cut every wire. Then she slashed the hose that connected the canister to the other line.

Without putting the cover back on, she ran back into the building. Entering the room where she'd killed Price, she barely noted his body was gone. She checked her watch.

It was 22:30

Peering through the peephole she saw Keane type. He had the headset on. "Got it?"

Keane pushed back from the keyboard, clearly happy. He scribbled some notes into a logbook, powered down the computer, and then walked to the door and turned off the lights as he left.

Leaving Scout alone in the dark.

Two kills.

London, England, 1618. 29 October

Mac's parents had taught him a harsh lesson: Going up against faith was breaking one's effort on a harsh, jagged, and immovable rock. Logic would not work.

Beeston, even though he was a member of the Time Patrol, believed in the prophecy. Mac's first instinct had been to tell Beeston of the Valkyries and that the Shadow had been manipulating Raleigh ever since a Valkyrie visited him, not an angel. Probably even saved his life here and there and now and then in some manner.

Then he remembered his parents and the way they had reacted to his brother's death and realized the possibility of changing Beeston's faith, and thus defusing the plot, in just a few hours, was futile, especially since it required Raleigh to actually lose his head. There had to be another way to maintain the timeline.

"Drink," Henry said, shoving another mug of ale Mac's way. It was an hour before dawn and if this was any indication of Raleigh's future, it looked drunken and sloppy. Except for Beeston. He was sitting at the other end of the table from Mac, arms folded, face somber. Waiting.

Most of the rest of the men were pretty plastered, but Mac had a feeling they had the capability of sobering up fast. The download had informed him of one interesting fact: People drank a lot of ale and wine and other fermented liquids for many centuries because it was actually safer than drinking the water. Apparently Ben Franklin had been pretty soused almost every single day and he'd managed to accomplish a thing or two.

Mac was evaluating possible courses of action as Henry was back to feeling him up under the table.

He could do it the Roland way: Plant a bomb and take out the scaffold and Raleigh. There was a precedent: Guy Fawkes, who'd been executed in the same exact place they were going to whack Raleigh. Fawkes had been part of the Gunpowder Plot of 1605 against King James. When the plotters got rolled up because of a tip from an anonymous letter, there was Fawkes underneath the House of Lords sitting on thirty-six barrels of gunpowder.

As an engineer and demo man, Mac would have loved to see what would have happened had Fawkes been able to fire the explosives.

Except Fawkes had been sentenced to be drawn and quartered and wanted no part of that, a perfectly understandable sentiment. So he threw himself off the scaffold and broke his neck, going out fast.

If only Raleigh would do that, Mac thought.

Henry was getting more daring the more he drank and the closer it came to chopping-hour, but Mac could care less. He was running out of time. It made sense that the Shadow had sent a Valkyrie to give Raleigh his three promises and who knew what other information? It explained a lot: Raleigh's willingness to put his life on the line as if possessed of boundless courage. Any man could be a world explorer with such promises tucked away.

So the first question was: How was Raleigh getting off the scaffold to the horses? Raleigh had only quizzed Beeston on the getaway from the scaffold. The Fawkes way? That hadn't turned out well either.

Or was the Shadow going to intervene somehow?

Mac doubted that. The idea had been brilliant so far. They didn't have to pop back up, because all the tools and motivations were in place. Beeston was going to attack the scaffold with these drunken fools. Allow them to get slaughtered while he made off with Raleigh. Mac's arrival was actually a confirmation of the prophecy.

What to do? What to do?

Roland's way was out. Might kill Raleigh, Beeston, and a bunch of other folks and thus change history. Raleigh had to die under the axe. Only him.

Mac realized he had to do it the Scout way. The smart way.

He accessed the download for information on beheadings. A curious note popped up: A clergyman accompanied the condemned up to the platform. At one beheading the priest had been so good at convincing a young man that he was going to a better life, that the fellow actually had tears of joy in his eyes at the thought of being rescued from the hell to which he'd believed he was condemned. That the pearly gates were wide open for his treasonous ass. He took the axe willingly.

Nope. Raleigh already believed he was right, so that wouldn't work. Mac accessed information about the way it was supposed to happen.

A chaplain had been sent to Raleigh in the same room where Mac had met Raleigh earlier. The chaplain later wrote about the encounter, dousing any last hope Mac had of "conversion" via faith:

"He was the most fearless of death that ever was known; and the most resolute and confident, yet with reverence and conscience. When I began to encourage him against the fear of death, he seemed to make so light of it that I wondered at him . . . He gave God thanks, he never feared death; and the manner of death, though to others it might seem grievous, yet he had rather die so than of a burning fever. I wished him not to flatter himself, for this extraordinary boldness I was afraid came from some false ground. If it were out of a humour of vain glory, or carelessness of death, or senselessness of his own state, he were much to be lamented. He answered that he was persuaded that no man that knew God and feared Him could die with cheerfulness and courage, except he were assured of the love and favour of God unto him; that other men might make shows outwardly, but they felt no joy within; with much more to that effect, very Christianly so that he satisfied me then, as I think he did all his spectators at this death."

A few things left out there, Mac thought. Like three promises from a so-called angel.

An interesting conundrum.

The Shadow had convinced Raleigh of a reason to live. Even the priest had walked away shaking his head. But according to the account, the priest was not the last one to see Raleigh before he was led to the scaffold.

Mac had to give Raleigh a reason to die.

Leverage. It was always about leverage.

———————

Andes Mountains, Argentina, 1972. 29 October

"The days are short," Correa told Moms. It was barely three thirty in the afternoon and the sun was already at the western horizon. "It will be a very long night."

They were now less than three hundred meters from the broken fuselage, edging their way down, bit by bit. They'd spotted some movement in the last couple of hours. A person slipping out from the wreckage to urinate every so often. But little else. Moms understood some of what those inside were feeling: exhausted, hope barely a flicker, unwilling to leave even the rough "comfort" of the interior of the plane. Given their condition, they would have the greatest difficulty stirring themselves for even the most basic needs. Moms had seen strong soldiers fold during Winter Warfare training. The cold and altitude and hunger sucked the will out of a person.

"Do you know from which direction the avalanche comes?" Correa asked.

Moms accessed the data. "There are no photos of it, but the survivors say it came in the open end of the fuselage."

Correa pointed past the plane to a slope. "From there then.

We should be all right here. From what I felt in the snow as we came down from the ridge, this side is relatively secure."

They were slightly higher than the plane, on the far side of the slope to which he had just pointed and in the shadow of a large rock outcropping. Neither had mentioned the hope that the other Yeti had died of its wounds. They were both experienced soldiers and knew better than to allow themselves that comfort.

They spent as much time searching the surrounding terrain as they did watching the fuselage. There was no reappearance of the Yeti or any other abnormal phenomenon.

Correa suddenly spoke through the cold silence. "You said this AIDS was 'gotten under control.' But not cured in your time?"

"Not cured yet," Moms confirmed.

"Is it restricted to homosexuals?" he asked.

Moms scanned back the way they had come. Their footprints had quickly been covered by snow. Visibility was less than a quarter mile and diminishing as darkness fell. "No. It's transmitted by some forms of sexual contact or any other way certain body fluids are exchanged; also from an infected mother to a child during pregnancy."

"To a baby?" Correa was shocked. "That is horrible. Babies can never be blamed for what befalls them."

"In my time," Moms said, "most who have it via sexual transmission are actually heterosexual, although many don't know that. It's a very large problem in Africa. And intravenous drug users can spread it by sharing a needle."

"You are breaking the rules," Correa said.

Moms turned her head toward him, startled. "What?"

"You are telling me of the future," Correa said. "Is it because I have no future?"

"I'm not a doctor." Moms shifted uncomfortably.

"You will be done with the here and now in . . ."—Correa looked at his watch—" . . . under eight hours. This is the rest of my life. Here and now. It would be comforting to know the future becomes better."

Moms had not considered that. Was the future from 1972 to her time actually better? "We're still around," she finally said. "Bad things happen, but there is no nuclear war. Many dire things people are predicting don't happen." *But 9/11 did happen*, Moms thought. And the never-ending War on Terror. And then there were Rifts, but it appears they had that one solved. Only to now face the Shadow. "The Time Patrol has done a great job."

"That is good to hear." He didn't sound encouraged. "Do you know what the motto of my Commando Group is?" He didn't wait for an answer. "*Stirps Virilis*. Latin. There are some variations of ways to translate it, but essentially 'manly character.' Perhaps there is some irony in that."

Moms thought of Mac, who'd hidden who he was for so long. "It takes a lot to be a real man. I think you've shown that."

Correa smiled. "And you, my friend, are a real woman. A leader. Your team is fortunate to have you."

Moms looked back at the remains of the plane. No one had appeared from inside the fuselage for a while. With darkness, the survivors were hunkered down inside.

"It will not be long now," Correa said. "Does your history record the time of the avalanche?"

"The accounts from the survivors just say it was after dark. Pretty much everyone was asleep, essentially passed out from hunger and exhaustion when it hit."

The snow was beginning to fall more heavily and there was a mist in the air.

The air was split by what sounded like a sonic boom.

"It is coming," Correa said.

They looked across, beyond the plane, but there was only darkness masked by falling snow. A sound grew louder, like a row of locomotives charging toward them.

As quickly as they saw the avalanche, a roiling sea of snow, it washed over the fuselage and spent itself, dying out less than a hundred feet from where they were hidden. The plane was gone from view.

"Most who die in there, will do so from suffocation," Correa said. "It takes about three minutes."

It was abnormally still now after the roar of the cascading snow. Moms had to force herself not to charge down the hill and start digging. It was an irrational thought, not only because of the imperative of the Time Patrol, but also because if she'd wanted to save those inside, she could have done so earlier.

"This sucks," Moms muttered.

"It is a difficult task," Correa understated. "Perhaps some of the eight were crushed when the snow came in the open end. They would have died instantly."

Moms spoke, as much to distract herself as to impart information. "One of those who survives does so because of what might be considered a miracle. Nando Parrado survived the initial plane crash but suffered a closed brain injury. They thought he was dead so they put him outside with the other bodies. But that saved his life, because the freezing temperatures kept his brain from swelling."

"He survived the accident by accident," Correa said. "Did he survive this?" he nodded toward the buried plane.

"Yes." Moms was going to say more, to tell her partner of the courageous journey that Parrado and one of the other survivors would make, crossing the Andes into Chile to summon help.

But that was in the future.

"Those who suffocated are now dead," Correa said, having kept a silent count.

"Whatever will happen, will happen soon," Moms said.

Eglin Air Force Base, Florida, 1980. 29 October

They'd made over two kilometers, but the mist hadn't dissipated. Sound was muted, as if the mist not only blocked light, but also noise. Everyone in the patrol was in the here and now; their pasts of no importance other than their training and combat experience. Their future was immediate: survival.

Eagle knew they were a team now because of the reason men always fought: for each other. One could wave the flag, make speeches about duty and country, but it always came down to fighting for the guy next to you. These were combat vets who knew the only way they were getting out of this swamp alive was to work together.

But they were down two; the Dirty Dozen was now an even ten.

Eagle was feeling some time pressure. Despite the mist, he could tell it was getting late in the day. He had to be in position near the airfield before the final flight of Credible Sport, or else it wouldn't be the final flight.

While Eagle had no doubt most in the know wanted the mission to go forward, as an objective observer from the future, he thought the plan was a stretch at best. It was one of those plans where everything would have to go just right or everything would go very wrong. It was almost as if nothing had been learned from the disaster at Desert One. There they'd relied on the helicopters with a low margin of error and it had failed; now they were relying on a single plane to do something never before attempted under combat conditions. As a pilot, Eagle knew how many ways the soccer stadium landing and takeoff could go awry. While all the concern was about the distances involved, a simple thing like a car parked in the field, or even goal posts, could initiate disaster.

Eagle also had the knowledge that the hostages would be released in three months without loss of life, when Ronald Reagan took office. For those in this present, the hostage situation looked like it was never going to end, a continuing national embarrassment with each day added to the total.

Hammersmith held up his fist once more.

Eagle saw why: Less than five feet away was a sandy road. For a Ranger, a road like this was a "danger" area. There was a Protocol to crossing such an area. Flankers were to be sent out, left and right. A team of two men sent across to reconnoiter the far side, etcetera, etcetera, etcetera.

There was no time for that. Plus, visibility in either direction down the road was less than ten meters.

Hammersmith looked at Eagle and raised an eyebrow in question. "The southern end of the airfield is about two hundred meters that way," he added in a low voice, pointing at an angle across the road.

Eagle signaled for the rest of the squad to come on line. Then he pointed ahead and pumped his fist. On line, the ten charged across the road.

And before they were halfway across the narrow road, a Valkyrie swooped in on either end and slashed at the flankers, decapitating one, nearly decapitating the other, but dealing enough of a blow to send arterial blood spurting from the neck.

Four men turned right, four turned left, and all opened fire. "The eyes!" Eagle yelled. "M203s!" he added.

The Valkyries on either side were two feet off the ground. Each was seven feet tall, totally encased in hard white armor with a featureless white face except for two red bulges that marked the eyes. Flowing red "hair" went over their shoulders. A foot-long blade appeared on the end of each finger. The electric monsters plowed ahead, into the second man on each flank. Both were shredded and died, having gotten off only a few shots.

But Caruso was on target with the M60, firing a sustained burst at the Valkyrie on the right, splintering the red bulbs. The creature let out a howl and halted its assault, hovering.

On the left, Hammersmith dove, rolling under a slashing hand and grabbing the M203 off a body. He fired a sustained burst, emptying the 5.56 rounds in the rifle magazine into the creature's back while quickly backpedaling.

He wasn't running away. He was gaining separation distance so that the 40 mm grenade in the launcher below the gun barrel would have arming distance.

Eagle ran forward as Caruso desperately reloaded another belt of ammunition into the M60. Aiming carefully, on semiautomatic, Eagle fired his M16, sending 5.56 mm rounds into the cavities that had once been covered by the red bulbs.

Hammersmith yelled a warning to one of the squad he passed as he backed up, but the man didn't understand and there wasn't time. Hammersmith fired. The 40 mm grenade spun out of the tube and armed a millisecond before striking the Valkyrie. It exploded at the neck, blowing the thing's head off. Caught in the blast, the man Hammersmith had warned was knocked to the ground, bleeding profusely.

Eagle reached the motionless Valkyrie. He tore a grenade off his web gear, pulled the pin, and then jammed it in the hole where the right red orb had been. It barely fit in, but it fit.

Eagle stepped back.

There was a muffled explosion.

And then the suit was rapidly pulled back into the mist as if on a bungee cord, disappearing.

Eagle wheeled. The other Valkyrie was also floating motionless. Then it too zoomed backward, out of sight. But the head remained on the ground.

Hammersmith was attempting to stop the bleeding on the wounded man. Eagle checked the severed head. He could see the stump of a spine sticking out of the bottom. From where, from when, Eagle had no idea, although he had to assume they were from the Shadow.

But even as he watched, the head and armor also crumbled inward just like the chimera. This would be a puzzle for Doc to work on when Eagle got back and gave his after-action review.

If he got back.

Hammersmith cursed and sat back on his heels. His hands were covered with blood, but the soldier he'd been working on was obviously dead.

They were down to five.

"Hey!" Caruso called out. "The fog is clearing."

And it was. As if it had lost all its power, the mist was dissolving.

Eagle looked at his watch. It was running once more. "The gate is closed."

"The what?" Caruso asked.

"Let's move out," Eagle ordered.

Manhattan, New York, 1929. 29 October

"So?" Lansky asked.

Frakking Dane, Ivar thought. *Frakking support personnel.*

"Tell me friend," Lansky continued, "how do you have a bank note that wasn't printed until next year?" Lansky asked. He tossed the bill onto the table, next to the stack and the note.

The answer to this wasn't in the download.

There was no answer other than the truth, and Ivar knew he couldn't tell the truth.

Lansky began to shake his hand. "Yes, you must keep your secrets. But here is the conundrum for you. The fact is we will torture you, and you will most likely give up your secrets. I have never seen a man who does not eventually speak, who will not eventually giving up everything he loves and holds dear when enough pain is inflicted. So what you are trying to do is futile."

Ivar thought that was a lie: history recorded numerous people who had died rather than give up what they knew or believed. Of course, he'd never actually *seen* someone do that and he had a feeling Lansky had seen quite a few people tied to this chair do the opposite.

And even if such people existed, Ivar strongly doubted that he was one of them.

Lansky continued. "But your real problem is this. Your friend, the courier, is dead. You will be dead, unless you talk. And that money, and that list, is mine. I do not have to buy the stocks indicated. Or I could buy them but I most certainly do not have to tie those stocks to that account. I assure you that Bugsy, Frank, and certainly 'Lucky' would be most upset with me if I did so.

"At the very least, I will use our money as I see fit." He smiled. "And some of these stocks sound quite attractive today. But the rest? Eh. Why should I care? Unless you tell me why I should care. So who are you? Where are you from? And most importantly, Mister Ivar, *when* are you from?"

Ivar's mouth dropped open in shock.

Lansky was surprised he was surprised. "I am a man who has lived a hard life, Mister Ivar. I grew up on the streets. Luciano saved my life five times before we were eighteen. I've survived these past years among very tough people. As a Jew, it has not been easy. These Italians are hotheaded. The Irish mob, not much better. I live in a very dangerous world, which makes me a realist. I deal with the facts as they are presented to me, not as I wish them to be."

He reached over and picked up the bill. "This could be a forgery, in which case, the forger is stupid. But it is not. I've seen the work of the best forgers. This is real. Ergo, this is a note from a Treasury Department printing a year from now. When are you from?"

Ivar kept his mouth shut tight.

There was a thud at the door. "Excuse me," Lansky said. "Don't go anywhere." He went over. Ivar could hear the door creak open and then shut. Lansky came back and resumed his seat.

"My friend. I control your fate. Unless we have a frank conversation, not only will the most unfortunate fate I have promised befall you, your mission with this money will fail. And, since it seems of some import to you, Bugsy will kill Joseph Kennedy." Lansky cocked his head. "In fact, I think we should wipe out the entire Kennedy family." He pulled a note out of his pocket. "Ah

yes. Mister Kennedy and his loved ones live up in Bronxville.
Not a very far car ride away—294 Pondfield Road. Those roads
up there can get confusing, but I believe Mister Siegel can find it."

"You can't do that," Ivar said.

"Ah. It speaks. And why can't I?"

"Kennedy is important."

"He's a crook," Lansky said. "Just like us. Except he hides it
behind being a lawyer, going to the right country clubs, and rubbing elbows with the big shots. Why is he so important?"

"He isn't," Ivar said. "His sons are."

Lansky glanced down at the paper, and then back up. "He's
got three sons. Which one is important?"

Ivar knew he was on the razor's edge and he was going to lose
a ball either way. "Can I trust you?"

Lansky didn't laugh or point out the foolishness of Ivar's asking that while bleeding and tied to a chair. "Yes. What you tell me
stays in here," he pointed at his head, "the rest of my life."

"Joe Kennedy will have four sons," Ivar said. "One will die
in a war."

"What war?"

"Not important right now."

"All right," Lansky ceded.

"The other three will enter politics. Two will be assassinated."

"Bad luck family," Lansky said.

"But not until after one is elected a senator and the other
becomes president."

The room was silent for a while.

Lansky finally nodded. "All right. Let's say I believe you. It's
crazy, but you know, it doesn't hurt me if you're making this up.
It will hurt you. So. What are you? Some guy from the future, you
know all this?"

"Yes."

Lansky laughed. "This gets better and better. All right, mister future man. You know what happens to me?"

"Yes."

"How do I get whacked? By who?"

"You don't," Ivar said. "You die a natural death, an old man."

"Now you're lying," Lansky said, but there was a hint of uncertainty, more hope, in his voice. "I die in prison?"

"No. You never go to prison. You get arrested, you get tried, but you never get convicted."

"You got a good story," Lansky said. "I bet you tell it to all the guys who tie you up and threaten to kill you. You wouldn't tell me if I did get whacked, would you?"

"I'm telling the truth."

"Lucky? How does he do?"

"He gets killed."

That didn't surprise Lansky. "Figures. Benny?"

"Killed."

"Frank?"

"Dies at home, a natural death."

"Interesting," Lansky said. He checked his watch. "I'm taking our money out of this pot."

Ivar waited.

"This son of Kennedy, who becomes president. Is he a good president?"

"He saves the world from"—Ivar was about to say nuclear war—"having a very, very bad war that might wipe out just about everyone on the planet." Of course, Ivar realized, he got the United States in a smaller war that killed a bunch of people too, but he figured that wasn't relevant right now.

Lansky laughed. "This is a great story. Great. All right. Here's what I'm gonna do. I don't like gambling. Think people who do are schmucks. I'm going to play the odds. I'm gonna send this money to my broker. Have him invest the balance, minus a two million finder's fee, as indicated and linked to that account. And I'm going to have him invest the finder's fee in the same stocks, but linked to my account. And I'm going to give Lucky and Benny and Frank back our money. That way, everyone's happy."

"What about me?"

Lansky headed for the door. "Two can keep a secret if one is dead. And that one ain't gonna be me."

WHAT WAS THOUGHT TO BE THE HEADQUARTERS OF THE TIME PATROL

Underneath the Metropolitan Museum of Art, New York City

"This is most unusual," Edith Frobish complained as she passed the DNA scanner leading into the cavern underneath the Met.

"You think?" Neeley replied. "There's no trace of Foreman since he left the President."

"Why would you think I know where he is?" Edith said as the steel door slid open.

"I don't think you do," Neeley said. "I think you can get me to where I think he is."

"Really," Edith protested. "I was doing important research for—"

"You were staring at a painting like you'd never seen one before."

"Ah!" Edith wagged a long finger at Neeley as they walked into the cavern. The HUB stood by itself, a spotlight on it. It was dormant, no gate open. "You have to understand the painting. And I was staring at the painting to see if it changed."

"How could it change?" Neeley asked.

"If history changed," Edith said. "If, perhaps, Sir Walter Raleigh was not executed on the 29th of October, 1618. It would stand to reason, his portrait might change also. Or even disappear. The replica I was looking at was one purchased for Thomas Jefferson by John Adams. Jefferson had a fascination with Raleigh, mostly based on his explorations of the Carolina coast. And, of course, the famous lost Colony of Roanoke. Jefferson owned copies of both *Sir Walter Raleigh's Essays* and Raleigh's *History of the World*."

"Right," Neeley said. She pointed at the HUB. "Can you get me to the Space Between?"

"Why do you want to go there?" Edith asked. "It's very dangerous."

"Because," Neeley said, "surveillance footage picked up Mister Foreman entering the museum above about eight hours ago. The guard out there," she indicated the last human defense in the hallway, "told me Foreman passed through and never came back out."

"Maybe he went back to the Possibility Palace," Edith suggested.

"I think he has other plans," Neeley said. "Get me to the Space Between."

Edith sighed and then walked over to the HUB. Its surface was covered with hieroglyphics. She ran her hands over the object, pushing here and there.

There was a noticeable surge of power in the room and then a gate appeared at the top of the ramp: a black rectangle, so dark it seemed to suck light into it.

"Keep it open until I get back," Neeley ordered. And then she walked up the ramp and into the gate.

The smell was familiar to Neeley, having been here before, via a gate in the Bermuda Triangle. Oily. Thick air. She was on a "beach" that ringed an inner sea. Black columns of varying diameters rose out of the dark water to a gray, misty haze overhead. More "gates." The one she'd come out of was just a few feet from the shore. Her feet were wet, but otherwise all was good.

Light came from above, not a single point, but diffused.

Neeley recognized the derelict and abandoned ships from her last visit. The five TBM Avengers from Flight Nineteen were parked wingtip to wingtip not far away. A piece of Foreman's history next to a Spanish galleon.

This was the spot where each member of the Nightstalkers had been given their "choice" by Dane. There was no time to explore. Neeley headed inland. Before she even crested the first dune of black sand, four samurai appeared, swords at the ready.

Neeley held her hands up.

One of them gestured for her to follow. Their quick appearance and acceptance of her presence indicated to Neeley that she was expected. Whether that was a good or bad thing remained to be seen.

They led her through draws, avoiding cresting ridges, moving tactically. They passed a gully with a trickle of water in it. Patches of brown soil with plants struggled to grow.

And then they reached a stone wall that rose up, slightly curving inward. The wall was pitted with shallow caves. There were dozens of people in and around the caverns, their garments indicating a spread across thousands of years of history.

A woman separated from the group and came toward Neeley. She wore a flight suit and had short curly brown hair.

"Neeley," she said, sticking her hand out.

"Amelia." Neeley shook the hand of the famed aviatrix. "Where's Foreman?"

Earhart frowned. "He came through several hours ago. He wanted to go to the Ratnik camp. I gave him an escort of a couple of warriors."

"Who else did you send with him?"

"My doctor," Earhart said.

"What does he want at the Ratnik camp?" Neeley asked.

Earhart cocked her head. "Come now. You wouldn't be here if you didn't know that. He wants to live."

The East Coast of England, 999 AD. 29 October

A dozen swords pointed at Roland, high odds against him, especially since he wasn't particularly trained on the use of his own sword. The men wielding those weapons were dressed in a mixture of pelts and hides or nothing at all. Some were painted, or it could be they were simply horrendously dirty.

They really smelled bad.

Roland missed his M240 machine gun, his M4, his pistol . . . a grenade perhaps?

"I will kill as many as possible." Roland spoke in a low voice to Tam Nok, his sword at the ready. "You make a break for it. Get to the chapel. Hide the girl."

"I can hear you," one of the berserkers said. "You will die quickly and so will she if you resist." He stepped forward. "You are our prisoners."

"I don't think so," Roland said. He lifted his sword, but Tam Nok put a hand on his forearm.

"We go with them," she said.

For Roland to give up his sword was like parting with one of his limbs, but he realized she was right. He might kill some, but not all, and then this mission ended here, now, and the vision he'd glimpsed would bring the deaths of many more. As long as they were alive, they had a chance.

He dropped the sword. One of the berserkers picked it up. Another grabbed Roland's arms and tied his wrists behind his back. The rope was tight and dug into his skin, but Roland barely noticed it.

"Come," the leader said.

Led like animals, Roland and Tam Nok were pulled forward through the mist.

They came over a low rise, and in a gully were thirty more berserkers. Roland could smell them before he saw them. One of the group, a tall, thin man with a naked torso and a wolf skin covering his waist and below, turned to them. His body was criss-crossed with innumerable scars. He was missing one eye, a gaping socket surrounded by scar tissue.

The other eye peered at the two of them, as if deciding how to slice a prime piece of meat. "I am Halverd One-Eye." He grinned, as if his obvious name were a joke.

Screams echoed out of the mist from somewhere ahead. Women, children crying out. Men pleading. Vikings yelling in exultation. The primal agonized cries of the mortally wounded.

"Bring them," Halverd ordered.

Roland realized they were getting closer to their objective, the chapel inside the monastery, although the mode of that approach needed some improvement given he was weaponless and his hands were tied.

The guide ropes were pulled. Roland and Tam Nok stumbled forward as the berserkers strode over the edge of the gully. Below them, flames flickered from straw roofs set on fire. Bodies littered the ground in front of the monastery. The gates were wide open, indicating either poor security or a vain attempt by the inhabitants to throw themselves on the mercy of the Vikings.

The sounds of the assault came from inside those gates, behind the three-meter-high wall surrounding a large building.

Roland was a bit surprised at the action of the berserkers. They were spreading out, no yelling, no running, just long purposeful strides. Halverd was in the middle, in the lead, and Roland and Tam Nok were prodded along right behind him.

They passed the first bodies. Men, women, and children. The slaughter was indiscriminate. Halverd reached the open gates and paused. He then signaled, left and right. A contingent of a half dozen berserkers disappeared into the growing darkness in either direction.

This was not some unorganized melee as the ambush had been.

Then Halverd gestured with his sword at the gate and the remaining berserkers rushed through. He looked over his shoulder and smiled once more at Roland and Tam Nok, and then led them through into the courtyard.

The Vikings were caught in midpillage, so the initial assault was heavily in favor of the berserkers. Vikings were cut down from behind even as they were killing monks and villagers.

Roland tested the ropes binding his wrists, but couldn't get them to budge. He looked at Tam Nok, but she was staring at the horror unfolding before them.

Roland considered ripping free of the man holding the end of the rope and charging Halverd. Perhaps he could batter the man into the ground with a bull rush?

Hrolf the Slayer appeared with a solid squad of Vikings, forming a shield wall in front of a large doorway that led into the monastery. The battle became more balanced now and Roland had hope that the shield wall would hold.

But then the flank parties Halverd had sent earlier appeared *behind* Hrolf and the squad, coming from inside the monastery. Surrounded, Hrolf and surviving Vikings began to fight back-to-back.

Halverd seemed uninterested in all of this. He walked around the swirling battle, the two controlling the ropes forcing Roland and Tam Nok to follow. Just before they entered, Roland saw Hrolf go down, an axe sticking out of the top of his head.

Candles flickered here and there, intermittingly lighting the stone interior. Halverd didn't hesitate. He stepped over a monk, whose head had been savagely separated from his torso. He turned right at a junction where several bodies were clustered. Tam Nok was bumping against Roland as they maneuvered around this, and he felt her half turn her back to him and then a sharp pain as a blade scraped along his arm, drawing blood. He couldn't see what she was doing in the dark, but then again, neither could the two guards. The blade went from his flesh to being jammed into the knot binding his wrists together. Stumbling their way down the stone corridor behind Halverd, Tam Nok was trying to cut Roland's wrists free.

Roland saw the stone hall widen ahead to a tall set of wooden double doors. Two Vikings were standing guard and they spotted the berserkers. Halverd stopped. "Attack," he ordered the two holding the ropes. They let go and ran forward.

Tam Nok increased her speed, cutting through the rope as a brief battled erupted. By the time she was done, everyone was dead except Halverd. He finished slicing the throat of one of the Vikings and stood up, turning to face them when Roland placed the blade of Tam Nok's dagger against his throat.

"You'll never get inside," Roland said.

Surprisingly, Halverd smiled, a cheerful fellow for a berserker. "I do not wish to go inside. That is *your* task."

Roland had been ready to cut the berserker's throat when the import of those words struck home. "Who are you?"

"Halverd of the Patrol," the berserker leader said. He looked past Roland at Tam Nok. "You picked the wrong man to lead you here. In fact, you led the wrong man directly to the wrong place, but fate is strange in that way. We are all here now. I suppose that is what is supposed to happen."

Roland tossed the knife back to Tam Nok and grabbed an axe from one of the bodies. He pulled open one of the large doors. Numerous candles lit the interior of the chapel, just like his vision. The nun was cowering in the corner, holding up her cross, pleading for mercy. But now what had been just a dark silhouette in the vision became a man: Ragnarok.

"Do not touch her," Roland warned.

Ragnarok spun about, Skullcrusher in his hands. He was splattered with blood. He nodded. "Ah, the strange one from another place and another time. You fools brought me here. I suppose I should thank you for that. Go back to your bitch."

"You do not get her." Roland pointed at the nun. "Your men are all dead. The berserkers have killed them all."

Ragnarok shrugged. "A small sacrifice for what will come of this." He nodded toward the nun.

"Your death will come of this," Roland said and then he charged.

He swung the axe and it hit Ragnarok's own swing, the two heavy heads of metal clanging loudly. Roland's arms shivered from the impact and he almost dropped the axe.

Ragnarok seemed unaffected and he shoved his axe forward, the flat top slamming into Roland's chest, knocking the wind out of him. As Roland gasped for breath and brought the axe up to defend himself, Ragnarok exclaimed in surprise.

He turned, staring down at the slender form of Tam Nok. Her dagger was stuck in his side and seemed more an unexpected irritant than a serious wound.

Roland took advantage of the moment and attacked.

Ragnarok swung back to him and blocked his swing, the impact knocking the axe from Roland's numbed hands.

"You're a fool," Ragnarok said as he lifted Skullcrusher to deliver a final blow.

A blow that never landed as a half dozen arrows snapped past Roland and into Ragnarok's chest. The Viking staggered back a single step, looking down at the shafts protruding from his body.

Halverd was next to Roland. "I am not impressed with what has been sent from the future to deal with this," he said as if commenting on the weather.

A group of berserkers were next to him, their bows already notched for a second volley.

Ragnarok was shaking his head. "No. No."

Then he fell to his knees.

Tam Nok stepped forward and slid her dagger across his throat. Blood spurted forth and he tumbled forward, dead at their feet.

"It's done," Roland said.

"No," Halverd said. "It is not done." He was looking at the nun.

"Surely you—" Tam Nok began.

Halverd signaled and the second volley went into the nun, pinning her against the wall. The cross tumbled from her lifeless hand. Tam Nok took an involuntary step back, shaken by the ruthless act.

Halverd turned to Roland. "My time is a dark and vicious era. I don't know of yours." He nodded at Tam Nok. "You believed the wrong man. And you, my large friend, must understand there is no mercy in time. There is only the time that must be protected. She was half of a dangerous equation. It is best to eliminate both elements."

"She had the Sight," Tam Nok said. "The blood of a Defender in her veins."

"What?" Roland was a bit behind.

Halverd turned for the door. "I wish both of you well."

"Wait," Tam Nok said.

Halverd turned. It seemed as if he were looking at her with not only his one eye, but also his dead socket.

"Let me come with you?" Tam Nok asked. "This was my task and it is done."

"Not done well," Halverd said

Roland stepped up. "But it *is* done. And it would not be so if she hadn't shown me the vision of possible futures. You were standing outside, waiting for me to come in and deal with this."

Halverd frowned. "I would have entered if you had not shown up."

"But *you* didn't," Roland said. "So it has turned out as it had to turn out. The mission has been accomplished and Tam Nok was a key element in that."

Halverd nodded. "Her vision could be useful." He smiled. "As I have only one eye, an extra set will be helpful." He looked at Roland. "And you, warrior, I wish you a safe journey back to whence you came."

And then they were gone, leaving Roland alone amid the bodies.

━━━━━━━━

Los Angeles, California, 1969. 29 October

The place was a hole in the wall. Literally a hole in the wall. Either they didn't have health inspectors in 1969 or the city didn't know this place existed. The smell reminded Scout of the alley that Luke had taken her into.

Luke. He seemed forever ago as Scout slumped into a seat, her back to the brick wall, her front to the hole in the wall that seemed to be the only way in or out. It was filled with students eating with relish stuff that looked like relish. Old relish. No kale, no arugula, no finely raised baby leaves of anything.

Scout had a beer in front of her, still in the bottle, because no way would she trust anything supposedly washed in this joint. The drinking age was eighteen in most of the country in 1969, but not California. When Prohibition was repealed in 1933, California made the age twenty-one and stuck with it.

But no one cared here. No asking for a driver's license, just money.

Scout was surprisingly hungry. She yearned for a Big Mac at a time when that would have actually consisted of real meat and real Mac, whatever that was. She was willing to put a lot on the line for a mission, but eating here wasn't one of those things.

Besides, checking her watch, it wouldn't be long before she was gone from 1969.

So much for the age of free love. The year 1969 would always be associated in her memory with death.

Her cheek throbbed from the cut, but it hadn't been deep and she'd gotten the blood to stop seeping out of it.

Some guy sat down across from her and tried to strike up a conversation above the sound of music blaring out of a jukebox. "Where you from?" "What's your major?" Scout didn't answer but it didn't bother the guy. He started talking about himself, which made him both a narcissist and an asshole. As he rambled on she knew he was lying. His voice had the sing-song cadence of a story memorized and now being regurgitated. And he was trying way too hard.

She assumed this was the backup third stringer. He was very bad at it.

Or maybe she was so much better?

There was the briefest of lulls as the 45 changed over on the jukebox, a little scratchy sound, and then Grace Slick was singing "White Rabbit."

Scout finally spoke. "She wrote that in an hour, you know."

He didn't seem surprised or care. "Really?"

"And the Airplane becomes a Starship."

That seemed to puzzle him and she wondered where and when he really came from. No Jefferson Airplane or Starship in his timeline? Of course, without the former, there probably wouldn't be a latter.

"You like music?" he asked.

"Someone doesn't?" Scout returned.

"How do you know all this?"

Read it on Wikipedia? Nope. Got it downloaded into my brain by a machine. "I heard it somewhere."

Scout was growing weary of the game.

"You want to blow this place?" he asked. "I've got some good weed in my room. And a reel to reel."

Seriously, was this accurate in 1969? Why didn't guys just say, "Hey, let's do it right here?" Scout wasn't so sure free love was a good idea.

He was cute, just like Luke, and she considered his proposal, but not at all in the way he would be imagining.

Did she want to kill another person tonight?

She glanced at her watch and there were only a few more minutes.

She thought about a short story she'd read once about time travel. Some scientist had invented a time machine in his basement. But it only went back forty years and traveling was limited to a one-block radius. She liked the idea of such strict rules better than Dane's vagaries of the variables. The inventor didn't see much upside to going back forty years until he mentioned to his wife there was a butcher shop just down the street forty years ago inside his time bubble.

Suddenly nice thick pork chops and steaks were right there and within their small budget. And that was it. They were perfectly happy with good, cheap meat. Scout liked the simple story and how happiness really was in the small things.

She seemed to have food on her mind a lot, and Nada could have told her that after the shock of killing wears off, the body reacts in very strange ways. Frasier could have told her that she was subconsciously seeking some form of solace and how that was manifesting itself in hunger. Regardless of her reason, Scout was sure her mother would disapprove of her hunger.

Whatever.

There were no small stories here. Just this sap's tale of lies and whether he was going to stay alive.

He was asking again, a slight irritation in his voice.

Scout leaned across the table and spoke through Grace Slick's singing. "What is with you people? You failed. Why are you still bugging me?"

The guy blinked. Then his eyes hardened and Scout knew he was a killer. The big difference now, though, was that she was too. She had the stiletto in her hand and she slid her hand under the table and pressed the point into his crotch. Those killer eyes widened, tinged by the flicker of fear. He had to wonder where the A and B team were.

"Sure you want to fool around?" Scout asked.

And then the place and the man were gone and everything went black for Scout.

London, England, 1618. 29 October

Mac looked up at the execution platform. Raleigh was dressed in a doublet, a black embroidered waistcoat, black taffeta breeches, a ruff band, and ash-colored silk stockings over which he wore a black velvet gown.

It was daylight, roughly 8:00 a.m. A contingent of guards had accompanied Raleigh out of the gatehouse and then spread out around the scaffolding. They seemed more focused on keeping the crowd away than guarding the prisoner. The crowd filled the yard.

A cluster of nobles were on horseback and Mac wasn't surprised to see Beeston among them with two of the other conspirators. Beeston had offered Mac a mount, but he'd declined, knowing he needed to get as close to the scaffold as possible along with the other conspirators, whose job it would be to rush the platform.

That wasn't Mac's intent.

One of the officials on the scaffold called out for quiet, and a hush settled over the crowd. The official gestured and Raleigh stepped forward to make a statement.

It was no Gettysburg Address of a mere 272 words.

Raleigh spoke for three quarters of an hour, addressing the various charges against him. During it he mentioned that he wanted his friends to be sure to hear, so Beeston, two other conspirators, and several other knights and lords were allowed to mount the scaffold to be nearer his voice.

Pretty slick, Mac thought.

The speech covered the past, as Raleigh tried to put to rest allegations and rumors that had been made about him. It was as if he were laying the groundwork for future acts, and Mac knew that was exactly what he was doing. Raleigh finally wound up his speech. He knelt to pray, but Mac caught the sideways glance he gave to Beeston. The Nightstalker also noted his drunken compatriots in the crowd elbowing their way forward. One had taken the bridle of Beeston's horse and another horse, and was slowly moving the animals closer to the scaffold.

Raleigh stood and gave away his hat and some money. He shook hands with all who had come up onto the scaffold and they all came back down, except Beeston. Raleigh even shook hands with the two sheriffs.

Then he took off his cloak and doublet. He turned to the executioner and asked to see the axe. An odd request, and the axe man was hesitant.

"I pray thee," Raleigh insisted, "let me see it."

The executioner held out the weapon and Raleigh ran his thumb along the blade. "This is sharp medicine," Raleigh said, "but it is a physician for all diseases."

Turning to face the crowd, Raleigh then went to each corner of the scaffold, kneeling, and asking for them to pray for him.

This is better than pro wrestling, Mac thought. Raleigh was putting on a great theatrical performance and an excellent camouflage to lull the guards' suspicions that anything amiss was afoot.

As Raleigh came to the corner closest to Mac, barely four feet away, and with only a guard between the two, Mac spoke in a voice that didn't carry far, but far enough.

"Croatan!"

Raleigh was startled. He was still on his knees, but his head snapped up and he looked directly at Mac.

"You abandoned them," Mac said, "and for that, God requires punishment. As you know from the prophecy I am his hand here on Earth to bring you God's word through time. You will not lose your head today for treason. You will lose your head today for abandoning those colonists who trusted you."

Mac could see that Raleigh registered the words, but was not shaken, so he went in with the final blow. He pressed forward between the two guards. "Your wife has no promises nor a prophecy. Take the axe now or she pays your fee to God for abandoning those in Roanoke."

Raleigh's eyes grew wide. He opened his mouth to speak and Mac held up a single finger to hush him, and then pointed at the executioner's block. "Take your fate and she will be spared God's vengeance."

Mac knew that was the last person Raleigh had met before coming out here: Elizabeth Throckmorton, the one-time maid of honor to Queen Elizabeth. The woman whom Raleigh had secretly bedded, married, and had a child with, facing the Queen's wrath afterward. Only a great love would cause a man like Raleigh to offend the Queen to which he owed everything.

Leverage.

Raleigh stood and for the first time his confidence seemed shaken. One of the sheriffs stepped up next to him and asked him something, pointing at Mac. Raleigh shook his head. He put his right hand to his temple and pressed. A twitch rippled just underneath that eye.

Raleigh looked over his shoulder to the waiting executioner and the block. Then back at Mac. Then over at Beeston. He gave the slightest shake of his head to his chief conspirator. Then he walked over to the block. Mac could see Beeston, confused, waiting for a signal, his hand under his cloak on the hilt of his sword.

But Raleigh gave no other signal.

The executioner asked Raleigh if he would like a blindfold.

Raleigh refused.

Beeston edged forward, but one of the sheriffs put out an arm.

The executioner spread his cloak on the ground for Raleigh to kneel on. But first, the axe man knelt and asked Raleigh for forgiveness.

Raleigh put both hands on the man's shoulders. "When I stretch forth my hands, dispatch me." Then he knelt and put his head on the block.

"Thou should face east!" someone cried out from the crowd. "East for our Lord's arising."

Mac saw that Beeston was confused. One-Hand was up on the scaffold now next to Beeston, whispering harshly in his ear, probably urging him to strike. But such was Raleigh's power over the man that he would not act without the proper signal.

Raleigh lifted his head off the block, clearly perturbed. "So the heart be right, it is no great matter which way the head lie." Nevertheless, he got up and without fully straightening, scuttled around the block and lay in the other direction.

"A moment for prayer," Raleigh said in a low voice, heard only by those closest to the platform. He raised his head slightly and caught Mac's eyes. Mac nodded. Raleigh closed his eyes and put out his arms.

But the executioner hesitated.

Raleigh pulled his arms in and then out again.

And still no blade.

"Strike, man, strike!" Raleigh insisted.

And the axe fell. Slicing *almost* all the way through, but there was no hesitation in the follow-up blow and the head sprung free of the body.

The eyes were open and staring directly at Mac from the floor of the scaffold. The lips were still moving in silent prayer.

And then the cloud of death faded out the life in the eyes.

The body remained exactly as it had been, not falling over. Blood, more blood than one would think a person could have in them, covered the scaffolding.

The head was lifted up by the hair. Walked to each corner of the scaffold. Without the customary words: "Behold, the head of a traitor," but in silence, almost respect.

To Mac it seemed the bloodlust of the crowd disappeared as quickly as the life in Raleigh's eyes. A collective moan swept over the yard.

A voice cried out: "We have never had such a head cut off!"

Mac realized something wet was on his forehead. He went to wipe it off and it was blood, Raleigh's blood, having pulsed across the platform immediately after the arteries were severed.

The head was put in a red leather bag while the body was wrapped in a black cloak. Beeston finally pushed his way forward and took the leather bag. He paused, holding Raleigh's head, and looked down at Mac. His eyes were brimming with tears. He sighed and then turned away, walking down the stairs, off the scaffold to a black coach drawn by two white horses. The body had already been bundled into it.

And with that, Sir Walter Raleigh, favorite of Queen Elizabeth, searcher for El Dorado, abandoner of Roanoke, and receiver of the prophecy, fulfilled his place in the timeline.

Andes Mountains, Argentina, 1972. 29 October

It began an hour after the avalanche.

The snow had lightened somewhat, as if the avalanche had taken its strength. But a strange mist began to creep across the valley. Moms had seen snow fog before, but this was different. A grayish white.

"That is not natural," Correa said.

There was a smell, one Moms had encountered before. Oily, slightly nauseating. She'd experienced it in the Space Between, the place between her timeline and other timelines that weren't directly connected. Where Amelia Earhart and her band of outcasts from various times and timelines fought their lonely battle.

"They're coming," Moms said, not exactly sure who "they" were, but assuming more of the Yeti were about to arrive.

She searched her area of responsibility, but visibility was diminishing even further, down to less than fifty feet.

"We have to protect the plane," Correa said.

"Let's go," Moms agreed.

They stood and moved forward, side-by-side, rifles at the ready.

Moms spotted the first Yeti too easily coming in from the left, plowing through the snow with a shuffling gait, twenty feet away and closing quickly.

"Contact left," Moms said as she brought the M14 to her shoulder and aimed. She fired, the round missing her target, hitting the thick ridgeline of bone above the creature's right eye. But her second round was dead on, directly into the eye socket. With a twisting fall, the beast collapsed into the snow and remained still.

"One down," Moms informed Correa, who was maintaining security in the other direction.

They'd both come to a halt while she fired. She glanced forward. The mound that represented the crashed plane still wasn't in sight. She had a vision of a Yeti bursting into the cramped interior, surprising the double survivors of the crash and the avalanche, and finishing them off. "Let's move," she ordered. She noticed the creature she'd just killed implode slowly and silently into dust.

Shoulder to shoulder, she and Correa continued forward.

"Contact," Correa said in a calm voice even as he fired. Once. Twice. Three times.

On the third shot, with nothing dangerous in her field of vision, Moms swung about to support him.

There wasn't a need for a fourth shot as another Yeti collapsed into the snow.

"It's too easy," Moms said. "Too obvious."

"Indeed," Correa said.

"There's something more coming." Moms halted as the mound of snow indicating the plane appeared twenty feet away. The mist was thicker, more tangible.

"This is evil," Correa said, echoing what Moms was feeling. "And it is still here," he added as the Yeti he'd just killed disintegrated.

There was no sound from inside the buried fuselage. About the only positive aspect of being buried by the avalanche was that the survivors inside were well insulated from the outside world, from both the cold and sound.

"Watch the snow," Moms said. It was waist deep where they stood. She recalled the rattlesnake possessed by a Firefly that attacked during the *Fun in the Desert* outside of Tucson. "Something could be coming through it."

She spotted it first. "Contact!" Floating about two feet above the snow fifteen feet away and closing: a green, elliptical sphere, roughly three feet long by two in diameter, an oversized football. Two black bands diagonally crisscrossed its surface. Moms didn't wait to see more detail.

She fired three rounds in rapid succession, each hit producing a puff of black liquid. The thing reacted, diving front point first into the snow. Moms fired where it had disappeared and then pulled back her aim, peppering the snow in front of her as the entity burrowed toward her.

"Contact!" Correa yelled, and she could hear the sound of his suppressor as he fired.

The sphere burst out of the snow right in front of Moms. She had a snapshot glimpse: The two black belts were moving, churning, with bands of small, sharp barbs like teeth. The apex of those two bands hit the muzzle of her rifle even as she pulled the trigger.

The tip of the suppressor was ripped up, the rifle torn from her hands. Metal was shredded as the bands did their work. From the widest part of the sphere, a thin sheet of green snapped open like a sail, catching the metal and then wood as the rifle was destroyed.

Moms wasn't standing still.

She drew Nada's machete with one hand and a grenade with the other as the remains of the rifle were snapped back, caught in the sail, and it snapped shut as quickly as it had opened.

This was a killing thing, designed specifically for that purpose. Whether machine or animal didn't matter.

Moms had to kill it.

"Backing up," Moms yelled to Correa. He was at her shoulder, still firing at something as they retreated.

Done with the rifle, the sphere moved toward Moms. She jabbed the point of the machete at it. The weapon was deflected off the churning bands.

Moms jabbed harder and the machete was ripped from her hand, metal getting shredded and tossed backward as the green sail snapped open once more to take the remains.

Which is exactly what Moms wanted as she pulled the pin on the grenade and tossed it into the sail.

"Grenade!" she warned Correa.

But there was no need for worry as the sail snapped shut, grenade caught inside along with the remains of Nada's machete.

A muffled explosion, the sphere expanded all around ever so slightly, and then it fell into the snow, the bands stopping.

Moms didn't bother to verify, pulling her pistol and turning to support Correa.

The sphere he'd been firing at reacted to her success by turning away and heading directly toward the mound of snow and the people inside. Moms didn't want to imagine what would happen if it burrowed through the snow and got in there among the survivors.

She added her bullets to those from Correa's FN FAL. "A mine," she shouted as she joined him, chasing the sphere as it headed toward the hump of snow.

As Correa reached into the pouch on his vest, Moms used every ounce of energy she had to push herself over and through the dense avalanche snow to try to catch up to the elliptical sphere. Correa was next to her. Moms knew they wouldn't make it, that the thing would beat them through the snow and into the plane and then literally into the survivors.

Correa thrust his free hand out, barely touching the rear point of the sphere, but that was enough. The black strips abruptly reversed and ripped into his fingers, pulling him forward. Moms grabbed the back of his pack, pulling him back.

She succeeded just as Correa's hand was done; flesh, blood, and bone being churned into a rough mist. The green "sail" snapped open to absorb the ghoulish remains.

Correa tossed an armed mine into the sail with his remaining hand.

The sail snapped shut. A muted explosion. The sphere dropped into the snow.

Everything remained frozen for a moment, and then as the sphere imploded as the Yeti had done, Moms ripped a cravat off her gear and wrapped it around Correa's forearm, cinching it tight to stop the arterial bleeding.

Satisfied she'd closed that off, she grabbed him by the back of his collar and dragged him back. He slid over the snow and she dug with every ounce of energy until she reached a depression underneath a large rock outcropping about two hundred meters from the plane.

She propped Correa up on his pack and sat down wearily.

She knew the time was close to midnight, when she turned into the Time Patrol version of a pumpkin.

Correa spoke, his face pale from loss of blood. "Tell me my friend. I believe I deserve to know some of the future. At least the future here." He nodded down toward the plane. "They probably never heard us. Muffled by the snow. Desperate with their own plight. Trying to dig each other out."

Moms broke the rules and spoke of the future. "They'll eventually poke through the snow. Get air. Break out in three days. They learned a while back by transistor radio that the search was called off. Now they will truly realize if they stay here, they will die from starvation, the weather, or something like the avalanche. This will give them the impetus to send someone to go for help.

"Three of them will head west since they think they are already in Chile. They'll send one back because they don't have enough food to make it. Enough human flesh. Even though they've gained eight bodies because of this latest tragedy.

"The two will make it. Summon rescue. At first the world will be shocked at the news of the cannibalism. But then, when the complete story of their ordeal comes out, it will be one of the greatest tales of courage in the face of extreme odds. Of human survival."

"And which of them will achieve something great?" Correa asked. His eyes were half-closed from exhaustion and blood loss. "So important the Shadow wanted to kill all of them?"

Moms shook her head. "The great thing is simply surviving and telling their story. They let people know that we can do so much more than we think we can when we have to. We can over-come the greatest odds."

"Ah," Correa said. He opened his eyes wider. "Hope. It is all about hope, not a single person doing something. Their story will give people hope. Hope is the enemy of evil. The enemy of this Shadow."

Moms realized that was it: It wasn't the lives saved. It was what those lives went on to do in the face of overwhelming odds and the story passed down.

The snow was tapering off. The grayish-white mist had dis-sipated with the destruction of the last sphere.

Correa spoke. "I am afraid, my new friend, that I am done."

Moms was not surprised, but a wave of deep sadness washed over her.

"It is not that I am giving up," Correa explained. "But my life was directed to this moment and we have succeeded." He peered at her. "You told me my disease, this AIDS, is transmitted by blood contact."

Moms nodded.

"But you didn't hesitate to bandage me," Correa noted. He looked at all the blood spattered on her. "I would suspect some would have hesitated."

"Some would," Moms acknowledged, thinking of the history of the disease and the fear it spawned among many when it wasn't understood, and even after it was. The opposite of hope: fear.

Correa pointed with his good hand, his only hand, toward the mound of snow. "They have hope and will spread it when they get rescued. But my future is bleak. You will be gone soon and I cannot make it out of the mountains with the blood I have lost."

"Don't lose hope," Moms said and regretted it. He wasn't giv-ing up. He was giving in. A huge difference.

Correa chuckled softly. "Nice try, Moms. I have done my duty and that is more than many can say."

Moms looked at her watch. Just a few minutes remained until her twenty-four hours in 1972 were done.

"It is very cold," Correa said.

Moms moved close to him, pressing her body against his and wrapping her arms around him.

"Would you pray with me?" Correa asked.

Moms cradled his head, pulling it tight in to her chest. "Certainly, my friend."

Correa murmured into her chest, his words muffled. It was Latin.

"Ave Maria, gratia plena, Dominus tecum. Benedicta tu in mulieribus, et benedictus fructus ventris tui, Iesus. Sancta Maria, Mater Dei, ora pro nobis peccatoribus, nunc, et in hora mortis nostrae. Amen."

And then he repeated it and she did too.

Moms tried to remember, to think back to that lonely house on the Kansas plains. Her mother had prayed. She remembered that. Prayers that were never answered.

But she tried anyway.

Correa paused in the reciting, pulled his head slightly away, and looked up at her. "What is your real name?"

Moms leaned over and whispered it in his ear.

He smiled. "That is a very pretty name." He reached inside his shirt and pulled out his dog tags. "Take them."

Moms took them.

"Remember my name," Correa said.

He began reciting the prayer again and Moms joined him.

And then all went black for Moms.

Eglin Air Force Base, Florida, 1980. 29 October

Eagle was on a "hill," as best this slight rise to the west of Wagner Field could be described given it was in relatively flat Florida. It was late in the afternoon and the sun was a quarter way down to the horizon behind them. Hammersmith was on his belly to Eagle's right, Caruso and the other two survivors forming a circular perimeter.

The mist was completely gone and visibility was good. The plans for Wagner Field had been downloaded into Eagle's brain, but he'd also been here before, piloting the Snake during some joint training with the Air Force's 1st Special Operations Wing, which was headquartered at Hurlburt Field, the headquarters of the entire Eglin reservation.

Constructed during the early days of World War II, Wagner was part of a series of airfields built on Eglin to train the thousands of pilots who shipped overseas to fight.

Originally, Wagner had been shaped like a triangle with a main 4,000-foot strip running north-south and another runway northwest-southeast. They were connected on their north ends by a taxiway, which also had a parking apron off of it. The north-south runway had since been extended another 3,500 feet south.

Eagle and the patrol were located just below where the north-south runway had been extended, on the west side. They were about fifteen feet above the level of the tarmac, and two hundred feet away, hidden in the low scrub trees the area surrounding the airfield was covered in.

"A dog and pony show," Hammersmith commented, indicating the group of obvious dignitaries clustered on a set of temporary bleachers.

"There's the plane," Eagle said, pointing north and offering Hammersmith his field glasses. It was on the junction of the angled runway and the taxiway, where a group of mechanics were working.

They'd taken a C-130 aircraft and modified it. The C-130 was still in widespread use in Eagle's time and he'd lost count of the number of times he'd parachuted out of one. It had four turboprop engines, two on each wing, a high tail, and a back ramp that could open up, with the ramp's top portion going up into the tail section. First fielded in 1956, the C-130 was the second longest serving aircraft in the Air Force, surpassed only by the venerable B-52, indicating its excellent design and usefulness in a variety of missions, from troop transport to aerial gunship.

Now it was being prepared for another unique task.

"What are they doing?" Hammersmith asked.

"Loading the rockets," Eagle answered. "It's been retrofitted with eight rockets. They've got a total of eighty-thousand pounds of thrust to stop the plane as it lands and also fire a three-second burst so it touches down lightly. It also has rockets to help it take off."

"So an updated example of Doolittle's B-24," Hammersmith noted, and Eagle realized he hadn't thought of it that way. But Credible Sport was very similar to what Doolittle had been trying to achieve in concept—to take off from a very short distance, which was, in Doolittle's case, the deck of an aircraft carrier. Except Doolittle hadn't planned on landing back on the carrier. This C-130 would not only land and take off from a soccer field, it would land on an aircraft carrier with the hostages in order to get to medical treatment as quickly as possible.

The sound of helicopter blades caught Eagle's attention. A Huey helicopter came in from the south, flying low over the long runway and then banking and coming back to near the stands. It settled down.

Hammersmith handed the binoculars back to Eagle. "What now?"

Eagle scanned the area slightly to their northeast, a section of the north-south runway that had large flags marking distances. "That's where the plane's going to land, turn, and then take off," he said. "The size of the soccer field in Tehran."

"Not much," Hammersmith noted.

"No," Eagle agreed. It was years before the Osprey would take flight, followed by Eagle's own toy, the Snake, a tilt-wing aircraft that could easily land in that space much like a helicopter. He knew the mission couldn't go. Not just because his timeline said so, but because it had little chance of success. But he had to admire the spirit and inventiveness of the men who were planning it and going to conduct it. And he had respect for the pilots who were testing this jury-rigged technology. Flying a propeller-driven cargo plane with powerful rockets attached all around was a proposition fraught with disaster.

"So," Hammersmith said, "what's the plan?"

"The M21," Eagle said.

Hammersmith crawled over to one of the men and retrieved the sniper rifle. It was essentially an M14, the precursor to the M16. It fired a larger round, a 7.62x51 mm NATO. Over a thousand match-grade M14s had been modified. A fiberglass stock replaced the traditional wooden one. A 3-9 adjustable ranging scope was mounted on top. And the gun's twenty-round box magazine was loaded with National Match–grade ammunition.

Hammersmith handed it to Eagle, taking the binoculars back to be his spotter. "You a trained sniper?"

"I went through SOTIC," Eagle said as he put the stock to his shoulder and rested the barrel on his backpack.

"'SOTIC'?" Hammersmith asked, peering toward the plane almost two and half miles away at the northern end of the runway.

Eagle realized this was a few years prior to that school starting up at 10th Special Forces. "Special Operation Target Interdiction Course."

"So," Hammersmith said, "sniper school."

"A little bit different emphasis," Eagle said. "We focused on shooting more than just people. You can do a lot with a well-aimed shot at a complex system." Looking through the sniper scope, Eagle could see cameras mounted on the far side of the runway inside the marked landing area. There were a couple of fire trucks and ambulances parked over there.

Just in case.

"Like a plane." Hammersmith said.

"Like a plane," Eagle echoed. Even though his watch was working, it had lost the hours in the mist, so he wasn't certain when the final test flight of Credible Sport would take place.

"Target is moving," Hammersmith said.

Eagle was checking for security, but there didn't appear to be any. He had to remember; this was 1980, pre 9/11, still in the Cold War. The biggest concern they probably had was a Russian satellite high overhead taking imagery. Whether the Russians would warn the Iranians was another story. Eagle knew that when the Delta Force Commandos who'd trained for the original mission carried out rehearsals at Camp Mackall, outside of Fort Bragg, they tore down their training facilities or covered them up every time a Russian spy satellite passed overhead. Just in case.

Eagle scanned left. The modified C-130 was moving along the taxiway, toward the north end of the long runway.

The helicopter lifted and took a position to the east at about two hundred feet. The observers filed into the bleachers.

The C-130 reached the landing strip and turned right, continuing down the long runway. It finally came to a halt at a flag, right where the first camera was filming. Eagle knew that the decision had been made to do the assisted takeoff first, even though on the actual mission, the landing would come first, and then the takeoff from the stadium.

Engines revving, the rocket pods facing to the rear and down were opened from the fuselage. With a bright flash of light, the rockets were fired as the brakes were released. The C-130 leapt into the air with the assist of the three-second burn of those rockets. It accelerated upward, propellers grabbing air.

"Far out," Caruso said.

"Keep your eyes on your sector," Hammersmith ordered.

Eagle pulled his eye back from the scope and watched as the plane roared by.

The C-130 began a long, clockwise racetrack. It curved around, behind where the squad was, and to the north, banking around to reach the approach to the runway. Eagle put his eye back on the scope and zeroed in on the approaching plane. He was off on a gentle angle to its approach. He could see that the pods for the descent and retrorockets were open.

Eagle brought up the specs for the rocket-assist system from the download, even though he'd already run this through in his head many times. While a computer was technically in charge of firing the rockets, the test pilots had insisted that safety switches be installed in the cockpit to prevent accidental premature firing. The navigator had one for the vertical, descent-arresting rockets. Both pilots had a switch for the retrorockets.

The C-130 dropped down to three hundred feet of altitude, the height needed to clear the stands of the stadium. At the designated point, the plane rapidly slowed and descended.

Eagle could clearly see the pilots in the cockpit.

He shifted the reticles from the cockpit to a set of rockets on the right side of the plane. The pilots had the plane slowed to a hair above stall speed at eighty-five knots.

The navigator had control of the lifting rockets, because he also had a laser altimeter that could give him the most accurate reading of height above ground. Eagle knew the way it was supposed to play out. As the aircraft hit seventy-five feet, Eagle fired a single shot.

Seconds later at fifty feet, the navigator flipped his switch.

The lifting rockets didn't fire.

The plane was at full flaps, going very slow. Not enough speed to pull out of the landing.

Eagle fired again and the retrorockets fired prematurely, slowing the plane to almost a halt and blinding the pilots as they flared around the cockpit.

From twenty feet it dropped like a stone onto the runway. Eagle gave the test pilots credit in that they brought the plane down level.

It hit hard, the right wing breaking between the two engines. Flames were still flickering out of the retrorockets as a fire blossomed in the shattered wing, which was spewing fuel. The broken plane skidded, left wing now dragging into the tarmac as the weight shifted.

"Geez!" Caruso muttered. "What the hell did you do?"

More fuel was pouring out of the broken wing as the plane came to a halt. Four crewmen ran out of the back of the plane, but the three men in the cockpit were trapped.

Fire trucks were on the scene spraying foam, and a path was opened so the rest of the crew could escape.

"They're all okay," Eagle said, glad that his improvisation of history had produced the same result.

"What exactly did you shoot?" Hammersmith asked.

"It's complicated," Eagle said. "Suffice to say I cut one control and initiated another."

"So there won't be another rescue mission." Hammersmith said. Not a question, but Eagle responded.

"Things will turn out all right for the hostages." That was all he could say of the future. He thought of all that would happen between 1980 and his own time and realized it was both overwhelming and incredible. Who, today, would believe the Wall would come down in just nine years, ending decades of Cold War, without a shot being fired? Or the Gulf Wars? 9/11? The War on Terror?

It would make for a novel people would dismiss now as being too farfetched. But it was history in Eagle's time. He looked over at Hammersmith. "We're done."

"What now?" Hammersmith asked.

"I go back to my time," Eagle said.

Hammersmith nodded toward the other three survivors. "And them? Don't they know too much?"

"Who would believe them?" Eagle said. "Fighting monsters in the swamp?"

Eagle also knew that if any of those men talked about this, they'd probably get a visit from the Cellar, although he knew it was more likely they wouldn't be believed. They had their freedom; they'd protect that with their silence.

Hammersmith nodded. "I been thinking. I think I was told to pick these guys because they were expendable, right?"

Eagle shrugged. "I imagine so."

"But that means I'm expendable too," Hammersmith said. "And you," he added.

Eagle had been expendable so long it hadn't even crossed his mind.

"And," Hammersmith continued, "it means none of us mean anything for our future. Our future here, and your future in your time. I find that a bit . . ." He searched for the word.

"Disheartening?" Eagle offered.

"Yeah. I guess." Hammersmith got to his feet. "But I figured that out from my first tour in Nam. No one gave a crap. We were meat to be fed into the grinder. I suppose most wars require that meat. Including this one we're in."

Down at the airstrip, the firefighters were still battling the blaze.

"Hey," Caruso said as he came over. He stuck his hand out. "Thanks, Top."

Eagle automatically shook his hand, but had to ask. "For what?"

"For leading us."

"Got most of you killed," Eagle said.

"You didn't kill anyone," Caruso said. "You saved our lives." He nodded at the other two men. "You led us into the darkness and out again." He looked past Eagle. "And whatever that was about, you did it right. No one got killed down there. I gotta assume there's a higher purpose to all this."

"It was my job," Eagle began. "I had—"

"We should all be dead," Caruso said. "I ain't stupid. And I heard every word you and hardass here said. I don't know half of what you're talking about, and I know half of what I wish I knew but I know I'm alive. Because of you. Thank you."

And then the other two survivors came up and shook Eagle's hand.

Hammersmith watched this without comment.

"Let's go, guys," he ordered the other three men. Hammersmith indicated a direction. "We need to police up the bodies. Close that out. Leave no trace."

Eagle stood. He handed the M21 to Hammersmith. "Thank you."

Hammersmith took the rifle. "Your job is screwed. So is mine." He gave the ghost of a smile. "Good luck and good hunting, wherever and whenever you end up." He paused. "But thank you. I'd have followed you into the gates of hell and we got a glimpse of that, didn't we?"

And then they moved out. They were out of view in a minute and Eagle was alone. He sat down and waited.

Manhattan, New York, 1929. 29 October

Ivar was startled into alertness. He had no clue what time it was. It had been hours at least since Lansky had left with the money and the list. He was thirsty, tired, and scared. He hadn't been asleep as much as passed out from utter exhaustion.

He was very much regretting spilling the beans, so to speak, to Lansky, but what else could he have done? This mission had screwed the pooch from the start.

He also stunk. He'd been forced to piss in his pants.

Could it be near midnight? Would he get a reprieve?

The door creaked open and Ivar twisted his head, trying to get a view of whoever had entered. He could hear footsteps. Someone was right behind him.

Ivar braced for the bullet to the back of his head that would bring the blackness of death. He gasped as a piece of cloth was jammed in his open mouth. Another piece of cloth looped over and the gag was cinched into place.

Ivar tried to yell, to beg, but all that came was a muffled noise.

The person walked around. Lansky looked down at him. "The deals are done. You'll be happy to know your Mister Kennedy will be left alone. I will be a rich man, if your piece of paper is correct. And my partners are happy they got their money back. They do wonder where the rest went, but they trust me when I said we had to return it to the proper owners. They understand that I understand the way money works."

Ivar was trying to plead.

"Save it," Lansky said. He nodded toward the door and another man walked up next to him. A short, barrel-chested man with a scarred face. "This is Vincent. He has a particular talent that is useful in this case. He can't hear anything. Result of being too close to a bomb he planted. Unfortunate for him, useful for my purposes. So even if you somehow convince him to take your gag off, he won't understand anything you say. Not that he will take your gag off. He's very loyal. Like a dog." Lansky smiled, as he was one step ahead of Ivar's thoughts. "He also can't read. And he won't untie your hands anyway. So. It was very nice to meet you. Thank you for the positive prognosis for my future."

And then Meyer Lansky walked out of sight.

A hood was thrown over Ivar's face, and he was carried out of the room and into the trunk of a waiting car.

He was going for ride.

And it took a while. He knew they went over a bridge, so they were out of Manhattan. He was beginning to get hopeful that midnight would come and he would disappear out of this trunk.

But he'd been taken out of the car. Vincent had carried him on his broad shoulder down some steps, across something that creaked, and then onto what was obviously a boat, given the swell.

Then it got worse.

How long does it take concrete to set? Ivar wondered.

He'd worked in the lab enough, knew the compounds of the mixture around his feet, but there were variables. How much water versus mixture? The temperature was also a variable.

The rocking of the boat was making him sick. So was his impending death and the method. He'd thought they would use a steel tub, as in *Billy Bathgate*, but this was much more efficient and lower class. Each of his feet was stuck in a hole in a cinder block. Vincent had poured concrete in the holes a little while ago and was now sitting on the railing, staring blankly at Ivar. Once the concrete hardened, Ivar wouldn't be able to get his feet out, and the cinder block plus concrete was more than enough to take him down, down, down into the depths.

Really. He was going to sleep with the fishes.

Ivar tried with a mixture of grunts and jerking of his head toward his watch to get an idea what time it was. Vincent either didn't understand, didn't care, or didn't own a watch. Most likely all three.

Ivar had been loaded onto the boat in the dark, so that was good. But it was the end of October, so it got dark kind of early. The ride out into the middle of Long Island Sound had taken a while. Probably an hour.

Ivar had spent that eternity struggling against his bonds with no success, kicking at the lid of the trunk with similar results.

Then he pushed against the front of the trunk, trying to push through into the back seat. No luck. Meanwhile, his mind tried to calculate time with a desperation greater than he'd ever put into any of his physics problems.

Seriously. This was ludicrous.

Vincent stood up and came over. He knelt down and poked a finger at the concrete.

Ivar was wiggling his toes inside the cinder block and he still had some movement so he figured he still had some time. But Vincent flicked his finger. The outside was solid. It was hardening from the outside in.

Ivar remembered being told, most likely by Eagle who loved telling such things, that the concrete deep inside Hoover Dam was *still* hardening.

His feet weren't Hoover Dam.

Vincent stood up and folded his arms, looking down at Ivar. Ivar gave the best *let me live* look he could conjure up with his eyes.

Something Vincent had probably seen many times.

Vincent turned and walked over to the railing. He unzipped his pants and took a long piss.

Really? Ivar thought. He couldn't catch a break. Of course there were worse things in that dark water than Vincent's piss.

Maybe Vincent needed to take a dump? Maybe he'd go inside and take a long, satisfying dump? One could hope.

Vincent opened up a section of railing.

Ivar struggled against the tight ropes, pleading incoherently into the gag, body spasming.

Vincent didn't bother to pick Ivar up. Or untie him from the chair.

It obviously wasn't a near and dear piece of furniture to Meyer Lansky.

Vincent scooted the chair toward the opening in the railing.

Ivar's body was rigid, his screams muted. He was wiggling his feet in the cold concrete mix, feeling it squeeze in between his toes.

The front legs of the chair were now at the edge of the boat. Ivar felt the rope fall away as Vincent cut it.

Ivar was shaking his head: no, no, no, no, no.

And then he was tipped forward toward the roiling, black water. He took a gulp of air around the gag just before hitting head first, almost regretting doing that, because it would make it that much longer until death took him; and he was stunned from the shock of the cold water, and all was darkness, the concrete and cinder block pulling his feet; and he was plummeting down, the pressure increasing on his ears, on his chest. He couldn't move, he was going to—

Foreman was splayed out, facedown, on one of the tables that the Ratnik had used to harvest organs, flesh, muscle, bone, and pretty much whatever they needed from the people they "reaped" via gates.

A Valkyrie hovered over him and Neeley went to draw her pistol, but Earhart stopped her. "My doctor is in that suit."

"Who is Foreman?" Neeley asked as they walked up to the table. Earhart's samurai took defensive positions.

"He's the man in each timeline that serves through World War Two and who links the Time Patrol with the present," Earhart said.

"Is that Foreman"—Neeley indicated the man on the table, whose flesh was being cut by the Valkyrie—"the one from my timeline?"

"Does it matter?" Earhart said. "I'm not from your timeline. My understanding is that the version of myself from your timeline simply disappeared in flight. Never heard from again. But, yes, he is from your timeline."

The Valkyrie's claws were slicing, cutting, pulling, all very delicately.

"So they can save life as well as take it," Neeley said.

"They're sophisticated machines," Earhart said. "We captured several suits. They're preprogrammed with surgical capabilities. My doctor is removing Foreman's tumor, something a surgeon couldn't do without causing extensive brain damage and most likely killing him."

"He played us," Neeley said. "And he's still playing us. He hasn't told us the truth."

Earhart, surprisingly, laughed. "Of course not. He hasn't told *me* the truth. He's different. He sensed the Shadow when he was a young man in World War Two. Then he sensed it again with Flight Nineteen. I think he has a male version of the Sight. Because of that, he doesn't know whether what he sees is real or not. Unless he sees something that can fix the date for him, he doesn't know if he's seeing the past or the future. Or just possibilities. The Sight can be a blessing but also a curse. You have a bit of it yourself. That young girl with you, Scout, she has the most powerful I've felt, other than Sin Fen. And speaking of her—" Earhart pointed.

Sin Fen came striding up to stand next to them. "Very good," she said to Neeley. "Figuring out he would be here."

"It was logical," Neeley said.

"It was the Sight," Sin Fen said. She was a striking Eurasian woman of indeterminate age. "As you sensed he would be here doing this, I sensed you would come."

"I don't trust him," Neeley said. "Do you?"

Sin Fen nodded. "I do."

The Valkyrie lifted something out of the back of Foreman's skull.

"The tumor," Sin Fen said. "He'll have a few more years."

"Lucky us," Neeley muttered. "He plays games within games."

"And you don't?" Sin Fen said. "The Shadow is a formidable opponent, as the Time Patrol has been finding out for the past twenty-four hours. Let us hope all return safely from their missions."

That distracted Neeley, and she knew that was deliberate on Sin Fen's part. Was Roland all right? Would he be back? Scout? Moms? The rest of the team?

"And Dane?" Neeley asked, not willing to go quietly into the night of subterfuge and intrigue. "Is he from our timeline?"

"No," Sin Fen said. "He isn't. He's from another timeline. One where he fought the Shadow and lost. He's a refugee. And he understands what's at stake better than anyone from our timeline." Sin Fen reached out and put her hand on Neeley's shoulder. "Come with me. We'll go meet the team returning."

THE RETURN

Roland was sliding through the tunnel of time, forward. To his own time. There was something off to one side. Images appeared, like an old movie flickering on a black-and-white television.

Roland didn't quite understand or comprehend the changes to his history he was seeing in that other possibility if he had failed in his mission: a Reformation starting in the year 1015 AD instead of 1517. England becoming the religious center of Europe. A kingdom rising, one that sent crusaders across the world. The Catholic Church crushed, and a new warrior-religion taking its place.

Flames. Bodies. A worldwide Inquisition.

And then nothing.

Scout was sliding through the tunnel of time, forward. It was a very strange sensation, to be pulled through time with no control. And then she could see things. The tunnel she was in, things flickering on the walls: people rushing an embassy rooftop, desperate to get on board. Blindfolded hostages. Ronald Reagan. The Berlin Wall coming down and so much more. But then Scout realized she could see out of her own timeline. And there were other possible time tunnels flickering out there.

In one she saw a single massive computer housed in a large cavern, lines leading out from it around the entire world, every other machine wired into it. But then there were missiles being launched, nuclear explosions, humans desperately trying to break their machines free from the single point, the image flickering and then disappearing as she got closer and closer to her own time.

There was a light ahead of her and she knew her present awaited her.

And hopefully a good meal.

But she wasn't the same person she'd been twenty-four hours ago.

She wasn't sure that was a good thing.

━━━━━━━━

Mac began to slide through the tunnel of time, forward, a long journey from 1618, through the decades and centuries. He could see other tunnels all around. Possibilities. Some from even before the time he left, others popping into existence as he moved forward.

But the closest and most immediate was most likely the one that could have been, had Raleigh escaped the axe and rode off with Beeston to fulfill a different destiny.

And Mac panicked because what he was seeing was a timeline

where there was no Thirty Years' War. Where Germany wasn't dev-astated and splintered by religious strife and millions weren't killed.

Surely that was good?

But that tunnel grew darker and redder as he moved for-ward and then he saw something chilling: zeppelins with swas-tikas emblazoned on their sides at high altitude, floating over American cities. A mushroom cloud and Washington, DC, wasn't there anymore. And then that timeline pulsed into solid red and snapped out of existence.

And Mac was back in his own time.

Which still existed.

Moms slid through the tunnel of time, forward. To her own time. She was aware that there was another hazy, flickering tun-nel nearby. A possibility, she realized, branching out from 1972 if none had survived that crash and the ordeal in the mountains.

As Moms was pulled back to her time, she couldn't see spe-cifics of that possible timeline. She realized it wasn't about any particular event happening or not happening that was different about that timeline; it was that the spirit was lacking. The desire to live. Somehow, rippling out of the tiny spark of hope and resil-ience sparked by the survivors of that single flight, something essentially human was kept alive, and without it, that other tun-nel turned darker and darker and farther away.

And then it simply faded out of existence. It was a timeline that would have required many other things to happen besides no survivors from this incident, but it was a possibility.

It was a possible timeline that proved without hope, there is no future.

Eagle was sliding through the tunnel of time, forward. To his own time. There were several tunnels paralleling his, possibilities branching out from 1980 and a second rescue mission launched. One disappeared from view so quickly he didn't even get a chance to make anything out. That left two.

In another, Eagle caught a glimpse of President Carter greeting the hostages at Andrews Air Force Base, a ticker tape parade. And then Carter winning the election on the 4th of November. Defeating Reagan. And that tunnel grew bright for a short period of time, and then suddenly ceased into absolute blackness, with no clue as to what had caused it to end.

The remaining tunnel showed a smoldering C-130 in the soccer stadium. Hundreds of dead Iranians. American hostages kneeling, being shot in the back of the head. The tunnel was moving away, heading in a different direction. Eagle tried to follow, but it was all too hazy, and soon it was just a thread in the distance.

One of so many possible threads in time.

Ivar returned to light with someone pounding on his chest. He looked up at Doc and tried to speak, but instead, vomited seawater.

"There's a story here," he heard Moms say.

"Nice shoes," Roland said.

But all Ivar could do was reach up and grab Doc, pulling him down, wrapping his wet arms around Doc's skinny body, just needing to feel a human, to feel life.

AFTERMATH

"Six for six," Dane said. "Excellent."

The Nightstalkers were seated around the table in their team room. Some the worse for wear. Scout sported a bandage on her cheek. Roland was breathing shallowly, nursing a pair of broken ribs, but he barely noticed because Neeley was sitting next to him and all he could do was stare at her like a puppy, a ferocious attack-dog puppy, in love. Moms had a tinge of frostbite here and there. Ivar was still shivering, a blanket over his shoulder, as much from his near death as from his plunge into Long Island Sound in late October.

Scout seemed strangely distant, eyes a bit unfocused.

Mac's head was down, deep in reflection.

It was Eagle who was the most composed. He'd checked each of them as they came back, making sure they were attended to. Getting the cinder block and concrete off Ivar's feet and administering treatment for his lacerations. Making sure Scout's cut was tended to as well. Ensuring hot coffee and food was supplied. Getting them boring but clean gray jumpsuits into which they could change from their era garments.

Sin Fen was standing next to Dane. She was looking over the group, peering at each as if she saw into their recent experience and what it meant. Each had given a brief after-action report to Dane and Sin Fen. And now they were together once more as a team.

Sin Fen turned to Dane. "It was different than we anticipated."

Dane didn't agree. "We anticipated it would be different."

"Cut the crap," Eagle said. "This isn't over, is it?"

"No," Dane said. "The Shadow will try again."

"So what did we learn?" Eagle asked. He nodded at Sin Fen. "Tell us."

Sin Fen spread her hands. "I've listened to your brief summaries of your day in the past. Your October 29th. And I can see"—she paused—"the effect. On each one of you and on the timeline."

She pointed at Mac. "Your mission was compromised years, decades, before you even went, by the prophecy the Shadow gave to Raleigh. A brilliant plan. But you were more brilliant in figuring out how to stop it from culminating. But we need to be aware that the seeds of a ripple can be planted many years before it comes to fruition on a specific day of the six cascade days."

Next she focused on Roland. "It was brutal, what you went through."

Neeley squeezed Roland's hand and he flushed bright red.

"There is a truth you must all know that bears on what Roland experienced," Sin Fen said. "You met Tam Nok, who is sister to me, although she lived long before me. She is one with the Sight. A descendant of the line of the survivors of Atlantis. Of the Defenders of Atlantis."

That got everyone's attention.

"But there are others from this line of survivors. Ragnarok had some Atlantean blood in him. As did the nun. If they had come together and produced a child, well, Roland, the vision Tam Nok gave you showed the catastrophe that would be."

"Is that why the nun had to die?" Roland asked.

"Whether she had to die or not," Sin Fen said, "is not for us to ponder. She died. That cascade event was stopped."

Roland slumped back in his chair and Neeley put her arm around his shoulder.

"Moms. In a way, your mission had the least concrete possibilities for a ripple or cascade event. None of the survivors of that crash have directly changed history. But you were most correct in understanding that emotion, particularly hope, is very, very powerful. When Atlantis fell, it was the mental and emotional power of those last Defenders and the warriors with them who managed to stop the Shadow from complete victory. They all died, but they kept the timeline alive."

Moms nodded, but all she could think about was Pablo, life fading from him, just before she was pulled back. She had his dog tags on her hands, fingers rubbing against the metal. She would remember his name.

"Eagle," Sin Fen said, "what you had to do went against everything you've been trained for. As a pilot, it was anathema for you to crash that plane. But you never questioned it. That means you are now the team sergeant of the Nightstalkers. Nada is gone. You are taking his place."

Everyone turned to look at Eagle, shaken out of their own situation by that.

Eagle shook his head. "No one can replace Nada. He was—"

"The glue that held the team together," Sin Fen said. "The team still needs that. And you are it." Sin Fen moved on, no more discussion on that subject. "Ivar. You came the closest to not making it back."

"You think?" Ivar said.

"But your mission is also an example of how the Shadow can appear to be going for one objective, Black Tuesday, and have something else entirely as the target: the Kennedys. We must all keep this in mind."

Dane spoke up. "It's like we said in the mission briefing. Don't get focused on one thing. The Shadow can, and will, attack in unexpected ways."

"What about the money?" Ivar asked. "I don't understand that."

Sin Fen and Dane exchanged a glance. Dane spoke. "Don't worry about it."

Which caused the members of the team to all exchange a look. They'd been in this situation before. Secrets within secrets.

"And the most unexpected," Sin Fen said, turning to Scout. "The Internet being initiated was not the objective of the Shadow for your mission."

"I was the objective," Scout said in a low voice. She was looking down, her fingers running along the edge of a leather belt she held in her hands.

"Yes," Sin Fen confirmed. "You were. The Shadow went to a great amount of trouble to come after you."

"And failed," Dane said.

"Why me?" Scout asked, looking up.

"Because you are the future," Sin Fen said. "You have the Sight, but there is something more to you. Something I've never sensed before."

"Hope," Moms said. "We knew you were special when we first met you in North Carolina."

"Yeah," Roland said. "Nada saw it right away. I thought he was nuts, but he wanted you on the team."

Scout's eyes grew moist. "But Nada—"

"Did the right thing," Moms said. "It's all as he would have wanted. Everything is just right."

"For the moment," Dane cautioned. "There are always more days."

ABOUT THE AUTHOR

Photo © 2004 Bob Mayer

Bob Mayer is a *New York Times* bestselling author, graduate of West Point, former Green Beret (including commanding an A-Team), and the feeder of two yellow labs, most famously Cool Gus. He's had over sixty books published, including three #1 bestselling series: Area 51, Atlantis, and the Green Berets. Born in the Bronx and having traveled the world (usually not the tourist spots), he now lives peacefully with his wife and his labs at Write on the River, Tennessee.

MORE WORLDS TO EXPLORE

For more on the following, I recommend these books:

The six-book Atlantis series: Tells the story of *another* Earth timeline that faced the Shadow and fought a battle against it covering centuries. We meet Tam Nok, Sin Fen, Foreman, Dane, Amelia Earhart, the Ones Before, Corpse-Loddin, and the Space Between.

The books cover a battle in the present and great battles in the past, such as Little Big Horn, Isandlwana, the 300 Spartans at Thermopylae, Gladiators in the shadow of Mount Vesuvius, and more.

The Nightstalkers series: The Fun in North Carolina. The Fun in the Desert. And a history of the Nightstalkers and how they dealt with the Rifts, a president who cannot tell a lie, and more! Where the Nightstalkers first encounter Scout in a gated community in North Carolina.

Shit Doesn't Just Happen: The Gift of Failure. This is a nonfiction series based on the Rule of Seven and how it applies to various catastrophes in history, such as Titanic, Little Big Horn, Air France Flight 447, The Last Czar, and many more. These books are also broken down into Kindle Shorts—quick reads, each focused on a single event titled: *Anatomy of Catastrophe.* One of those covered is the crash of Uruguayan Flight 571: *Alive! Perseverance Triumphs over Tragedy.*

And, of course, if you're interested in how Hannah and Neeley came together, The Cellar series consists of *Bodyguard of Lies* and *Lost Girls.*

FOR MORE TIME PATROL STORIES AND INFORMATION ABOUT THE CHARACTERS, THE POSSIBILITY PALACE AND MORE, GO TO

www.coolgus.com/bobmayertimepatrol.com

ALSO BY BOB MAYER

Nightstalkers Series
Nightstalkers
*Nightstalkers: The Book of
Truths*
Nightstalkers: The Rift
Nightstalkers: Time Patrol

The Area 51 Series
Area 51
Area 51: The Reply
Area 51: The Mission
Area 51: The Sphinx
Area 51: The Grail
Area 51: Excalibur
Area 51: The Truth
Area 51: Nosferatu
Area 51: Legend

The Green Beret Series
Eyes of the Hammer
Dragon Sim-13
Cut Out
Synbat

Eternity Base
Z: The Final Countdown
Chasing the Ghost
Chasing the Lost

The Shadow Warrior Series
The Gate
The Line
Omega Missile
Omega Sanction
Section Eight

Atlantis Series
Atlantis
Atlantis: Bermuda Triangle
Atlantis: Devil's Sea
Atlantis: Gate
Assault on Atlantis
Battle for Atlantis

Psychic Warrior Series
Psychic Warrior
Psychic Warrior: Project Aura